# Frank Merriwell's Bravery

## BURT L. STANDISH

Author of the celebrated "Merriwell"
stories, which are the favorite reading of
over half a million up-to-date (1904)
American boys.

### BOOKS FOR ATHLETICS

LONDON
IBOO PRESS HOUSE
86-90 PAUL STREET

Frank Merriwell's Bravery

BURT L. STANDISH.

BOOKS FOR ATHLETICS

Layout & Cover © Copyright 2020 iBooPress, London

Published by
iBoo Press House

3rd Floor
86-90 Paul Street
London, EC2A4NE UK

t: +44 20 3695 0809
info@iboo.com II iBoo.com

ISBNs
978-1-64181-937-4 (h)
978-1-64181-938-1 (p)

Printed in the United States

# Frank Merriwell's Bravery

## BURT L. STANDISH

Author of the celebrated "Merriwell"
stories, which are the favorite reading of
over half a million up-to-date (1904)
American boys.

BOOKS FOR ATHLETICS

# Contents

# CHAPTER I.

## TWO TRAVELERS.

ell, that's a pretty nervy piece of business!"

It was Frank Merriwell who spoke the words, more to himself than to any one else.

Frank was westbound, from Oklahoma City at the time, continuing the extensive tour mapped out after his Uncle Asher had died and left him so much money.

As readers of former books in this series know, Frank was not making the tour alone. Professor Scotch, his guardian, was with him as was also Barney Mulloy, his old schoolmate from Fardale. But, as the professor and Barney had not wanted to stop at Oklahoma, they had gone on ahead, leaving Frank to catch up with them later.

The "nervy piece of business" to which Frank referred was the following account of a hold-up published in a leading Oklahoma newspaper:

"BLACK HARRY'S LATEST STROKE.

"HE HOLDS UP AN EXPRESS TRAIN, AND SHOOTS AN EASTERN BANKER.

"As we go to press, an imperfect account of Black Harry's latest outrage reaches us from Elreno. Ten days ago this youthful desperado was unknown to fame, but within that number of days he has left a red trail from the Texas Panhandle to the Canadian River. He began by raiding Moore's ranch, and killing a cowboy, and he and his band of desperadoes, which he calls his 'Braves,' have robbed and plundered and burned and murdered at their own sweet will, till the climax was capped last night by the holding up of the northbound express on the Chicago, Rock Island and Pacific, shortly after leaving Chickasha and crossing the Washita. Between Chickasha and Minco is a twenty-mile stretch of desolate track, and a better place for a train hold-up could not be found.

"Just how the express was stopped we do not know at present, but the trick was accomplished, and Black Harry and his Braves boarded the cars. Strangely enough, they did not attempt to enter the express car, but were satisfied to go through the train hastily and relieve the passengers of their valuables. In this work, Black Harry took the lead; but Mr. Robert Dawson, an Eastern banker, who happened to have quite a sum on his person, objected, and snatched the mask from the young ruffian's face. Before the eyes of Miss Lona Dawson, who was traveling with her father, Black Harry deliberately shot the banker down, and then relieved him of his watch, diamond pin, and pocketbook, having first re-covered his face with the mask.

"The robbers made a hasty but very thorough job of it, leaping from the train at a signal from their boy leader, and quickly disappearing in the darkness. But Black Harry's face was seen fairly by the banker's horrified daughter, and by several other passengers, so there will be no trouble in identifying him if he is captured. Sheriff Kildare, of Canadian County, is aroused, and Burchel Jones, an Eastern detective, has promised to round up Black Harry within a very short time. Let us hope, for the good of the Territory, that the young ruffian's career may be quickly terminated, and that he may receive his just due at the hands of the law.

"Mr. Dawson was taken to Elreno, where a surgical operation was performed. He is still alive, but his chance of recovery is small. His daughter, who seems to be a girl of spirit, has stated that, if her father dies, she will know no rest nor spare no expense till Black Harry is run to earth."

The article terminated abruptly, showing it had been hastily written, and had been inserted at the last moment before publication.

"Truly an outrage!" Frank continued. "It would be a good scheme to organize a hunting party, and give this Black Harry a run for it."

"Just my idea," said an oily voice, as a man slipped into the seat beside the young traveler, without as much as saying "by your leave." "The people out here do not seem to mind these things. I suppose they are used to them."

Frank glanced the speaker over, with a pair of searching, brown eyes. He saw a slender figure in a well-worn suit of gray. The striking features of the man's face were his eyes and his nose. His eyes were too near together, and his nose was long and pointed. He was smooth-shaved, and there was a cunning, foxy look about his face.

Frank did not seem in any hurry about speaking; he continued

8

to inspect the man, who moved restlessly beneath the scrutiny, and said:

"I have not been very long in this country, but I have noted the peculiarities of the people. They do not seem to have time to bother much about an affair like this train hold-up, and the shooting of an occasional tenderfoot, as they call all Easterners. If they should happen to capture Black Harry, they would give him their full attention for a short time—a very short time. They would be pretty sure to lynch him, as they would consider that the easiest way of disposing of him, and they would not consider it worth while to spend time in giving him a regular trial. To be sure, this train robbery and tragedy occurred in Indian Territory, but I understand that Hank Kildare, the sheriff at Elreno, has offered three hundred dollars reward for the capture of Black Harry himself, and fifty dollars each for his men. Er—ah—ahem! My name is—Walker. I am from Jersey."

Frank bowed.

"How do you do, Mr.—er—ah—Walker. I presume that what you say about Black Harry's chances, if he is captured, is quite true—he will be lynched."

"Oh, it is not certain, of course; he might obtain protection by officers of the law. But he would stand a good show of being lynched. And Elreno is the worst place in Oklahoma for him to show his face in at present."

"I should presume it might be. Dawson, the wounded banker, is there?"

"And his daughter—can she identify this young desperado the moment she sees him?"

"Without doubt."

"Black Harry will be very foolish if he goes to Elreno."

"He is not likely to go there, I fancy."

"I don't know about that. He is a dare-devil fellow."

"So it seems."

"And he might take a fancy that Elreno would be the last place where he would be expected to appear, and so he would go there."

"He might do that."

"Now, in your own case, if you were Black Harry, for instance, you might put on a bold face, and show yourself in Elreno, while everybody outside that town would be on the lookout for you."

"Possibly, you are right."

"I think such a trick would be very like Black Harry. He might go so far as to take the train to Elreno from some place that would make it seem that he could not have been in the locality where the hold-up was committed. If he were to come into Elreno on this train, for instance, it would be a blind."

"How far is Oklahoma City from the place where the train was robbed?"

"Between thirty and forty miles, direct."

"That distance could be made on horseback between the time of the robbery and this morning—do you think so?"

"Well, it is very likely. What do you think, Mr.—ah—er—I beg your pardon?"

"My name is Frank Merriwell."

"Really?"

Walker lifted his eyebrows in a very odd manner, which Frank did not fail to observe.

"You appear as if you doubted me," came a trifle warmly from the lad's lips, while the color rushed to his cheeks.

"Oh, not at all—not at all! You are in Oklahoma on business?"

"No, sir."

"Not?"

"No."

"Pleasure?"

"Yes, sir."

"How? Traveling?"

"I am."

"Alone?"

"No."

"Didn't notice you had company."

"I have not, at present."

"H'm! Ha! Your friends—are they on this train?"

"No, sir."

Walker elevated his eyebrows again. His nose seemed longer and more pointed than ever. It was a nose that reminded the boy of an interrogation point. It seemed built to thrust itself into other people's business.

"Ha! Not on the train?"

"No."

"You expect to meet them?"

"Yes."

"Where?"

"In Elreno."

"How many of them?"

"Two."

"No more?"

"No."

Frank was answering curtly, and his manner announced his dislike for his inquisitive companion. Still, he was courteous and cool, holding himself in check.

"I presume your companions are older than yourself?" questioned the prying Jerseyite, his small eyes glistening.

"One is; the other is a boy about my age."

"Ha! H'm! Just so. You are from the East, I presume?"

"Yes, sir."

"It seems to me that I have seen you before, but I cannot remember where it was. And I do not remember your name. Do you mind giving me the names of your traveling companions?"

"Not at all. They are Professor Horace Orman Tyler Scotch, of Fardale Military Academy, sometimes known as 'Hot' Scotch, as he has a peppery temper, and the initials of his first three names form the word 'hot.' The other is Barney Mulloy, a youth who was born in Ireland, and has not recovered from it yet. The latter was a classmate of mine at Fardale, and he is traveling with me as a friendly companion, which he can afford to do, as I pay all the bills."

"Haw!" exclaimed Walker. "You must have money to burn!"

"No, I have not. My uncle left me a comfortable fortune, and his will provided that, in order to broaden my knowledge of the world, I should travel in company with my guardian. He selected Professor Scotch as a proper man to become my guardian, and specified that I might take along a schoolmate as a companion, if I so desired."

"Re-e-markable!" cried Walker. "A most astonishing will! And how does it happen that you have become separated from your guardian and friend?"

"We were going through to Texas on the Chicago, Rock Island and Pacific. I wished to visit Guthrie, the capital of Oklahoma, and they did not care to do so. I left them at Caldwell, in Kansas, with the understanding that they were to proceed to Elreno, and wait for me there."

"H'm!"

Walker's nose seemed pointing at the boy like an accusing finger. Doubt was expressed all over that foxy face.

"You tell it well," said the man, with another queer lifting of his thin eyebrows.

"What do you mean by that?" demanded the youth, sharply, wheeling squarely toward Walker. "Do you insinuate that I am not telling the truth?"

Before Walker could reply, a commotion arose in the seat directly behind them.

11

# CHAPTER II.

## "HANDS UP!"

w! Thay, weally, this ith verwy impudent, don't yer know!" drawled a languid voice. "What wight have you to cwout yourthelf into a theat bethide a gentleman, thir?"

"I don'd seen der shentleman anyvere," replied a nasal voice, a voice that had the genuine Jewish sound.

"Thir! Do you mean to thay I am no gentleman, thir?"

"Vell, I don'd mean to say nodding aboud id. I don'd vant to hurd your veelings."

"You insulting w'etch!"

"Don'd get excided, mein friendt."

"Will you leave thith theat, thir?"

"Cerdinly I vill—ven I leaf der drain."

"I thall call the conductor!"

"Don'd vaste your preath—peckon to him."

"Thir, I would have you understand that my name ith Cholly Gwayson De Smythe."

"Vell, I vos bleased to meed you. Anypody vould be pleased shust to dake a look ad you."

"Thir!"

"My name vas Solomon Rosenbum, vid the accent on der bum. Shake handts vid yourself."

By this time everybody in the car was staring at the Jew and the dudish fellow beside whom Solomon had taken a seat. The latter was a youth of uncertain age, with an insipid mustache, a sallow face, and spectacles of colored glass, which seemed to indicate that he had weak eyes. He was dressed, as far as possible, in imitation of an English tourist.

The Jew, who had given his name as "Solomon Rosenbum, vid der accent on der bum," was a rather disreputable-looking man of about thirty, having the appearance of the Jew peddler, and carrying a pack, which he had stuffed down between his knees and the back of the next seat, thus completely fencing in Cholly De Smythe.

"Will you wemove yourthelf fwom this theat?" squawked the dude, in a flutter.

"Say, mein friendt, you vas nervous. Now, I dell you vat you do vor dat. Shust dake a pottle of Snyde's Shain-Lighdning Nearf Regulardor. Id vill simbly gost you von tollar a pottle, dree bottles vor dwo tollars. I haf shust dree pottles left. Vill you dake 'em?"

Solomon began to untie his pack.

"Stop it!" squealed Cholly, in terror. "I don't want your nawsty stuff, don't yer know!"

"Berhaps I know petter dan vat you do. I haf studied to pe a horse toctor, und I make a sbecialty uf shack-asses."

"You wude thing!"

The other passengers in the car were enjoying all this, and the laughter that had begun with the first passage between the two now threatened to swell to a tumult.

"Uf one pottle don'd gure you, der dree pottles vill—or kill you, und nopody vill mindt dot."

"Go'way!"

"Vill you half der dree pottles?"

"No, thir!"

"Veil, dake von uf dem ad sefenty-fife cends."

"Get out!"

"I alvays haf von brice vor all uf mine goots, und I nefer make a bractice uf dakin' off a cend; but I see dat you vas on der verge uf nerfus brosdration, und I vant to safe your life, so I vill sell you von pottle vor a hellufer-tollar."

"I don't want it—I won't take the nawsty stuff!"

"Dat vas too sheap at hellufer-tollar, but in your gase I vill make an eggsception, und you may haf von pottle vor a qvarter. Dake id qvick, before I shange my mindt."

"Help! Take the w'etch away!"

"Moses in der pulrushes! Vat you vant? Vas you dryin' to ruin me? Dot medicine gost me ninedy-dree cends a pottle, und I don'd ged a cend discoundt uf I puy dwo pottles. Dake a pottle ad dwenty cends, und I vill go indo pankrupcy."

"Conductaw! Conductaw!" squawked Cholly.

"What is all this noise about?" demanded the conductor, as he came hastily down the aisle and stood scowling at Cholly.

He had overheard all that passed, and he was enjoying it as much as any of the passengers.

"Conductaw," said the dude, with great dignity, "I wish you to instantly wemove this verwy insolent cwecher. He cwoded in thith theat without awsking leave."

"Have you paid for a whole seat?"

"I have paid one fare, thir, and ——"

"So has this gentleman. He is entitled to half of this seat, if he chooses to sit here. Don't bother me again."

The conductor walked away, and Cholly looked at Solomon, faintly gasping:

"Thith gentleman! Gweat Scott!"

Then he seemed to collapse.

Solomon grinned, and lifted his hat to the conductor. Then he turned to Cholly.

"Vill you half a pottle uf der Nearf Regulador ad dwendy cends?"

"Let me out!" gurgled the dude. "I will not stay heaw and be inthulted!"

"Set down," advised the Jew. "You ain'd bought a pottle uf medicine, und I can'd boder to mofe vor you."

Cholly fell back into his seat, giving up the struggle. He turned his head away, and looked out of the window, while Solomon talked to him for ten minutes, without seeming to draw a breath. Cholly, however, could not be induced to purchase a single bottle of the "Nearf Regulador."

All through this, Mr. Walker had not seemed to remove his keen eyes from the face of the boy at his side. The lad apparently enjoyed the affair between the Jew and the dude as much as any one in the car, laughing merrily, and seeming quite at ease.

Somehow, Walker did not seem to be pleased at all. He appeared like a man with a very little sense of humor, or he had so much of grave importance on his mind that he did not observe what was going on behind him.

When Cholly De Smythe had collapsed, and the Jew had ceased to talk, the boy squared about in his seat, and seemed to settle to take things in the most comfortable manner possible. He pulled his hat over his forehead, and continued his perusal of the newspaper.

This did not satisfy his seat mate.

"You seem to be very interested in that paper," said Walker.

"I am," was the curt return, and the boy continued reading.

"You are not much of a talker."

"You are."

"H'm! Ha! I am; I am very sociable."

"So I observed."

"I have been wondering what we would do if a band of robbers was to hold up this train."

"I am sure I cannot tell what I would do. I scarcely think any person can tell what he would do in such a case till he meets the emergency."

"I presume you go armed?"

"In the West—yes."

Walker's thin nose seemed to resemble a wedge which he was driving deeper and deeper with each question.

"Would you mind permitting me to look at your revolver?"

"Yes."

The boy uttered that word, and remained silent, without offering to take the weapon out.

Walker coughed.

"H'm! Ha! I think you misunderstood me."

"I think not."

"I asked you if you would mind letting me look at your revolver."

"And I said I would mind."

"Oh!"

The Jew's voice sounded in Walker's ear.

"I haf a revolfer vat I vill sell you sheep. Id vas a recular taisy, selluf-cocker, und dirty-dwo caliber. Here id vas, meester. Id vas loated, so handle id vid care. Vat you gif vor dat peautiful revolfer, meester?"

Walker took the weapon, glanced into the cylinder, to see that it was actually loaded, and then suddenly thrust it against the head of Frank, crying, sharply:

"Hands up, Black Harry! You are my prisoner!"

# CHAPTER III.

## A THRILLING ACCUSATION.

The words rang through the car, startling the passengers, and causing them to stare in astonishment at the man and the boy.

The man with the revolver was quivering with excitement, while Frank, at whose head the weapon was held, seemed strangely calm.

Exclamations were heard on all sides.

"Black Harry!"

"Is it possible?"

"Not that beardless boy!"

"It's a mistake!"

"If that's Black Harry, his Braves are near, and there is liable to be some shooting before long."

"Sufferin' Moses!" came from the Jew, who owned the revolver. "Ish dat der ropper vat ve read apout der baper in? Stop der cars! I vant to ged off!"

"What do you mean by this crazy act?" calmly demanded Frank, looking straight into Mr. Walker's eyes.

"I mean business, and I am not going to fool with a fellow of your reputation a minute! If you don't put up your hands, I'll send a bullet through your head immediately!"

"Then I shall put up my hands, for I have no fancy for having the top of my head blown off."

Up went the boy's empty hands.

"That's where you are sensible," declared the man with the foxy face. "I have dealt with your kind before, and I know better than to let 'em monkey with me. I am a man with a reputation for catching criminals. At the sound of my name, the professional crooks in the East tremble."

"Walker does not seem to be such a very terrible name."

"Walker—bah! That's not my name!"

"No?"

"Not much!"

"Pray, what is your name, then?"

"I am Burchel Jones, the famous detective," declared the owner of the gimlet eyes, swelling with importance. "Out in this country the fools call me a tenderfoot, but I will show them the kind of stuff I am made of. When they want to catch their desperadoes and robbers, they should send for a tenderfoot detective."

The boy laughed outright.

"You are more sport than a barrel of monkeys," he said, merrily. "What do you think you have done, anyway?"

"I have captured Black Harry, the terrible desperado, who has been giving them so much trouble out here of late."

"You think I am Black Harry?"

"I do not think anything about it—I know it."

"How do you know it?"

"By your face."

"Have you ever seen Black Harry?"

"Yes."

"When?"

"Last night."

"Where?"

"On the northbound Chicago, Rock Island and Pacific express."

"You were on that train?"

"I was, and I saw Black Harry's face when he was unmasked by Robert Dawson—saw it distinctly. You are Black Harry!"

"You were never more deceived in all your life. My name is Frank Merriwell, as I can easily prove."

"Your real name may be Frank Merriwell, but you are the boy desperado who is known as Black Harry, and you are the chap who shot Mr. Robert Dawson."

The detective spoke with conviction, and it was plain that he really believed what he said. The boy began to look grave, as the situation was not exactly pleasant.

"You came from Elreno to Oklahoma City on the first train this morning, did you?" asked the youth.

"I did."

"How did it happen that you took this train back?"

"I spotted you. The moment I saw your face I knew you, and I shadowed you till the train started. I boarded the train with the determination to capture you. I seldom fail when I have resolved on a thing, and I did not fail this time."

"Then this is no joke?"

"You will find it is no joke."

"Well, I can't ride from this place to Elreno with my hands held above my head, as you must very well know."

"Of course you can't. I'll have to put the irons on you. Here, young man, hold this revolver to his head while I handcuff and search him."

He spoke to Cholly De Smythe, who had been watching, with staring eyes, his jaw dropped, and a look of amazement on his face.

"Haw?" squawked the dude, aghast. "What ith that you want, thir?"

"Take this revolver, and hold it to this boy's head. If he moves, shoot him as if he were a dangerous dog."

"Good gwacious!" gurgled Cholly. "I nevah touched a wevolver in awl my life! You will hawve to excuse me, thir."

"If you are determined to treat me as if I were a mad beast, I beg you to let some one who knows something about firearms handle that revolver," said the captive. "I will give you my word not to make any trouble if you lower the weapon."

"Your word does not count with me," declared the crafty detective. "I wouldn't trust you a second—not a second."

"I can show you my card, letters, and other papers to prove my claim that I am Frank Merriwell, a traveler."

"Black Harry would be likely to have such letters and papers ready for just such an emergency. That trick will not count."

"Oh, well, don't fool around with that loaded gun held up against my head! Put on the irons, and give me a chance to rest my arms. Hurry up!"

"Shust led me dake dat revolfer, mine friendt," said the voice of the Jew. "Uf dot poy tries any funny pusiness, he vill be deat, vid der accent on der deat."

"Can I trust you?" cautiously asked Burchel Jones.

"Vell, I dunno. You can uf you vant to. I alvays make a bracdice uf doin' a cash pusiness."

After some hesitation, the tenderfoot detective decided that he could not do better than trust Solomon, and the revolver was surrendered to the Jew.

"Don'd you vink!" commanded Solomon, as he screwed the muzzle of the weapon up against the lad's head. "Uf you do, you vas a deat poy!"

The detective searched the youth, removing a handsome revolver from one of his pockets. That was the only weapon found anywhere on his person.

Burchel Jones was disappointed, for he had expected to find "guns" and knives concealed all over the lad.

"Oh, you're slick—you're slick!" he said. "But you can't fool me. I know how to deal with rascals like you. I have handled hundreds of 'em—hundreds upon hundreds."

"You must be a very old hand in the business," said the captive, with a laugh. "Still, you seem to need assistance to capture a boy, who has made no offer to resist you, although he knows very well that you have no legal right to arrest him."

"Oh, you are ready with your tongue—altogether too ready."

Having searched the lad, Jones produced some manacles, and snapped them on the wrists of his prisoner.

"There," he said to Solomon, "you needn't hold the revolver to his head any longer. I have him foul now."

"Dank you," nodded the Jew. "You vas much opliged vor der use of my revolfer."

"Of course, of course."

"V'y you don'd puy dot revolfer, den, und gif a poor man a drade?"

"Oh, get out. I don't want it any longer."

"Vell, I am glad uf dat, vor it vas long enough alretty. Uf you like id so vel, v'y you don'd bought id?"

"I have one of my own."

"Vell, haf dwo. I gif you a drade on dat revolfer. I sell you dat revolfer vor elefen tollar."

"Don't want it."

"Ten tollar."

"Don't want it."

"Nine."

"No."

"Eight."

"Say, shut up! I wouldn't take it for five!"

"Vell, you may haf him vor your tollar, und dot vas less dan haluf vat id vas vort'. Shall I put a biece uf baper roundt id?"

"I won't buy it at any price."

"Moses in der pulrushes! Do you vant me to gif him to you? I vill dake tree tollar, und dat vas der rock-pottom brice. Here you haf him."

But the detective still declined to take the weapon, which made Solomon exceedingly disgusted and angry.

"You vas der meanest man vat I nefer met!" he cried. "Uf I hat known how mean you vas, I vouldn't helluped you capture dot ropper! I hat better do pusiness vid der ropper anyhow."

19

Burchel Jones was well satisfied with himself. At Yukon he sent a dispatch to Hank Kildare, the sheriff at Elreno, saying:

"Have captured Black Harry. Bringing him in irons. Have Miss Dawson at station to identify him when train arrives.

Burchel Jones,

"Private Detective."

Jones was surprised at the quiet manner in which Frank had submitted to arrest, but he felt that the lad had been cleverly taken by surprise, and had seen by the eye of the man with the revolver that the best thing he could do was to give in without a struggle.

The boy saw it was quite useless to attempt to convince the man that any mistake had been made, and so, after the first effort, ceased to waste his time in the vain struggle. He remained calm and collected, much to the dismay of the some nervous passengers, who were certain the train would be held up by Black Harry's Braves, who would be on hand to rescue their chief.

Jones heard one man declaring over and over that he knew the train would not reach Elreno without a hold-up, and the detective immediately declared:

"If an attempt is made to rescue Black Harry, it will be very unfortunate for Harry, as I shall immediately shoot him. I do not propose to let him escape, to continue his career of crime and devastation."

The boy smiled, in a scornful and pitying way.

When the train drew into Elreno, a great crowd was seen on the platform of the station, and, for the first time, a troubled look came to the face of the youthful prisoner.

"The whole town has turned out to see Black Harry and the man who captured him," said Jones, swelling with importance.

Frank said nothing; he knew well enough that such a crowd was dangerous in many cases. What if it were generally believed that he was, in truth, Black Harry, and the mob should take a fancy to lynch him? His chance of escaping a speedy death would be slim, indeed!

The train stopped, and, with his hand clutching the boy's shoulder, Jones descended to the platform.

"Thar he is!"

The cry went up, and the crowd surged toward the two.

"Stan' back hyar!"

A man that was six feet and four inches in height, and weighed at least two hundred and fifty pounds, forced his way through the throng, casting men to the right and left with his muscular arms. He had a hard, weather-tanned face, and looked as if he did not fear the Evil One himself.

"Are you Burchel Jones, ther detective?" asked this man, as he loomed before Jones and his captive.

"I am, sir," was the dignified reply; "and this is Black Harry. I surrender him to you, and claim the reward offered for his capture."

"Thet ther skunk known as Black Harry?" said the giant sheriff, in evident surprise. "He don't look like a desperado. Wal, we'll soon settle all doubts on thet yar point, fer Miss Dawson is hyar, an' she will recognize him ef he is Black Harry. Come on, boy."

Kildare, the sheriff, for such the giant was, again forced a path through the crowd.

In the station door, a woman and a girl were standing. The girl was not more than seventeen, and was very pretty, despite the traces of grief upon her face.

Kildare led the boy up before the woman and girl, and he spoke to the latter:

"Take a good, squar' look at this yar kid, Miss Dawson, an' see ef yer ever saw thet face afore."

The girl looked at Frank, and then fell back, horror and loathing depicted on her face. She stretched out one hand, with a repellent gesture, as if warning them to keep him away, and with the other hand she clutched at her throat, from which came a choking sound. The woman offered to support her, but she sprang up in a moment, pointed straight at the youthful captive, and literally shrieked:

"He is the wretch who shot my poor father!"

# CHAPTER IV.

## FOR LIFE AND HONOR.

A sudden, mad roar went up from the crowd on the station platform. They swayed, surged, struggled, and shouted:

"Lynch him!"

That cry was like the touching of a torch to dry prairie grass. Men climbed on each others' shoulders; men fought to get nearer the prisoner, and the mob seemed to have gone mad in a moment.

"Lynch him!"

A hundred throats took up the shout, and it became one mighty roar for blood, the most appalling sound that can issue from human lips.

The face of the menaced boy was very pale, but he did not cower before that suddenly infuriated mob. He showed that he had nerve, for he stood up and faced them boldly, helpless as he was.

Burchel Jones, the detective, looked as if he would give something to get away from that locality in a hurry.

A black scowl came to the face of Hank Kildare, and his hands dropped to his hips, reappearing from beneath the tails of his coat with a brace of heavy, long-barreled revolvers in their grasp. The muzzles of the weapons were thrust right into the faces of the men nearest, and the sheriff literally thundered:

"Git back thar, you critters, or by thunder, thar'll be dead meat round hyar! You hyar me chirp!"

Lona Dawson, the banker's daughter, was badly frightened by the sudden outbreak of the mob, and, with her older companion, she retreated into the waiting-room of the station.

"Death to Black Harry!"

A man with strong lungs howled the words above all the uproar and commotion.

"Bring the rope!" screamed another.

And then, as if by magic, a man struggled to the shoulders of those about him, waved a rope in the air, and yelled:

"Hyar's ther necktie fer Black Harry!"

And then, once more, there was a roar, and a surge, and a struggle to get at the handcuffed boy.

"Stiddy!" sounded the voice of Hank Kildare. "Back! back! back! or, by the eternal skies, I'll begin ter sling lead!"

But twenty hands seemed reaching to clutch the lad and drag him away. The sheriff saw that he would not be able to retain his prisoner if he remained where he was.

"Inter ther station, boy!" came from the giant sheriff's lips. "It's yer only chance ter git clear o' this yar gang!"

"Howly shmoke!" cried a familiar voice just behind the handcuffed youth. "Pwhat are they doin' wid yez, Frankie, me b'y?"

"Yes," quavered another voice, likewise familiar, "what is this crazy mob trying to do? This is something appalling!"

"Barney! Professor!" cried the boy, joyously. "Now I can prove that I am what I claim to be!"

"I've got him!"

A big ruffian roared the words, as he fastened both hands upon the manacled lad, and tried to drag him into the midst of the swaying mob.

"Thin take thot, ye spalpane!" shouted the Irish boy, who had appeared in company with a little, red-whiskered man at the door of the station.

Out shot the hard fist of the young Irishman, and—smack!—it struck the man fairly in the left eye, knocking him backward into the arms of the one just behind him.

"It's toime ye got out av thot, me b'y," said Barney Mulloy, as he grasped the imperiled youth by the collar, and drew him into the waiting-room of the station.

"That's right, that's right!" fluttered the little man, who was Professor Scotch. "Let's hurry out by the back door, the way we came in. We were detained, so we did not arrive in time for the train, but we came as quickly as we could."

"And arrived just in time," said Frank. "I am in a most appalling position."

"Well, well!" fluttered the professor. "You can explain that later on. Let's get away from here."

"Look!"

Frank held up his hands, and, for the first time, his friends saw the irons on his wrists. They cried out in amazement.

"Pwhat th' ould b'y is th' m'anin' av thot?" demanded Barney Mulloy, in the most profound astonishment.

"It means that I have been arrested; that's all."

"Pwhat fer?"

"Robbing, shooting, murdering."

"G'wan wid yez!"

"This is no time to joke, Frank," said Professor Scotch, reprovingly. "Are you never able to restrain your propensity for making sport?"

"This is a sorry joke, professor. I am giving you the straight truth."

"But—but it is impossible—I declare it is!"

"It is the truth."

"Who arristed yez?" asked Barney, as if still doubtful that Frank really meant what he was saying.

"A private detective, known as Burchel Jones. He surrendered me to the sheriff of Canadian County, Hank Kildare. That's his voice you can hear above the howling. He is trying to beat the mob back, so he can get me to the jail before I am lynched."

"Before you are lynched!" gurgled the little professor, in a dazed way. "What have you done that they should want to lynch you?"

"Nothing."

"Pwhat do they think ye have done?" asked Barney.

"I presume you have heard of Black Harry?"

"Yes."

"Well, they say I am that very interesting young gentleman."

Small man though he was, Professor Scotch had a deep, hoarse voice, and he now let out a roar of disgust that drowned the stentorian tones of Hank Kildare.

"This is the most outrageous thing I ever heard of!" fumed the professor, in a rage. "Somebody shall suffer for it! You Black Harry! Why, it is ridiculous!"

Barney Mulloy seemed to regard it as extremely funny, for he laughed outright.

"Thot bates th' worruld!" he cried. "But it's dead aisy ye kin prove ye're not Black Harry at all, at all!"

"I don't know about that. I have been identified."

"Pwhat's thot?"

"I have been recognized by a person who has seen Black Harry's face."

"Who is that fool person?" demanded Scotch, furiously. "Show me to him, and let me give him a piece of my mind!"

"There is the person."

Frank pointed straight at Lona Dawson, who was regarding him with horrified eyes from a distant corner of the waiting-room.

"Thot girrul?"

"The young lady?"

"Yes."

"Who is she?"

"Miss Dawson, daughter of Robert Dawson, the banker, whom Black Harry shot during the train hold-up last night. Dawson tore the mask from the young robber's face, and she saw it. A few moments ago she declared that I was the wretch who shot her father."

The girl heard his words, and she started forward, panting fiercely:

"You are! You are! I will swear to it with my dying breath! I saw your face plainly last night, and I can never forget it. You are the murderous ruffian from whose face my father tore the mask!"

Professor Scotch was fairly staggered, but he quickly recovered, and swiftly said:

"My dear young lady, I assure you that you have made the greatest mistake of your life. I know this boy—I am his guardian. It is not possible that he is Black Harry, for——"

"Were you with him last night?"

"No. We were——"

"Don't talk to me, then! Black Harry or not, he shot my father!"

"But—but—why, he would not do such a thing!"

"He did!"

It seemed that nothing could shake her belief.

"Av yez plaze, miss," said Barney, lifting his hat, and bowing politely, "it's thot same b'y Oi have known a long toime. Oi went ter school with thot lad, an' a whoiter b'y nivver drew a breath. He'd foight fer ye till he died, av he didn't git killed, an' it's nivver would he shoot anybody at all, at all, onless it wur in silf-definse. Oi give ye me wurrud thot is th' truth, th' whole truth, an' nothing but th' truth."

The girl was unmoved.

"I have sworn to avenge my poor father!" she declared. "He shall not escape!"

"It is useless to talk here," said Frank. "She believes she is right, and her mind will not be changed till she sees the real Black Harry at my side. It must be that the fellow is my double, and so my life will be in peril till he is captured, and meets his just deserts. From this time on for me it is a fight for life and honor."

# CHAPTER V.

## HURRIED TO JAIL.

A t this moment another wild roar rose outside the station, telling that something had again aroused the mob:

Hank Kildare was in the doorway, blocking it with his gigantic form, his long-barreled revolvers holding the crowd at bay, while he hoarsely cried:

"You galoots know me! Ef yer crowd me, some o' yer will take his everlastin' dose o' lead!"

They dared not crowd him. He could hold them back at that point, but there were other ways of reaching the interior of the waiting-room, where the prisoner was.

"Ther back door!" howled a voice. "We kin git at him thet way!"

"Hear that?" fluttered Professor Scotch. "They're coming, Frank! We must get out before they get in that way! Quick!"

He caught hold of the boy, and started to urge him toward the rear door; but Lona Dawson placed herself squarely in their path, flinging up one hand.

"Stop!" she cried, her eyes flashing. "You cannot pass! You shall not escape!"

A look of admiration came into Frank's eyes, for she was very beautiful at that moment.

"As you will," he bowed, gallantly. "I may get my neck stretched by remaining, but your wish is law."

"Well, I like that!" roared the professor, in a manner that plainly indicated he did not like it.

"Av ye choose ter make a fool av yersilf, Frank, it's not yer friends thot will see ye do it in this case!" cried Barney.

The Irish lad grasped Frank by one arm, while the professor clutched the other, and they were about to rush him toward the door, for all of any opposition, when the door flew open with a bang, and a man pitched headlong into the room. This person carried a bundle, which burst open as he struck the floor, scattering its contents in all directions.

"Moses in der pulrushes!" exclaimed the nasal voice of Solomon Rosenbum, and the Jew sat up in the midst of the wreck. "Dat vas vat I call comin' in lifely, vid der accent on der lifely!"

"The dure!" shouted Barney. "They're coming round to get in thot way!"

The frightened station agent thrust his head out of an inner office, and said:

"The door can be braced. The brace is just behind it."

Not a moment was to be lost, for the mob was at the very door, and would be pouring into the station in a moment. Barney sprang for the heavy brace, but he would have been too late if it had not been for the singular Jew.

Solomon leaped to his feet, sprang for the door, and planted his foot with terrific force in the stomach of the first man who was trying to enter, hurling that individual back against those immediately behind.

"Good-tay!" cried the Jew. "Uf I don'd see you some more, vat vos der tifference!"

Slam! The door went to solidly. Bang! The bar went against it, being held in position by heavy cleats on both door and floor.

"Holdt der vort!" rasped Solomon, with great satisfaction. "Dot was very well tone. I didn't vant dose beople comin' und drampin' all ofer mine goots. Id vould haf ruint me."

The mob beat against the door, howling with baffled rage.

"Thot wur a narrow escape, Frankie, me b'y!" said Barney.

"That's what it was," admitted Frank, who realized that his chance for life would have been less than one in a thousand if the crowd had burst into the room.

"Vell, I don'd sharge nodding vor dat, uf you puy a goot pill uf goots vrom me," said the Jew.

"The window!" came from Professor Scotch. "They are about to come through the window!"

Crash! Jingle! Jangle! The window was smashed, and the mob was seen swarming toward it.

Suddenly, Solomon Rosenbum sprang toward the opening, a revolver in his hand.

"Holdt on, mine friendts!" he cried, waving the weapon. "Uf anypody dried to get in py dis vindow, he vill ged shot, vid der accent on der shot!"

"Begobs, thot is roight!" shouted Barney Mulloy, as he suddenly produced a "gun," and took his place at Solomon's side. "Kape off, me jools, av ye want ter kape whole skins!"

The mob hesitated. Thus it had been baffled at every turn, and the mad heat of the moment was beginning to subside. Still, it could be aroused again in a twinkling.

Hank Kildare alone could not have protected his prisoner from the crowd, but he had done all one man could possibly do. Now, of a sudden, he retreated into the station, closing and bolting the door.

"That," he said, with a breath of satisfaction, "so fur, everything is all right. An' now it is ter see ef——"

He was interrupted by pistol shots outside, and bullets began whistling in at the broken window.

With an exclamation of anger, the fearless sheriff flung his massive body into the window, roaring:

"Hold up thar, you critters! Don't you know anything a tall? Thar is ladies in hyar, an' yer might shoot 'em ef yer keep flingin' lead round so promiscuous like!"

"We want Black Harry!" yelled a voice.

"Wa-al, ye'll hev ter want!" returned the sheriff. "You galoots know me purty well, an' ye know I ain't in ther habit o' talkin' crooked. I tells yer right yar an' now thet ye can't hev Black Harry. I offered ther reward fer ther critter, an' I'm goin' ter hold him, you bet! He'll be lodged in jail, ur Canadian County will be minus a sheriff!"

It was plain that his words impressed them, but they were reluctant to give over the hope of lynching the boy prisoner.

"Look yere, Kildare," said a thin, wiry, iron-jawed man, who wore a huge sombrero and leather breeches, "I'm Bill Buckhorn, o' 'Rapahoe, an' thet's a place whar we don't 'low no critter like this yere Black Harry ter go waltzin' round more then sixteen brief second by ther clock. We ketches such cusses, an' then we takes 'em out an' shows 'em how ter do a jog on empty air. Over in 'Rapahoe we allows thet thar is ther way ter dispose o' sech cases, and I'm ready ter show you people o' Elreno ther purtiest way ter tie a runnin' knot in a hemp necktie. Whatever is ther use o' foolin' around an' dallyin' with ther law when it's right easy ter git rid o' critters like this yere Black Harry without no trouble a tall, an' make things lively in ther town at ther same time? Pass him out, sheriff, an' I'll agree not ter do ye ary bit o' damage!"

"Wa-al, you are kind!" returned Kildare, contemptuously. "You're mighty kind, an' I allows thet I 'preciates it. I reckons you galoots over in thet forsaken, 'way-back, never-heard-of hole called 'Rapahoe sets yerselves up fer a law unto ther rest o' Oklahoma an'

28

all other parts o' creation! You allows thar don't nobody else but you critters know what is right an' proper, an' so you has ther cheek ter come over hyar an' tell us what ter do! You even offers ter show me how ter tie a runnin' knot in a rope, an' I will admit thet I've tied more knots o' thet kind then you ever heard of! Take my advice, my gentle stranger frum 'Rapahoe, an' go get right off ther earth, afore something happens ter yer which yer won't like none whatever!"

This bit of sarcasm was appreciated by the assembled citizens of Elreno, and they raised a howl at Bill Buckhorn, scores of voices hurling derisive epithets at the lank stranger.

Buckhorn grew intensely angry, and he howled:

"You galoots make me sick! You're short on fer hawse sense, an' thet's plain enough!"

"Take a tumble!"

"Puckachee!"

"All right! All right!" cried the man from 'Rapahoe, waving his hands, each of which clutched a huge revolver. "You kin run yer blamed old town ter suit yerselves, an' I allows thet Black Harry fools yer all an' gits erway! I hopes he does, an' I draws out o' this yere game right now."

He thrust his revolvers into leather holsters made to receive them, and strode away, forcing a passage through the crowd, and pretending not to hear the derisive epithets hurled at him.

Hank Kildare smiled, with grim satisfaction.

"Thet wuz ther best thing could hev happened," he muttered. "It took their 'tention erway fer a minute, an' now it's likely I kin talk them inter reason."

He tried it, without delay. He urged them to disperse, promising that Black Harry should be lodged in Elreno jail, and properly tried for his life.

"This yar lynchin' is bad business," concluded the sheriff. "I will allow thet I hev taken a hand in more than one lynchin' party, but I'm derned 'shamed o' it. Law is law, an' no gang o' human critters has a right ter take ther law in their han's. I hev swore never ter let one o' my prisoners be lynched, ef I kin help it, an' I'll set 'em free, an' furnish 'em with guns ter fight fer their lives, afore I'll see 'em strung up by a mob. At ther same time, I'd ruther be shot then forced ter do such a thing."

Kildare was so well known that every one who heard him felt sure he was not "talking wind," that being something he never did.

There was muttering in the crowd. The worst passions of the

mob had been aroused, and now it hated to be robbed of its prey.

"Hank Kildare means whatever he says," declared more than one. "He'll fight ter hold Black Harry."

Some cursed Kildare, and that aroused the anger of the sheriff's friends, so it seemed at one time as if the mob would fall into a pitched battle among themselves.

"Let 'em fight," muttered the giant, who still held the broken window. "Ef they git at it, I'll find some way ter slip 'em and put my man inter ther jail."

But they did not fight. Kildare called on them to disperse, and a few went away; but a great crowd lingered in sullen silence outside the station, waiting and watching.

"They want ter git another look at Black Harry," muttered the sheriff, knitting his brows. "Ef they do thet, they're likely ter break loose again, like a lot o' wild tigers. How kin I make 'em disperse, so I kin kerry him ter ther jail?"

"I will appeal to them," said a musical voice at his elbow.

He turned, and saw Lona Dawson there.

"You?"

"Yes. It is possible they will listen to me."

"They mought. I'd clean forgot you wuz hyar. Go ahead an' try yer luck, little one."

He stepped aside, and she appeared in the window. The moment she was seen, all muttering ceased in the crowd, and every one gave her attention.

"Gentlemen," she began, speaking clearly and loud enough for all to hear, "you must confess that I have as much interest as any one here in seeing this youthful ruffian brought to justice. I do not wish to see him lynched, but I wish him to receive such punishment as the law may give him."

"Ther law is slow!" cried a voice.

"An' it often fails!" came from another direction.

"In this case there is no reason why it should fail, for there is proof enough to convict Black Harry. It will not fail."

"He may escape from jail."

"That is not likely. Now, for my sake, I ask you all to disperse— to allow the officers to take Black Harry to jail. If you do not disperse, I shall remain here, and I will protect the prisoner with my own body and my life, for I am determined that he shall be legally tried and properly punished."

There was a moment of silence, and then a voice shouted:

"Thar's stuff fer yer, pards! Ther leetle gal has clean grit, an' I'm fer doin' as she asks. Who's with me?"

"I am!" a hundred voices seemed to roar.

"Then come on. Good-by, leetle gal; we're goin'."

Every head was bared, and the crowd began to disperse with swiftness, so that, in a very few minutes, all had departed.

Then came the deputy sheriffs, with horses, and arrangements for conveying the prisoner to the jail were swiftly completed.

Frank had advised the professor and Barney not to be too out-spoken, for fear they might also be arrested. He advised them to keep quiet, but to work for him to the best of their ability, and lose no time.

A handshake, a hurried parting, and the boy was borne away to jail.

# CHAPTER VI.

## SOLOMON SHOWS HIS NERVE.

he jail at Elreno was a wooden building, hastily constructed in the feverish days of the early boom, with many weak points and few strong ones.

Not for long were prisoners confined there, as "justice" in the new Territory moved swiftly, and an arrest was quickly followed by a trial.

Hank Kildare and the guard moved swiftly with their prisoner, avoiding the most public streets, and taking the boy to the jail by a roundabout way.

It was well they did so, for, although the mob had dispersed, at the request of Miss Dawson, the street along which it was believed the sheriff would take Black Harry was thronged with citizens eager to get a square look at the boy outlaw, who had become famous within ten days.

It is possible that Frank might have been taken along that street without trouble, but it is much more likely that the sight of him would have aroused the mob once more, and brought about another attempt at lynching.

In fact, Bill Buckhorn, the man from 'Rapahoe, had gathered an interested knot of tough-looking citizens about him, and he was dilating on the "double derned foolishness" of wasting time over a person like Black Harry by taking him to jail and giving him a trial.

"Over in 'Rapahoe we hang 'em first an' try 'em arterward," boastingly declared the man in leather breeches. "We find that thar is ther simplest way o' doin' business. Ef we makes a mistake, an' gits ther wrong galoot, nobody ever kicks up much o' a row over it, fer we're naterally lively over thar, an' we must hev somethin' ter 'muse us 'bout so often.

"Now, ef we hed ketched this yere Black Harry—wa'al, say! Great cats! Does any critter hyar suspect thar'd been any monkey business with thet thar young gent? Wa'al, thar wouldn't—none whatever. Ef we couldn't found a tree handy, we'd hanged him ter ther corner o' a buildin', ur any old thing high enough ter keep his feet up off ther dirt.

"Hyar in Elreno, ye'll take ther varmint ter jail, an' it's ten ter one he'll break out afore twenty-four hours, arter which he'll thumb his nasal protuberance at yer, an' go cayvortin' 'round after ther same old style, seekin' whomsoever he kin sock a bullet inter. Then you'll hate yerself, an' wish ye'd tooken my advice ter hang ther whelp, sheriff or no sheriff. You hear me chirp!"

There were others who thought the same, and it was hinted that Hank Kildare might not be able to take his prisoner to the jail, after all.

Burchel Jones, the private detective, was in the crowd, and he hustled about, loudly proclaiming that he was the man who captured Black Harry. Bill Buckhorn heard him, stopped him, looked him over searchingly.

"Look hyar!" cried the man from 'Rapahoe. "Is it a straight trail ye're layin' fer us?"

"What do you mean by that?" asked the man with the foxy face, in a puzzled way.

"Dern a tenderfoot thet can't understand plain United States!" snorted Buckhorn. "Ther same is most disgustin', so says I! Ye've got ter talk like a Sunday-school sharp, ur else ther onery critters don't hitch ter yer meanin'. Wat I wants ter know, tenderfoot, is ef yer tells ther truth w'en yer says yer roped Black Harry."

Jones stiffened up, assuming an air of injured dignity.

"The truth! Why, I can't tell anything but the truth! It's an insult to hint that I tell anything but the truth!"

"W'at relation be you ter George?"

"George who?"

"Washington."

"Sir, this attempt at frivolity is unseemly! Why should it seem remarkable for me to capture Black Harry?"

"Ef a galoot with his reputation let an onery tenderfoot like you rope him, it brings him down in my estimation complete!"

"I took him by surprise. I clapped a loaded revolver to his head, and he could do nothing but put up his hands."

"Wa'al, you might ram a loaded cannon up ag'in my head, an' then I'd shoot yer six times afore you could pull ther trigger," boasted Buckhorn. "Black Harry ain't got no license ter live arter this, an' I thinks it's ther duty o' ther citizens o' this yere town ter git tergether an' put him out o' his misery."

"That ith wight," drawled a voice that seemed to give the man from 'Rapahoe an electric shock. "The w'etch ith verwy danger-wous, and I weally hope you will hang him wight away, don't yer know. It ith dweadful to think that the cwecher might get away and stop a twain that I wath on, and wob me of awl my money—it ith thimply dweadful!"

"Great cats!" howled Buckhorn, staring in amazement at the speaker. "Is thar ary galoot hyar kin name thet critter?"

"Uf anypody vill name id, I vill gif id do 'em!" cried a nasal voice, and Solomon Rosenbum, with his pack, newly bound up, was seen on the edge of the crowd, having just arrived.

"My name, thir, ith Cholly Gwayson De Smythe," haughtily de-clared the dude. "I do not apweciate youah inthulting manner, thir. I demand an apology, thir!"

"Apology!" howled Buckhorn, looking savage. "Of me?"

"Ye-ye-yeth, thir," faltered Cholly, shivering.

"Wa'al, I'll be derned!"

"Do you apologize, thir?"

"Ter a thing like you? No!"

"Then I'll—I'll——"

"What?"

"Thee you lataw, thir."

And the dude took to his heels, breaking from the crowd and running for dear life, literally tearing up the dust of the street in his frantic effort to get away in a hurry.

"Haw!" snorted Bill Buckhorn. "See ther varmint go! I reckon I'll hurry him up jest a little!"

Then the man from 'Rapahoe jerked out a big revolver, and sent three or four bullets whistling past Cholly's ears, nearly frighten-ing the poor fellow out of his clothes.

Buckhorn supplied the revolver with fresh cartridges, at the same time observing:

"Over in 'Rapahoe such a derned freak as thet thar would be a reg'ler snap fer ther boys. They'd hev more fun with him then a funeral. Somehow, this yere place seems dead slow, an' it makes me long ter go back whar thar is a little sport now an' then."

"Vell," said the Jew, with apparent honesty, "v'y don'd you go pack? Maype uf you sdop a vile, you don'd pe aple to do dat."

"Haw? What do you mean, Moses?"

"My name vas nod Moses."

"Wa'al, it oughter be, an' so I'll call yeh thet."

"All righd, Mouth; led her go."

"Wat's thet?" shouted Buckhorn, surprised. "Whatever did you call me jest then, I want ter know."

"Mouth."

"Mouth!"

"Dat vas righd."

"Thet ain't my name."

"Vell, id oughter peen; your mouth vas der piggest bart uf you."

Buckhorn literally staggered. He looked as if he doubted his ears had heard correctly, and then, noting that the crowd was beginning to laugh, he leaped into the air, cracking his heels together, and roaring:

"Whoop! Thet settles you, Moses! You'll hev a chance ter attend your own funeral ter-morre!"

The Jew quietly put down his pack, spat on his hands, and said:

"Shust come und see me, mine friendt, und I vill profe dat your mouth vas der piggest bart uf you."

"I ain't goin' ter touch yer with my hands," declared the man from 'Rapahoe, once more producing the long-barreled revolver; "but I'll shoot yer so full o' holes thet ye'll serve fer a milk-skimmer! Git down on yer marrerbones an' pray!"

"Look here, mine friendt," calmly said the Jew, as the crowd began to scatter to get out of the way of stray bullets, "uf you shood ad me, id vill profe dat you vas a plowhardt und a cowart. Uf you shood ad me, der beople uf dis blace vill haf a goot excuse to holdt a lynchings."

"Wa'al, I'm good fer this hull derned county! This town is too slow ter skeer me any ter mention. Git down!"

"Uf I don'd do dat?"

"I'll shoot yer legs out from under yer clean up ter ther knees!"

"Vell, then, I subbose I vill haf to—do this!" Solomon had seemed on the point of kneeling, but, instead of doing so, he ducked, leaped in swiftly beneath the leveled revolver, caught Buckhorn by the wrist, and wrenched the weapon from his hand, flinging it aside with the remark:

"I don'd vant to peen shot alretty, und, if you try dat again, you vill ged hurt pad, vid der accent on der pad!"

Buckhorn seemed to be stupefied, and then, uttering another roar, he lunged at the Jew, trying to grapple Solomon with his hands.

"I'll squeeze ther life out of yer!" snarled the ruffian.

"Oxcuse me uf I don'd lofe you vell enough to led you done that," said the Jew, nimbly skipping aside. "Your nose shows you vas a greadt trinker; shust dry my electric punch."

Crack! The knuckles of the Jew struck under the ear of the

man from 'Rapahoe. It was a beautiful blow, and Buckhorn was knocked over in a twinkling, striking heavily on his shoulder in the dust of the street.

The fall seemed to stun the man in leather breeches, but he soon sat up, and then, seeing Solomon waiting for him to rise, he asked:

"Whar is it?"

"Vere vas vat?"

"Ther club you struck me with."

"Righd here," said the Jew, holding up his clinched hand.

"Haw! Ye don't mean ter say you didn't hit me with a club, or something like a hunk o' quartz?"

"Dat vas der ding vat I hit you vid, mine friendt. Shust ged up, und I vill profe id py hitting you again."

"Say!"

"Vell?"

"I don't allow thet I'm as well as I might be, an' I ain't spoiling' fer trouble none whatever. I'm onter you. You're a perfessional pugilist in disguise. If you'll let me git up, I'll go right away and let you alone."

"Vell, ged up."

"You won't hit me when I do so?"

"Nod if you don'd tried some funny pusiness."

Buckhorn struggled to his feet, keeping a suspicious eye on Solomon all the while. He then picked up his revolver, but made no offer to use it, for the Jew was watching every movement, and he noted that Solomon had one hand in his pocket.

"A critter thet knows tricks like he does, might be able ter shoot 'thout drawin'," muttered the man from 'Rapahoe. "I don't allow it'd be healthy ter try a snap shot at him."

A roar of laughter broke from the spectators, as they saw the ruffian put the revolver back into its holster, and turn away, like a whipped puppy.

"Hayar, you mighty chief from 'Rapahoe," shouted a voice, "do yer find this yar town so dead slow as yer did? Don't yer 'low yer'd best go back ter 'Rapahoe, an' stay thar? Next time, we'll set ther dude tenderfoot on yer, an' he'll everlastin'ly chaw yer up!"

"How low hev ther mighty fallen!" murmured Buckhorn, as he continued to walk away.

# CHAPTER VII.

## IN JAIL.

reat was the disgust of the crowd when it was found that Hank Kildare had taken his prisoner to jail without passing along the main street of the town. It was declared a mean trick on Hank's part, and some excited fellows were for resenting it by breaking into the jail at once and bringing the boy out and "hangin' him up whar everybody could see him."

The ones who made this kind of talk had been "looking on the bug-juice when it was red," and they finally contented themselves by growling and taking another look.

In the meantime, Frank found himself confined in a cell, and he began to realize that he was in a very bad scrape.

Throughout all the excitement at the railroad station, he had remained cool and collected, but now, when he came to think the matter over, his anger rose swiftly, and he felt that the whole business was most outrageous.

Still, when he remembered everything, he did not wonder that the mob had longed to lynch him.

Black Harry was a youthful desperado of the worst sort. He had devastated, plundered, robbed, and murdered in a most infamous manner, his last act being the shooting of Robert Dawson, the Eastern banker.

And Lona Dawson, the banker's daughter, had looked straight into our hero's face and declared that he was Black Harry!

"It is a horrible mistake!" cried Frank, as he paced the cell into which he had been thrust. "She believed she spoke the truth. This young outlaw must resemble me. I cannot blame her."

The manacles chafed his wrists.

"Are they going to leave those things on me, now that they have me safe in jail?" he cried.

His door opened into the corridor, and he called to the guard, asking that the irons might be removed.

"I believe Hank has gone fer ther key," said the guard "He didn't take it from ther detective what put them irons on yer."

"Will they be removed when he returns with the key?"

"I reckon."

"Then I hope he will hurry. I am tired of carrying the things."

He turned back, to pace the cell once more.

"This is a flimsily-constructed building," he said. "It would be an easy thing to break in here and drag a prisoner out. I escaped death at the hands of the mob because I had friends at hand to fight for me, and because Hank Kildare is utterly fearless, and was determined to bring me here. But the whole town may become aroused, and to-night—— What if Robert Dawson should die!"

The thought fairly staggered him, for he knew the death of the wounded banker would again inflame the passions of the citizens, and a night raid might be made on the jail.

"They would stand a good show of forcing their way in here, and then it would be all up with me."

It was a terrible thing to stand in peril of such a death. Frank felt that he could not die thus; he would live to clear his honor.

But what could he do? He was helpless, and he could not fight for himself. Must he remain impassive, and let events go on as they might?

"I do not believe fortune has deserted me," he whispered. "I shall be given a chance to fight for myself."

It seemed long hours before the sheriff appeared, accompanied by Burchel Jones, the foxy-faced private detective.

"Has he been disarmed?" cautiously asked Jones, as he peered at the boy through the grating in the door.

"Yep," replied Kildare, shortly. "Do you think I'm in ther habit o' monkeying with ther prisoners yar?"

"H'm! Ha! No, no—of course not! But, you see, this fellow is dangerous—very dangerous. He is not to be trusted."

"Wa'al, he's been mild as milk sense he fell inter my hands."

"Trickery, my dear sir—base trickery! By the time you have handled so many desperate criminals as I have, you will see through them like glass."

Kildare grunted.

"Now," continued Jones, with the wisdom of an old owl, "mark the curl of his lip, and the bold, defiant stare of the eye. Mark the covert smile on that face, as if he were really laughing at us now. All those things are significant—mighty significant. You do not dream of the treachery hidden beneath that boyish exterior; but I, sir, can see by his eye that he had rather cut a throat than eat a square meal. The peculiar shape of his lips denote blood-thirstiness, and his nose, which seems rather finely formed to the casual observer, is the nose of a person utterly without conscience. His forehead indicates a certain order of intelligence, but this simply makes him all the more dangerous. He has brain power and force, and that explains why he has succeeded in becoming a leader of desperadoes. That chin is a hard, cruel feature, while the shape of his ears indicates an utter disregard for anything sweet and harmonious of sound, like music. That is an ear which finds more music in the shrieks of murdered victims than in anything else."

Frank literally staggered.

"Great Scott!" he gasped. "I never before dreamed that I was such a villainous-looking creature!"

Kildare began fitting a key to the lock of the door.

"Are you sure he is disarmed?" asked the private detective.

"Yep."

"Well, you are at liberty to do as you like, but I should not remove those irons. It would be far better to keep them on him."

"Why?"

"Well, you see—that is—hum!—ha!—such a creature cannot be held too fast. There is no telling what he is liable to do."

Kildare gave a grunt of disgust, entered the cell, and removed the manacles from Frank's wrists.

"Thank you," said the boy, gratefully. "They were beginning to get irksome. I am glad to get them off."

"Ther man what calls hisself Professor Scotch has dispatched East fer yer," said the sheriff. "He sw'ars thar has been a mistake made, an' he kin prove you are what ye claim, an' not Black Harry at all."

"That can be easily proven," smiled Frank. "All we want is a little time."

"Trickery! Trickery!" cried Jones from the corridor. "They will do their best to get his neck out of the noose; but he is Black Harry, and I shall receive the reward for his capture."

"You'll receive it when it is proved thet he is Black Harry, so don't yer worry," growled Kildare, who had taken a strong dislike to the foxy-faced detective.

"He has been identified by Miss Dawson; that is proof enough."

To this Kildare said nothing; but he spoke again to the boy:

"Make yerself as easy as yer kin, an' be shore ye'll hev a fair show from Hank Kildare. Thar's talk in town about lynchin', but they don't take yer out o' hyar so long as I kin handle a shootin' iron. I'm goin' ter stay hyar ter-night, an' I'll be reddy fer 'em ef they come."

"Thank you again," said Frank, sincerely. "All I ask is a square deal and a fair show. I know it looks black against me just now, but I'll clear my honor."

Burchel Jones laughed, sneeringly.

Kildare said nothing more, but left the cell, locking the door behind him.

At noon Frank was brought an assortment of food that made his eye bulge. He asked if that was the regular fare in the jail, and was told it had been sent in by his friends.

"The professor and Barney, God bless them! I wonder why they have left me alone so long? But I know they are working for me."

It was late in the afternoon when Barney appeared, and was admitted to the cell. The Irish lad gave Frank's hand a warm squeeze, and cried:

"It's Satan's own scrape, me lad; but we'll get ye out av it if th' spalpanes will let yez alone ter-noight. Av they joomp yez, we'll be here ter foight ter ther last gasp."

"I know you will, Barney!" said Frank, with deep feeling. "You are my friend through thick and thin. But, say, do you think there is much danger of lynchers to-night?"

"Av Mishter Dawson dies, there will be danger enough, and, at last reports it wur said he could not live more than two ur thray hours."

# CHAPTER VIII.

## THE LYNCHERS.

When Barney returned to the hotel he found Professor Scotch in a very agitated and anxious mood.

"This is terrible—terrible!" fluttered the little man, wringing his hands. "How can we save him?"

"Phwat has happened now, profissor?" asked Barney, anxiously.

"I have received no reply to my telegrams."

"Kape aisy; the reploies may come lather on."

"And they may not till it is too late. I leaned out of the window a short time ago, and I heard a crowd talking in the street below. That horrible ruffian, Bill Buckhorn, was with them, and he was telling them how to make an attack on the jail. Some of the crowd laughed, and said Hank Kildare had been very slick about getting his prisoner under cover, but he would not be able to keep him long after night came."

"Av they make an attack on th' jail, it's oursilves as should be theer to foight fer Frankie," said the Irish lad, seriously.

"Fight!" roared Scotch, in his big, hoarse voice. "Why, I can't fight, and you know it! I can't fight so much as an old woman! I am too nervous—too excitable."

"Arrah! Oi think we have fergot how ye cowed Colonel La Salle Vallier, th' champion foire-ater av New Orleans."

"No, I have not forgotten that; but I was mad, aroused, excited at the time—I had completely forgotten myself."

"Forget yersilf now, profissor."

"I can't! I can't! It's no use! I would be in the way if I went to the jail. I shall stay away."

The professor was an exceedingly timid man, as Barney very well knew, so he did not add to his agitation by telling him that, while returning from the jail, he had heard it hinted that the boy prisoner had two friends in the hotel who might be treated to a "dose of hemp necktie."

The professor, however, suspected the truth, and he kept in his room. Danger could not keep Barney there, and, having reported the result of his conversation with Frank, he went out to learn what was going on.

Two persons very much in evidence since the arrival of the train were the Jew and the dude. The Jew had a way of insinuating himself into the midst of any little knot that was gathered aside from the general throng, and, if they were speaking guardedly, he seemed sure to hear what they were saying and enter into the conversation. As a rule, this was not what would be called a "healthy" thing to do in such a place and on such an occasion; but the report of Solomon's encounter with Bill Buckhorn, the Man from 'Rapahoe, had been circulated freely, and the Jew was tolerated for what he had done.

While he appeared very curious to hear anything that seemed like private conversation, the Jew did not neglect any opportunity to transact business, and he made so many trades during the day that the size of his pack materially decreased.

The dude seemed scarcely less curious than the Jew. He had a way of listening with his eyes and mouth wide open, but he lost no time in getting out of the way if ordered to do so. For all of his curiosity, he seemed very timid.

The day passed, and night came. Still Professor Scotch had received no answers to his telegrams.

Shortly after nine o'clock that evening, the report spread rapidly that Robert Dawson, the Eastern banker, was dead.

Immediately there was a swift and silent stirring of men—a significant movement.

"Thot manes throuble!" was Barney Mulloy's mental exclamation. "Th' sheriff should know av it."

The Irish lad believed that he was watched, but he hurried to the professor's room, telling him to lock the door and keep within till the storm was over, and then he slipped out of the hotel.

Barney did not hurry toward the jail at once, but he took a roundabout course, dodging and doubling, to bother any one who might attempt to follow him.

Finally, having doubled on his own course, he struck out for the jail.

There was a moon, but it was obscured at times by drifting clouds, something rather unusual in that part of the country for a night that was not stormy, and did not threaten to become so.

Coming suddenly to the main street of the town, which led straight from the hotel to the jail, Barney paused and listened.

He heard a sound that caused his heart to beat faster, while he held his breath and strained his ears.

Tramp! tramp! tramp! It was the swift and steady rush of many feet.

There was no sound of voices, but the crouching boy knew a body of men was approaching.

Barney drew back, concealing himself as well as he could, and waited.

Nearer and nearer came the sound.

A cloud passed from the face of the moon, and then the watching boy saw a band of men rushing swiftly past his place of concealment.

The men were masked, and all were armed.

They were moving straight toward the jail.

"Th' lynchers!" panted Barney. "They are afther Frankie! Oi must get to th' joail ahead av thim!"

He ran back along the side street till he came to another that led in the same direction as the one along which the mob was rushing. Turning toward the jail, he ran as he had never ran before in all his life.

On the front door of the jail was a push-button that connected by a wire with a gong within the building. A push on that button set the gong to clamoring loudly.

"Rattle-ty-clang-clang! rattle-ty-clang!

"Wa'al, what's thet mean?" growled Hank Kildare, as he leaped up from the couch on which he had been reclining lazily. "What derned fool is punchin' away at thet thar button like he hed gone clean daft! Hyar ther critter ring!"

Kildare looked at his revolvers, then picked up a short-barreled shotgun, and went out into the corridor that led to the door. Reaching the door, he shot open a small panel and shouted:

"Whatever do yer think ye're doin' out thar? Will yer stop thet thar racket, ur shall I guv yer a dost out o' this yar gun!"

"Mr. Kildare, is thot yersilf?" panted a voice, which the sheriff had heard before, and which he immediately recognized.

"Wa'al, 'tain't nobody else."

"Will yes be afther lettin' me in?"

"What's ther matter?"

"Th' lynchers are comin'!"

Kildare peered out, and the moon, which did not happen to be hidden at that moment, showed him the boy who stood alone at the door.

Clank, clank, clank!—the sheriff shot back the bolts which held

43

the door, open it swung a bit, out shot his arm, and his fingers closed on Barney Mulloy's shoulder.

Snap—the boy was jerked into the jail. Slam—the door closed, and the bolts shot back into place.

"Howly shmoke!" gasped Barney. "Is it all togither Oi am, ur be Oi in paces?"

"Ye're hyar," came in a growl from the sheriff's throat. "Now tell me w'at yer mean by wakin' me an' kickin' up all this yar row."

"Th' lynchers are comin'."

"How do yer know?"

"Oi saw thim. Less than thray minutes ago."

"Where?"

"Back a short pace."

"How many of them?"

"I didn't count, but it's a clane hundred, sure."

Kildare asked Barney several more questions, and he was satisfied that the boy spoke the truth.

The deputy sheriff had slept in the jail that night, and, together with the guard, he was now at hand.

"Look out fer this yar boy," directed Kildare. "One o' yer git ther hose ready. I'm goin' ter try my new arrangement fer repellin' an attack."

He rushed away.

The deputy sheriff, whose name was Gilson, opened a small square door in the wall of the corridor, and dragged forth a coil of hose.

"Pwhat are ye goin' ter do with thot?" asked Barney, in surprise.

"Wait, an' ye'll see," was the reply.

Then the deputy spoke to the guard.

"Tyler, be ready ter let ther prisoner loose if the mob breaks in an' gits past me. You kin tell by watchin'. You know it's Hank's order thet ther cell be opened an' ther poor feller give a chance ter fight fer his life."

"Where is he?" palpitated Barney. "Oi'll shtand by him till he doies!"

"Ye kin do better by stayin' hyar," declared the deputy. "Ye may be needed."

Bang! bang! bang!

The lynchers had arrived, and they were hammering on the door. The gong began to clang wildly.

"Open this door!"

"Why don't Hank turn on ther water up above?" came anxiously from the lips of the deputy. "Kin it be thet his tank on ther roof has leaked dry? Ef so, his new scheme fer repellin' an attackin' party won't work very well."

"Open this door!" shouted a commanding voice outside.

The deputy sprang to the small panel and flung it open.

"What d'yer want yere?" he demanded.

"We want to come in," was the answer.

"Wa'al, yer can't."

"We'll agree to stay out on one condition. If you will pass out something, we'll agree not to break in."

"What's ther something?"

"Black Harry."

"I reckoned so."

"Will you give him up?"

"No."

"Then we shall break down the door, and I warn you that it will be very unfortunate if any of us is injured. It might bring about the lynching of other parties besides Black Harry."

"Wa'al, I warn yer ter keep away from yere. We're goin' ter defend ther prisoner regardless, an' somebody's bound ter git hurt."

"For the last time, will you open?"

"No."

"Down with the door!"

Crash! crash!—the assault on the door began.

# CHAPTER IX.

## THE ASSAULT ON THE JAIL.

hy don't Hank put on ther water?" groaned the deputy sheriff. "Et'll be too late in a minute!"

Crash! crash! The assailants were using a heavy battering ram, and the door was beginning to give.

"Oi'm afraid it's all up with poor Frankie!" gasped Barney.

A wild yell came from the mad mob at the door.

"Death to Black Harry!"

Bang—splinter—crash! The door was breaking, and the battering-ram was being driven against it with renewed force.

There was one last great shock, and down went the door before the assault.

"No water yet!" cried Gilson. "Now it is too late!"

He flung down the hose, taking to his heels before the gang of masked men that swarmed into the doorway.

Barney Mulloy heard a hissing noise, and then he leaped forward and caught up the nozzle of the hose. He turned the large stop-cock, and a bar of water shot out, striking the leader of the lynchers in the neck, and hurling him, gasping and stunned, back into the arms of those behind.

"Hurro!" trumpeted the Irish lad, in delight, his blood aroused. "Come on, an' git washed off th' face av th' earth!"

This method of defense proved unpleasantly surprising to the attacking party. The stream of water swept men off their feet and flung them, half-drowned, back from the doorway into the night. In less than half a minute Barney had cleared the doorway.

"Hurro!" he shouted, once more. "This is th' kind av sport! We'll howld th' fort till th' last drop av warther is gone!"

There was a lull, and Hank Kildare came panting to the side of the lad with the hose. When he saw the broken door an exclamation of dismay came from the lips of the sheriff.

"Something wuz ther matter, so I couldn't turn ther water on," he said. "An' now they've got ther door down!"

"But Oi bate 'em off!" shouted the Irish lad, triumphantly.

"They'll come in when ther water fails."

Barney had not thought of that, and his feeling of triumph turned to anxiety and dismay.

"Pwhat kin we do?"

"Where is Gilson?"

"Th' spalpane run whin the dure wur broke."

"We might fight, but what if we did shoot down a few o' ther critters? It w'u'dn't stop 'em, an' we'd hev killed somebody. Stay hyar—hold 'em back long as yer kin."

"Pwhat are ye goin' ter do?"

"Git ther prisoner up onter ther roof. Mebbe we kin hold 'em back from gittin' up thar."

"All roight. Oi'll do me bist here."

Kildare ran back along the corridor and disappeared.

Of a sudden rocks began to whistle about Barney's head, and then one struck him, knocking him down. The nozzle of the hose fell from his hands, and he lay prone and motionless on the floor.

Wild yells of savage delight broke from the mob.

Then, with a clatter of hoofs, a band of masked horsemen came tearing down the street, whirled into the open space before the jail, and began shooting into the mob. The horsemen were dressed in black, and every man was masked.

"It's Black Harry's Braves!" screamed a voice that was full of fear.

Twenty voices took up the cry, and the mob, utterly demoralized, broke and ran in all directions.

Some of the masked horsemen sprang from their animals and dashed into the jail, springing over the prostrate body of the unconscious Irish lad.

Kildare was removing Frank from his cell when those masked men came upon them. In a moment the boy had been torn from the sheriff, and the men whirled him away.

Out of the jail rushed Black Harry's Braves, the boy was placed astride a horse, and away they went, with him in their midst.

Frank had believed them lynchers, and he thought them lynchers as they bore him away.

"It's all up with me," he mentally said.

But his hands were free, and he was watching for an opportunity to escape. He meant to make one more effort for life, if given an opportunity.

Through the town tore the wild horsemen, yelling like so many fiends, shooting to the right and left.

Out of Elreno they rode, and then the man on the right of Frank leaned toward the boy, saying:

"We came just in time, chief. If we'd been ten minutes later, the lynchers would have had you sure."

"The lynchers?" gasped the bewildered boy. "Why, you——"

"They had the door down when we reached the jail, but a dozen shots set them scattering."

"But—but—I don't understand."

"We didn't mean to strike before midnight, but Benson brought word that they were liable to lynch you, and so we lost no time in getting here. We rode twenty miles like we were racing with an express train. You must allow we did a good job this time, chief."

"Chief? Why I——"

Frank stopped short, choking the words back. At last he realized who these men were.

They were Black Harry's Braves, and they believed him to be Black Harry!

He reeled upon the horse he bestrode.

"What's the matter?" asked the man, quickly. "Are you hurt any way?"

"No."

The boy's voice was hoarse and unnatural.

"What can I do?" he thought. "How long will it be before they discover their mistake? I must keep up the deception, and I may find an opportunity to escape."

In a moment he had recovered his composure. As old readers know, Frank was a boy of nerve, and he began to feel very well satisfied with the situation.

"I have escaped lynching," he thought, "and these men believe me their leader. I am out of jail and now I shall be given a chance to fight for my life and honor. In order to prove my own innocence, I must capture Black Harry. This may lead me to the opportunity."

But for one thing his heart would have been filled with exultation. That one thing was the memory of Barney Mulloy, whom he had seen lying prone and motionless just within the broken door of the jail. Had they killed his faithful friend?

He feared the Irish lad had met death while trying to hold back the lynchers.

The outlaws did not seem to fear pursuit, and they slackened their pace somewhat as soon as they were out of town.

"Where shall we go, chief?" asked one.

Frank was at a loss to answer, for he knew that a slip might be-

48

tray him, and he was determined to be on his guard all the time. His hesitation was observed, and the man said:

"I reckon it will be safe to return to Cade's Canyon for a while."

"I reckon so," said Frank. "We'll go there."

"I warned you that you would make a mistake if you ventured into Elreno," said the talkative outlaw, "but you were determined to have another look at that girl, and so you took chances. Girls have caused more trouble in this world than everything else combined."

"That's right," admitted Frank, who was wondering what girl the fellow meant.

"Did you see her?" asked the man, with a sly chuckle.

"Oh, yes, of course."

"Ha, ha! I like the way you say that, chief. No offense, but Benson said you saw her in the railway station as soon as you landed in Elreno."

Now Frank knew that Lona Dawson was meant.

"Yes," he said, "she was there, and she informed the public in general that she had seen me before."

"I don't suppose you will bother with her any more, and so we'll move on as soon as possible, and get out of this part of the country? It's getting right hot here."

"It is all of that," admitted Frank; "but I am not for running away, as if we were scared out."

"Well, you know our original plan."

"Certainly."

Frank spoke as if he knew it well enough, but he was wondering what it could be. However, the man soon explained.

"We are to carry the expedition through into Indian Territory, and disband when the Arkansas line is reached. Then we can scatter and defy pursuit, and we can come together at Ochiltree, in the Panhandle, at the time set."

Frank felt like thanking the fellow for the information.

"That's right," nodded the boy, speaking carefully; "but this little affair has made me rather mad, and I don't feel like running away so very fast."

"Especially from the girl."

"Hang the girl!"

Frank felt that it would not do to allow the fellow to become so familiar.

"You didn't talk that way after seeing her last night. Why, you were sorry we didn't carry her off when we left the train."

"Oh, well, a fellow has a right to change his mind. I have seen her by daylight."

"And she didn't look so well?"

"Hardly."

"Still, she is something of a daisy."

"She'll do; but I can't waste my time with her. There are others."

"Now you're beginning to talk right, chief. The boys felt a little doubtful of you when you went racing off after that girl, and they will be mightily relieved to know you have come to your senses."

Frank grunted, but spoke no word. During the entire ride, he talked as little as possible, but he kept his ears open.

# CHAPTER X.

## IN CADE'S CANYON.

The moon had swung far down to the west when the outlaws entered Cade's Canyon amid the mountains and finally reached an old hut, where they halted.

"You must be rather pegged, chief," said one of the men, addressing Frank.

"Well, I am not feeling too frisky," said the boy. "I didn't sleep much in Elreno jail, for I wanted to be wideawake when the lynchers came."

The men had removed their masks, but their faces were shaded by wide-brimmed hats, and Frank was not able to study their features. However, he had heard the voices of several, and he felt sure he would not forget them.

He was not going to be in a hurry about escaping. There was plenty of time, and he was beginning to believe that he must be the perfect double of Black Harry, else why should these men be thus deceived?

He wondered if none of them would detect the difference when daylight came.

"If they do—well, I can't be worse off than I was in Elreno jail. I'll have weapons, and I can fight. I may be able to make it hot for them before they down me."

Frank was reckless, and he felt a strange delight in the adventure through which he was passing. Somehow, now that he had escaped being lynched, he believed he would be successful in bringing Black Harry to book and proving his own innocence.

Frank's first care was to obtain some revolvers, and he was soon in possession of a pair of fine weapons. With these loaded and ready to his hand, he breathed easier.

Of course he had no idea of sleeping, but he entered the hut and looked the place over.

Morning was not far away, and the time soon passed, while

Frank pretended to sleep. At daybreak he was astir, and looking the place over.

The cabin was built in a strange spot, standing close to the verge of a chasm that opened down into the lower depths of the canyon, through which ran a stream of water.

Dan Cade, the man who had built the cabin there, was said to have been crazy. He had lived there years before the opening of Oklahoma to settlement, and had died there in that wild gorge. His only friends were the Indians, as he hated and mistrusted his own race.

It had often been remarked by those who passed through the canyon that no man in his right mind would have built a cabin in such a place. It looked as if the building was crouching on the verge of the chasm, preparing to spring headlong into the creek below.

Here the outlaws had camped.

Frank found a flight of stairs that led to the cabin loft. They were shaky, but he ascended to investigate.

There was a square door, shaped like a window, at the back end of the cabin, and this the boy opened. He thrust his head out, and found he was looking down the face of the bluff straight into the stream far below.

The light that shone into the loft revealed, to the boy's surprise and wonder, a coil of rope. He examined this, and found a stout clasp-hook at one end. The other end of the rope was made fast to a rafter.

For some time Frank wondered to what use old Cade had put the rope, but it came to him at last.

"With this he drew his water from the stream down there."

This seemed evident, as there was no other apparent means of procuring water.

The outlaws slept heavily, apparently fatigued by their exertions of the night. They had left sentinels in both directions, up and down the canyon, so that they could not be taken by surprise should they be followed by enemies.

The sun had not risen when Frank went forth into the morning air.

The horses were tethered near the cabin, and a half-blood Indian was watching them. As Frank approached, the half-blood peered out from beneath the blanket, which was drawn up over his head. The boy saw the fellow's beady eyes regarding him, and then the blanket was drawn closer, indicating that the Indian was satisfied.

Once more Frank thought that he must be the perfect counterpart of Black Harry, else he would arouse the suspicion of the fellow who owned those eyes.

Frank believed it would be an easy thing to mount one of the horses and ride away, as if he was going a short distance. He believed he could do so without being challenged or questioned, and the desire to attempt it was almost ungovernable.

Then came another thought.

Where could he go?

Surely he could not return to Elreno, for, now that he had been carried away by Black Harry's Braves, he was branded in that town as the youthful outlaw beyond the shadow of a doubt.

He did not know which way to turn, and the thought that his situation was most remarkable forced itself upon him. If he remained among the outlaws, they were liable to discover how they had been fooled, and that would make them furious. If he escaped and hastened to any of the nearby towns, it was pretty certain that he would be taken for Black Harry and lynched.

"This is a real jolly scrape!" thought the boy, ruefully. "What can I do?"

Well might he ask himself the question.

He walked a short distance down the canyon, and thought it over. The impulse was on him to get away as soon as possible, but his sober judgment told him that he would leap from the frying-pan into the fire.

Frank did not care to be lynched. He seemed helpless for the time. Although he longed to fight for his honor, he was unable to strike a blow.

The result of his walk was a determination to stay with the outlaws and keep up the deception as long as he could.

Black Harry himself must appear sooner or later, and Frank longed to see the young rascal whom he so much resembled.

Most boys would have improved the opportunity to get away, but Frank was not built of ordinary material, and it was like him to do the unexpected.

He strolled back to the cabin, seeming quite at his ease.

It was not far from sunrise, and the men began to stir. Several of them came out of the hut, and a fire was built.

Of a sudden, from far up the canyon, came the musical blast of a bugle, causing the outlaws to start and look at each other in surprise.

They listened, and it was repeated.

One of the men turned sharply on Frank, hoarsely crying:

"What does that mean?"

"I don't know," replied the boy, at the same time feeling for his revolvers, with the idea that there was trouble on hand.

"It is your signal!" burst from the man's lips. "And that means trickery! There is something wrong!"

"You're right!" cried several voices.

More of the braves came running out of the cabin, there was a hustling for arms, and the men prepared for trouble.

"My signal?" repeated Frank, to himself. "By that he must mean it is the signal of Black Harry! He is coming!"

Frank felt the blood tingling in his veins.

Black Harry was coming!

"Now," muttered Frank, "I shall have a chance to strike a blow for myself! Let Black Harry come on!"

# CHAPTER XI.

## BLACK HARRY APPEARS.

There was a clatter of hoofs, and a doubly burdened horse swept into view, bearing straight down upon the Braves, who were waiting as if ready to fight or take to flight.

The horse was foam-flecked, and it was plain he had been driven to the limit of his endurance.

The person who handled the reins was a youthful chap, and, as he came nearer, Frank gasped with surprise.

"Cholly Grayson De Smythe, the dude! Is it possible?"

In his arms, held upon the horse, was a bundle, like a human form, wrapped in a blanket.

The outlaws looked for a posse of armed men to follow the boyish horseman, but he was not followed, and he did not hesitate or turn back when he saw the party awaiting him.

Straight down upon them he rode, and Frank drew aside, shielding himself behind one of the men.

"It can't be possible!" muttered Frank. "It's ridiculous!"

Straight down upon the desperadoes rode the dude, seeming utterly fearless.

"Halt, thar!" cried one of the men, leveling a rifle at the young horseman. "Hold up, ur chaw lead!"

The youth gave a surge that flung the horse upon its haunches.

"Steady Bolivar!" his voice rang out. "Would you shoot me?"

"Who be you?"

"Don't you know me? Ha, ha, ha! Well, I do not wonder. I'll look different when I peel this mustache and wash off my make-up. I have her! See here, boys!"

The blanket was flung back, and the face of Lona Dawson, the banker's daughter, was revealed!

The girl was not unconscious, and she suddenly squirmed from the grasp of her captor, slipped from the horse, and ran into the midst of the outlaws, crying:

"Save me! Protect me!"

"Stop her, boys!" laughed the youth on the horse. "Don't let her get away. I've had trouble enough, and taken risk enough to get her."

"Wa-al, who be you?" roared one of the band.

"Who am I? Look here; do you know this sign?"

He made a swift motion with his hand, and nearly every man cried:

"The chief's sign! But you are not the chief! He is here with us! You are an impostor!"

"Am I? Look!"

He tore off a false wig, jerked away a false mustache, took a vial from his pocket, turned some of its contents in his hand, and seemed to sweep the make-up from his face.

The result was a wonderful transformation, and the face revealed was almost exactly like that of Frank Merriwell.

The men stared in bewildered astonishment.

"It is the chief!" gurgled one of them.

"Of course I am," laughed the unmasked youth. "You wasted your time in carrying off that other fellow who looks like me. Why didn't you leave him to be lynched? Then the fools would have thought they had put Black Harry out of the way."

"The other fellow?" repeated more than one of the men. "Who is the other fellow?"

"He is the fellow who looks like me," laughed Black Harry, for the new arrival was the boy chief of the marauders.

In the meantime, while this unmasking was taking place Frank had not been idle. He had longed to meet Black Harry face to face, but now he realized that his situation was perilous in the extreme. He must act at once.

But the sight of the captive girl and her appeal for aid had bestirred all the chivalry of his nature. He longed to do something to save her.

Swiftly moving near her, he suddenly caught her up, swung her over his shoulder, and, with her held thus, regardless of the shriek of terror that broke from her lips, he dashed straight for the open door of the hut.

Cries of amazement broke from the lips of the outlaws.

"There he goes!" shouted Black Harry. "That is the fellow who looks like me, and he has the girl! After him!"

The men leaped in pursuit.

Into the hut bounded Frank, and the door went to with a slam.

The foremost man, who flung himself against it, found it had been fastened.

"Well, we have him fast," said Black Harry, easily. "He can't get away in a thousand years. We'll dig him out at our convenience."

The men now gathered round their boy chief, eager to hear his explanation. It was difficult for them to realize that they had been deceived—that the boy they rescued from the lynchers at Elreno jail was not their leader.

"I was not fool enough to go into Elreno without disguising myself," said Harry. "I knew I should be recognized if I did. I fixed myself up in the outfit I just threw off, and, with this English tourist rig and a sissy lisp, I succeeded in deceiving everybody.

"You may imagine how surprised I was when I saw this other fellow, who is nearly my perfect double. He took the train at Oklahoma City, and I sat directly behind him. I was there when the private detective, Burchel Jones, who fancies he is so shrewd, arrested him.

"If they had lynched him, I could have disappeared, and it would have been thought that Black Harry had gone up the flume. But you fellows thought that I was in the scrape, and you came round in time to save him.

"I watched my opportunity to scoop the girl, and I have brought her here, although I was hotly pursued for a time, and I did not know but I'd have to drop her and get away alone. I succeeded in fooling the pursuers, and I arrived here at last.

"My double and the girl for whom I have risked so much are in that hut. I propose to break down the door and go in."

A wild shout came from the men. They were furious to think they had been so wonderfully deceived.

"Down with the door!"

"Drag him out!"

"Shoot him!"

With a hoarse roar of rage the Braves rushed toward the cabin, and flung themselves against the door, which went down with a crash, letting them into the hut.

# CHAPTER XII.

## A CHANCE IN A THOUSAND.

**F**rank, with his usual daring and gallantry, had resolved to make an effort to save the unfortunate girl—to rescue her from the clutch of Black Harry.

Having determined on such an attempt, he lost no time in catching her up and dashing into the hut with her in his arms.

Dropping her upon her feet, he whirled, slammed the door shut, found the wooden bar with which old Cade had made it fast, dropped the bar into its socket, and cried:

"Hurrah for us! This is the first step to freedom!"

Turning, he found the girl was leaning against the wall, staring at him in a wondering way, but without fear being expressed on her handsome face.

"I trust you are quite unharmed, Miss Dawson?" he said, swiftly. "My unsavory double has——"

"He has not harmed me," she broke in, swiftly, "but I feel that I have done you a harm I can never repair."

"Nonsense! How have you harmed me?"

"By declaring that you were the one who shot my father."

"You believed it when you said so, and that——"

"Yes, I believed it, but that is nothing that will lessen the injury I did you. And to think of the terrible peril in which I placed you! Then, when it was reported that father was dead, they were determined to lynch you."

"And your father is not dead?"

"He was not when I last saw him, and the doctor said he might come out all right."

"That is indeed fortunate."

"I heard them crying that he was dead, I saw them preparing to make an assault on the jail, and I left father's side to stop them if I could."

"Brave girl!"

"Then it was that I fell into the hands of this wretch who brought me here—the real Black Harry. He was waiting for an opportunity to capture me—he told me so. He told me how I had imperiled the life of one who was innocent, and he laughed at my horror and remorse. He is a heartless creature!"

"He seems to be all of that."

"And you have placed your life in greater peril for me—you did so after what I did to you! Why should you do such a thing?"

"Why, Miss Dawson, you were not to blame for thinking me Black Harry. The fellow is my double, and I ought not to have a double. Do you suppose I would think of leaving you in his power if there was any possible way for me to save you?"

"You are a noble fellow! But you cannot save me—you cannot escape yourself! They will soon break in here, and then——"

Frank was listening at the door, and he heard Black Harry complete his explanation to his Braves, heard their wild cries, and knew they were going to charge on the door.

"It will not stand before them!"

He looked around and saw the stairs.

"Up!" he cried to the girl. "Don't lose a moment!"

He motioned toward the stairs, and she ran toward them, hearing the roar that came from the outlaws as they made the rush for the cabin.

"Come!" she panted, looking over her shoulder, and seeing Frank with a revolver in either hand. "Don't stay there! They will kill you!"

"Up!" he shouted again. "I will follow!"

She sprang up the stairs, which creaked and swayed beneath her.

There was a great shock, and the cabin seemed to totter on the brink of the chasm. Then the door fell, and the ruffians swarmed into the cabin.

Frank Merriwell was right behind the girl, and he seemed to lift her and fling her into the loft.

"There they go!" rang the voice of the real Black Harry. "Up the stairs!"

"This is no time for talk!" cried Frank, as he crouched at the head of the flight, his teeth set, and the light of desperation in his eyes.

The braves came rushing up the stairs, and the boy above thrust out both hands, each of which held a revolver.

Frank fired four shots, and the smoke shut out the faces of the fierce rascals on the stairs. He heard cries of pain and the sound of falling bodies.

"I didn't waste my bullets," came grimly from his lips.

But what could he do now? He had repulsed them for the time, but they were in the cabin, and it would not be for long that he could keep them back. They would soon find a way to reach him.

He leaped to the swinging window and flung it open, thrusting the revolvers lightly into the side pockets of the coat he wore. He looked down into the depths of the chasm, through which ran the stream of water.

"It is a long distance down there," came hoarsely from the lad's lips. "I will try it! It is our last hope."

With a bound, he caught up the coil of rope, then he rushed to the window and flung it out. As one end was made fast to a rafter, it hung dangling from the window.

Frank looked out, and he saw that the rope reached to the stream of water.

At the same time, he heard Black Harry calling on his braves to follow him up the stairs.

"Come!" said Frank, hurrying to the side of the girl, and grasping her arm. "There is one chance in a thousand that we may do the trick and escape alive. We'll make a try for that chance."

She did not question him, she did not hold back, but she bravely trusted everything to his judgment.

Frank passed through the window in advance. He twisted the rope around one leg, and he secured a good hold on it with his hands. Then he said to the girl:

"Be lively now! Get through the window, put your arms about my neck, cling for your life, and trust to Frank Merriwell and Providence."

She did so, and they were soon descending the rope.

Frank went down, hand under hand, as he did not dare slide at first, knowing that his hands would be torn and bleeding, and that he must lose his hold before the bottom was reached. With the twist about his leg to aid him, he managed to sustain himself and his living burden very well.

The girl whispered in his ear:

"Courage! You are the noblest fellow I ever saw—the greatest hero in the whole wide world!"

He made no reply, for his teeth were set, and he was mentally praying for strength and time.

Down they went—down, down. And then, when nearly half the distance had been covered, a shout came from above.

"Here they are! Ten thousand fiends! They shall not get away alive!"

It was the voice of Black Harry himself.

"Oh, for a little more time!" panted Frank.

But no more time was to be given him. He heard the voice of the boy outlaw crying:

"Look up here, Frank Merriwell—look up! I have a little trick to show you."

Frank looked upward, and he saw Black Harry leaning far out of the window. A knife glittered in the hand of the young desperado.

"I am going to cut the rope!" came down to the ears of the boy and girl. "Poor fools! Did you think to escape me! You will go down to your death in the creek!"

Frank clung with one hand to the rope, although the strain was terrible. With his other hand he drew one of the revolvers from his pocket, lifted it, took aim, fired.

The weapon spoke just as Black Harry slashed at the rope.

There was a shriek of pain, a human body shot out from the window, and, as it went whirling downward, the rope parted!

Then down shot Frank and Lona to fall into the stream. They struck where the water was quite deep, and they were unharmed, although the girl was unconscious when our hero bore her to solid ground.

As for Black Harry, he struck where some jagged rocks reared their heads from the water, and he lay there, in a huddled heap, and dead, forever past harming any living creature.

And yet, as was afterward discovered by examination, he had not been touched by the bullet which Frank had fired up at him. He had been startled by the shot, had lost his balance, and had fallen to his death.

Frank was trying to restore Lona to consciousness when he heard the rattle of rifle and revolver shots, the sound coming down faintly from above. Following it there was wild and continued cheering, and still more shooting.

"It sounds like a battle," thought the boy. "I believe the outlaws have been attacked."

He was right. For all that he fancied he had thrown his pursuers from the trail, Black Harry had been tracked to Cade's Canyon. The guard was captured while the assault on the hut was taking place, and then Hank Kildare, at the head of the trailers, swept down on the astonished braves.

The battle was short and sharp, and but few of the outlaws escaped. Some were killed, and some were captured.

One of the captured ruffians told them where to find Black Harry, Frank and the kidnaped girl.

Lariats were tied together, and a line was made long enough to reach the bottom of the chasm.

Lona Dawson was drawn up first, and then Frank tied the rope about the body of his double, permitting them to draw him to the top of the bluff. Frank came up last, and he found the men from Elreno in a rather dazed condition.

"Is thar two Black Harrys?" asked one, staring at the dead boy, and then at his living counterpart.

"Moses in der pulrushes!" groaned Solomon Rosenbum, who was on hand. "There vas only von, und he vas deat, vid der accent on der deat. Dat leds me oudt, und I don'd vas aple to take him pack East vor murter."

"Take him back East for murder?" questioned a man. "What do you mean by that."

"I mean that he is wanted in the East, and I have been tracking him for the last two months," said the supposed Jew, suddenly speaking without a trace of accent.

"Who are you?"

"I am Burchel Jones, a detective."

"Burchel Jones! Impossible! Jones was the fellow who arrested this boy for Black Harry."

"That fellow was not Burchel Jones; he is an impostor, and he was working for the reward offered for Black Harry's capture. If he is in Elreno when we get back there, I shall have a little settlement with him."

Then Lona Dawson, who had recovered, told them how bravely Frank had fought for her, and the boy suddenly found himself regarded as a hero by the very ones who had been fierce to lynch him a short time before.

"Hurro!" cried Barney Mulloy, who was on hand. "Oi knew ye'd come out at th' top av th' hape in th' ind, Frankie, be b'y!"

And the delighted Irish boy gave his friend a "bear's hug."

It was a triumphant party that returned to Elreno. Lona Dawson was restored to her wounded father, the body of Black Harry was placed on exhibition, and Frank was cheered and stared at by admiring eyes wherever he went.

The bogus detective heard what had happened in time to leave the place and avoid meeting the real Burchel Jones.

Robert Dawson did not die from his wound. He recovered in time, but, as he lay on his bed, with his daughter restored to him, he held out a hand to Frank, who had been summoned to that room, saying, fervently:

"God bless you, young man! My daughter has told me

everything. You shall be rewarded by anything it is in my power to give you."

Frank laughed, his face flushing, as he gallantly returned:

"Mr. Dawson, I have already been rewarded by the pleasure it gave me to be of service to your daughter in a time of peril."

A week later Frank and his friends continued their journey westward, where fresh adventures awaited them.

# CHAPTER XIII.

## A THRILLING RESCUE.

"No, sir!" roared Professor Scotch, banging his clinched fist down on a rough wooden table that stood in the only "hotel" of the town of Blake, Utah. "I say no, and that settles it!"

"But," urged Frank, who sat opposite the little professor at the table, "wait till I tell you——"

"You have told me enough, sir! I do not want to hear any more!"

Barney, who sat near, could restrain his merriment no longer.

"Begobs!" he cried; "th' profissor is on his ear this toime, Frankie, me b'y. He manes business."

"That's exactly what I do!" came explosively from the little man's lips. "It is my turn now. You boys have been having your own way right along, and you have done nothing but run into scrape after scrape. It is amazing the troubles you have been into and the dangers you have passed through. Several times you have placed me in deadly peril, and but for my coolness, my remarkable nerve, my extremely level head, I must have been killed or gone insane long ago."

Both boys laughed.

"Allow me to compliment you on your remarkable nerve, professor," chuckled Frank. "You are bold as a lion—nit."

The final expressive word was spoken in an "aside," but the professor heard it, as Frank had intended he should.

"Laugh, laugh, laugh!" shouted the little man, in a hoarse tone of voice. "The time has passed when you can have fun with me; I decline to permit you to have fun with me. I have decided to assert myself, and right here is where I do it."

"Ye do thot, don't yez, profissor!" cried the Irish lad, in a way that made the little man squirm.

"You can bet I do! Judging by the past, any one would think Frank my guardian. They'd never dream I was his. He has gone where he pleased, and done as he pleased. Look where he has dragged me! Where is this forsaken hole on the face of the earth? It's somewhere in Utah."

"Blake is very easily located," said Frank, glibly. "Any schoolboy will tell you it is in Eastern Utah, on the line of the Grand Western Railway, at the point where the railroad crosses Green River. You are a little rusty on such things, professor, and so you fancy everybody else is as much a back number as yourself."

"Back number!" howled the little man, leaping into the air and dashing his hat to the floor. "That is more than I can endure. You have passed the limit."

Neither of the boys had ever before seen him so far forget his dignity without greater provocation, and they were not a little surprised.

"Steady, professor," laughed Frank. "Don't fly off the handle."

"Howld onter yersilf, profissor," chuckled Barney. "Av ye don't, ye may get broken."

"This is terrible!" cried the professor, his face crimson with anger. "Frank Merriwell, you are an ungrateful, reckless, heartless young rascal!"

"Oh, professor!"

Frank seemed deeply touched. He grew sober in a moment, out came his handkerchief, he carried it to his eyes, and he began to sob in a pitiful way.

Behind the handkerchief the mischievous lad was laughing still.

The professor rushed about the room a moment, and then he stopped, staring at Frank and beginning to look distressed.

"That I—should—ev-ev-ever live—to—see—this sad—hour!" sobbed the boy, with the handkerchief to his eyes. "That I should be called ungrateful and heartless by a man I have loved and honored like—like a—a sister! If my poor uncle had not died——"

"Goodness knows you cannot feel worse about that than I do!" came from the little man's lips. "I suppose he fancied he was doing me a favor when he appointed me your guardian and directed that I should accompany you as your tutor in your travels over the world. Your tutor indeed! Why, you insist on giving me points and information about every place we visit. You do exactly as you please, and it is a wonder that either of us is alive to-day. You have dragged us through the most deadly perils, and now that I object when you want to go ranting away into a wild and unexplored region of Southern Utah, where you say there dwells the last remnant of the murderous and terrible Danites, you—you—you——"

"What have I done?" sobbed Frank.

"Why, you've—you've said——"

"What?"

"I don't remember now; but I'd give seventeen million dollars if Asher Merriwell, your uncle, was living and had to travel around with you!"

"Now my heart is broken!" came mournfully from behind that handkerchief.

That was more than Scotch could stand. He edged nearer Frank, who fell face downward on the table, still laughing, but pretending to quiver with sobs.

"There, there, there!" fluttered the little man, patting the boy on the shoulder. "Don't feel so bad about it."

"I—I can't help it."

"Oh, I didn't mean anything—really I didn't. I'll take it back, and——"

"Your cruel words have pierced my tender heart as the spear of the fisherman pierceth the unwary flounder."

"I was too hasty—altogether too hasty."

"That does not heal the bleeding wound."

"Oh, well, say—I'll do most anything to——"

"Will you permit me to go on this expedition?"

"No, never!" cried the little man. "There is a limit, and that is too much."

"But you have not heard the story of this Walter Clyde, to whom I owe my very life," said Frank, pretending to dry his eyes with the handkerchief.

"You owe what?" shouted the professor, astonished. "How do you owe him so much?"

"Well, sir," spoke the boy, "it was like this: I had fallen into the hands of a band of murderous ruffians, and——"

"When did this occur?"

"At about half past six. Please do not interrupt me again. These ruffians, after relieving me of my valuables and wearing apparel, so that I was clad in nothing but a loose-fitting suit of air, proceeded, with fiendish design, to tie me to the railroad track."

"Terrible!" gasped Scotch, his face pale and horrified. "But where did this take place?"

"Directly on the line of the railroad. Will you be good enough not to interrupt! I was helpless in their power, and I could do nothing to save myself. I begged them to spare me, but they laughed at my entreaties."

"The wretches!" roared the little professor. "Ah! Er! Excuse me for breaking in."

"Having tied me firmly across the polished rails," continued Frank, growing dramatic in his method of relating the yarn, "they told me the express would be along in fifteen minutes, and then they left me to my fate."

"The dastardly scoun—— Beg pardon! Go on! go on!"

"I tried to wrench myself free, but it was impossible; they had tied the knots well, and I began to believe I was doomed. The rail sang beneath my head, and I knew the express was approaching at terrible speed."

"This is too much—too much!" groaned the little man, flopping down on a chair. "It actually overcomes me!"

"I fully expected the express would come over me," the boy went on. "I gave up hope. Looking along the track, I saw the engine swoop into view round a curve in the road. Down upon me with the speed of the wind it swept."

No sound but a groan came from the lips of Professor Scotch.

"Staring with horrified eyes and benumbed senses at the engine, I heard it shriek a wild note of warning. I had been seen! But the train was on a down grade, and it could not stop in time. I was doomed just the same."

The professor was ready to fall off his chair.

"Then," cried Frank, dramatically, "out along the side of the engine crept a boy, who carried something in his hand. That boy was Walter Clyde, to whom I owe my very life. The something he carried in his hand was a lasso, and with that he saved me."

"How—how could he do it?" palpitated the professor. "You were tied to the track!"

"Yes, but Walter Clyde is an ingenious fellow, and he saw how to get around that difficulty."

"But how—how?"

"Well, close beside the railroad was the stump of a great tree that had been cut down. I saw him point at it, and above the roar of the train I heard him shriek for me to lift my head and look at it."

"Yes, yes! Go on!"

"I saw him whirling the lasso-noose about his head, making ready for the cast, having first hitched the other ends to the cow-catcher of the locomotive."

"Well, well?"

"I lifted my head as high as possible, and I saw the noose shoot through the air. Excuse me while I shudder a few seconds!"

"Did he drag you from the track in time?" shouted the professor. "Did the noose fall over your head?"

"No," answered Frank; "but it fell over that stump, and, when the express reached the end of the lariat, having come so near that the nose of the pilot brushed my hair, the lariat brought up. It was a good stout rope, and it yanked that engine off the track in a second, and piled the entire train in the ditch. I was saved—saved by a brave boy, and only forty of the passengers on the train were killed."

Professor Scotch gasped for breath and sank from his chair to the floor.

# CHAPTER XIV.

## WALTER CLYDE'S STORY.

arney Mulloy had been holding on to keep from shouting with laughter, and now he exploded.

"Ha! ha! ha!" he roared. "Pwhat do yez think av thot, profissor? Thot wur th' narrowest escape ivver hearrud av, ur Oi'm a loier!"

"Send for the undertaker!" came in a hollow groan from the lips of the professor.

"You do not seem to feel well?" said Frank, hastening to the man's assistance. "What is the trouble?"

"If I die of heart failure you will be responsible!" fiercely grated Scotch.

"Doie!" cried Barney. "Whoy, ye'll live ter pick daisies on yer own grave, profissor."

"This is terrible!" faintly rumbled the little man, as he regained his chair, and began to mop cold perspiration from his face with a handkerchief.

There was a knock at the door.

"Come in," cried Frank.

The door opened, and a boy about seventeen years of age entered the room. He was a slender, delicate-appearing fellow, but he had a good face and steady eyes.

"Hurrah!" cried Frank. "Here is my preserver! Professor Scotch, permit me to introduce you to Mr. Walter Clyde."

The professor held out a limp hand to the boy, saying:

"Excuse me if I do not rise. Frank just robbed me of strength by telling how you saved his life by derailing an express train and killing forty passengers."

Clyde was quick to catch on. A faint look of astonishment was followed by a smile, and he said:

"Mr. Merriwell is mistaken."

"Ha!" cried the professor. "Then you denounce the whole story as false?"

"I said Mr. Merriwell was mistaken—but thirty-nine passengers were killed," said the newcomer, who had caught the end of Frank's yarn.

The professor came near having a fit, and Barney Mulloy held onto his sides, convulsed with merriment.

"I beg your pardon, Mr. Clyde," said Frank. "I may have stretched the yarn a trifle."

"Just a trifle!" muttered the professor.

"If I had used giant-powder instead of dynamite in blowing up the track," said Clyde, "it is possible there might have been a smaller loss of life."

"But you did not blow up the track at all," hastily put in Frank. "You yanked the train off the rails with a lasso."

"So I did! I was thinking of another case. In this instance, if I had not stood so far from the railroad——"

"But you were on the pilot of the engine."

"Was I? So I was. Excuse me if I do not attempt any further explanations."

Then the three boys laughed heartily, and the professor was forced to join in at last.

Having restored Scotch to good nature, Frank requested Walter Clyde to tell his story. Clyde's face clouded a little, and he slowly said:

"I will tell it briefly. Years ago, when I was a very small child, my father left his home in the East to make a trip to California. Business called him out there, and, on his way, he entered this Territory. He never reached California.

"My father had a deadly enemy—a man who had sworn to kill him some day. That man's name was Uric Dugan. Father had been instrumental in sending him to prison for robbery, but he had escaped, fled to the West, and, it was said, joined the Mormons.

"Fate led Uric Dugan and my father to meet in Utah. What happened then is known to Dugan alone. Months passed, and mother heard no word from father. She grew thin and pale and desperate. At length, a letter came to her. It was from Uric Dugan.

"That letter told my mother that father had died in a living tomb, where he had been placed and kept by Dugan till he went mad. Dugan gloated over his frightful crime. He told how father had raved in his delirium, called wildly for his wife and his boy, and how her name was last on his lips when he died."

"The monster!" broke in Professor Scotch, who was intensely interested.

"He was in truth a monster," agreed Clyde. "The effect of that letter on my mother was terrible. It nearly drove her mad, and she was ill a long time. When she recovered, she took measures to find and punish Dugan, but she never succeeded. She learned, however, that Dugan, after joining the Mormons, had been one of that terrible organization known as the Danites. He had disappeared, and no trace of him could be found.

"The detective who was in my mother's employ was aided by an old guide, miner, and fortune-hunter in general, known as Ben Barr. Barr learned the whole story of my father's disappearance, and it happened that he knew Uric Dugan—that Dugan had once done him an injury. He took a great interest in the case, and did his best to trace the man. As I have said, Dugan was not found, nor did the detective learn anything further of my father.

"Years passed, and I grew up. The years wrought their changes in Utah, and the Destroying Angels ceased to be a menace to every Gentile in the Territory. The younger Mormons regretted that such an organization had ever existed, and had been in any way connected with the Mormon Church. Danites who had been powerful and feared, found their former friends turning against them. Even the Mormon Church pretended to denounce them. John D. Lee, chief in the Mountain Meadow butchery, was captured, tried, found guilty, and shot. There were others as guilty as Lee, and they, who had been the hunters, found themselves hunted. They fled to the mountains, hid, disguised themselves, changed their names, and did everything they could to escape retributive justice.

"It seems that Dugan was still with them, and he found himself a fugitive like the others. Somewhere in Southern Utah, west of the Colorado, and amid the wild mountains that are to be found to the north of the Escalante River, the hunted Danites found a home where they believed they would be safe from pursuit, and there the last remnant of the once terrible Destroying Angels are living to-day.

"In his wanderings, Ben Barr came upon this retreat of the Danites, and there he saw Uric Dugan, who is now the chief of the band. Barr barely escaped with his life, and he lost no time in writing to my mother, telling her what he had discovered.

"This was enough to revive old memories and set mother to brooding over it. Her health was not very good, and I am sure that she worried herself to death. Before she died she told me of a dream that had come to her for three successive nights. In that dream she had seen my father, and he was still living, although he was unable to return to her. Just why he could not return was not very clear, but it was because of Dugan.

"As she was dying, my mother called me to her side and told me of the dream. 'My boy,' she said, 'I know your father is still living, and I want you to find him. Something has told me that you will be successful. Promise me that when I am gone you will not rest until you have found him or have satisfied yourself beyond the shadow of a doubt that he is dead.'

"I gave that promise, and I am here to search for my father and for Uric Dugan. If father is not living, I may be able to avenge him, and that will set me at rest.

"By accident I was thrown in with Mr. Merriwell, and we became somewhat friendly. I told him my story, and he was intensely interested in it. He asked me to let him go along. I did not refuse, and he said he would obtain your consent. That is all."

"Young man," said Professor Scotch, "I sympathize with you, and I sincerely hope you may be successful; but I do not care to have Frank thrust himself into such perils as you may encounter on that search."

"Hold on, professor!" cried Frank. "Just wait and——"

Scotch waved his hand.

"The time has come for me to assert my authority," he said, sternly; "and I propose to assert it."

"You will not let me go?"

"No, sir!"

"All right. You'll be sorry, professor."

"That sounds like a threat, young man. Don't threaten me. This search looks like a wild-goose chase. How do you propose to reach this retreat of the Danites?" he asked, turning to Clyde.

"By cruising down the river in a strong boat which I have bought and provisioned for the trip."

"And did you boys think of going alone?"

"Oh no."

"Who was going with you?"

"Two explorers."

"Their names."

"Colton Graves and Caleb Kerney."

"What do you know about them?"

"Nothing, except that they wish to take a cruise through the canyons."

"Young man," said the professor, "let me give you a bit of advice."

But before he could do so there came a sharp knock on the door.

# CHAPTER XV.

## PROFESSOR SEPTEMAS SCUDMORE.

he door opened with a quick, jerky movement immediately after the knock, and, without waiting to be invited to enter, a tall, angular, thin-legged, knock-kneed man walked into the room with a peculiar movement that seemed to indicate that his legs were in danger of breaking at every step.

This man had a very long, thin neck, on which was set a long, narrow head, crowned with an out-of-date silk hat. He wore a suit of rusty black, a flaring high collar, that was sadly wilted and lay out over the collar of his coat, and a black string necktie, which was tied in a careless knot. His face was shaven smooth, and a pair of gold-bowed spectacles clung convulsively to the end of a long, thin nose.

"Excuse me," he said, in a high-pitched, cracked tin-pan sort of voice. "I seek a fellow laborer in the field of science. You know the Good Book says: 'Seek and ye shall find, knock and it shall be opened unto you.' I knocked—didn't stop for it to be opened—am in a hurry. Ahem! You"—pointing a long, slim finger at Scotch—"you must be the one I seek."

The little professor looked startled.

"What have I ever done to you?" he asked, hesitatingly.

"Not anything, my dear sir, but I believe you are Professor Scotch, are you not?"

"That is right; but I do not know you, sir."

"I am Professor Septemas Scudmore, of Pudville Classical Institute, in the State of Ohio."

"Never heard of you, sir."

"And I never heard of you till a few moments ago, when one of the polite and obliging citizens told me you were here, and asked me why I did not call on you, as you seemed to be a bigger fool than I am, and we might make good company for each other."

"What's that?" roared Scotch. "Who dared to say anything like that? The insulting wretch!"

Professor Scudmore waved a long, lank hand at the little man.

"Do not get agitated," he chirped. "It is not well for a man of your years. You should preserve a calm and even demeanor. Excuse me if I do not always follow my own teaching. We tutors never do."

Scotch stared at the strange man as if doubting his sanity.

"You seem to enjoy being called a fool!" he growled.

"Not at all—not at all. But I have been called that so much that I do not mind it. Genius is ever regarded as folly till it astounds the world. I am a man of genius. You may think that is boasting, but I assure you it is not. I am naturally modest—very modest. But I have found that, in order to be thought anything of by others, I must think well of myself. I am so exceeding frank and honest that I never hide my thoughts, therefore, I tell you candidly what I think of myself."

"Well, well!"

"It is possible you do not believe in this sort of thing—few do. Duplicity I despise. You are not a man of genius yourself, but you have led others to think you pretty smart, and you have succeeded in getting through the world thus far pretty easy. You are naturally slothful; in fact, I may say you are lazy, and you——"

"Hold on there!" thundered the little man. "You may be as frank as you please about yourself, but you had better be careful what you say about me!"

"Touchy, eh?" sniffed Septemas Scudmore. "Not strange at all. Studious inclination, close application to work, baffling researches, midnight oil—these things irritate the nerves and make a man crusty. But then, I don't think you ever hurt yourself by close application to work. You must be naturally irritable."

Professor Scotch pranced up and down the room like an angry bantam.

"Sir," he cried, "you are altogether too free with your mouth."

"The Scudmores are naturally generous, so I can't help it. Keep calm, sir. In some things we have an affinity. I can see it in your eye. I did not anticipate meeting an affinity out here in this wild and heathenish country."

"Affinity!" cried Scotch, scornfully. "A man with your tongue would be an affinity for a cackling old woman!"

"That is your hastily formed opinion. Permit me to warn you against forming opinions too quickly. It is a bad habit to get into, and——"

"Sir!" shouted the little man, "there is the door!"

Scudmore bowed profoundly.

"I noticed it when I came in," he chirped. "Very ordinary door, but I don't suppose we can expect anything better out in this wild section of the country."

Scotch was ready to tear his hair.

"Will you take a hint, or do you need a kick?" he bellowed, in his hoarsest tone.

"A man with hair and whiskers colored like yours should always beware of undue excitement. Don't think of kicking anybody, for you may lose your dignity. Speaking about aërial navigation, beyond the shadow of a doubt, I, Septemas Scudmore, A. M., B. A., LL. D., and B. C, have solved the problem. I say beyond the shadow of a doubt, and I mean exactly what I say. It is not a matter of fans and wheels——"

"I think it is a matter of wheels," broke in Scotch, "and they are in your head."

Scudmore waved one thin hand loftily, his nose high in the air.

"Peace, professor, peace," he said. "It ill becomes you to interrupt a fellow scientist. Hear me out."

"I had much rather see you out—of the door."

"I see you are skeptical—you doubt the practical and practicable value of my invention. But you shall be convinced—you shall be my fellow passenger on my first voyage through space."

"Not if I know myself!" shouted the little man. "You may be a fool, but——"

"There are others, sir—there are others. I beg you to grant me this favor. Think what an honor it will be to have it go abroad that you accompanied Professor Septemas Scudmore on his first voyage in his new airship."

"Oh, you make me very languid!" cried the little man, using a bit of slang which he had heard from the lips of one of his youthful companions.

"I am shocked—shocked beyond measure," declared the lank professor, sinking his chin upon his bosom and looking reproachfully over his spectacles at Scotch.

The three boys were enjoying this immensely. It was sport to Frank, who saw in Septemas Scudmore a character worth studying. Barney laughed heartily.

"Begorra!" cried the Irish lad, "it's shocked we all are. Th' profissor has gone crazy, sure."

"If I have, it is not surprising, after what I have passed through. It has been enough to drive any man insane."

"I fancy you are a person whose brain would not stand a severe strain," put in Scudmore.

"Oh, you do! Well, I have stood just all of this I can from you! There is the door—get out!"

"And you decline the honor I have attempted to confer upon you?"

"I decline to talk further with a crank. Get out!"

Septemas Scudmore shook his head dolefully.

"I will do as you have so politely requested; but you will regret this to your dying day. I shall hold no hardness against you. In fact, I am sorry for you, as you——"

The little man could stand no more, and he actually drove Scudmore from the room. When he came back, he found the boys laughing heartily, and this caused him to drive them out also.

"It is doubtful if he will consent to allow me to accompany you, Clyde," said Frank, when they were outside. "He is an obstinate man when he sets his mind on anything."

"Well," declared Walter, "I am sorry. We met by accident, and I took to you in a moment. When you had heard my story and expressed a desire to accompany me on my search for Uric Dugan, I was delighted."

"And I had no idea the professor would object. This is the first time he has done anything of the sort; but it is true that we have run into many perilous adventures, and he wishes to prevent such things in future."

"Whoy not run away an' go, Frankie?" asked Barney, whose thirst for adventure was whetted to a keen edge. "It's mesilf thot would loike to go hunting fer this colony av Danites."

Frank shook his head.

"I hardly feel like doing that," he said. "There is a bare chance that the professor will relent. We will wait and see."

"There can be little waiting," said Clyde. "I start in the morning. Everything is ready, and Graves and Kerney are eager to be off."

"Well, we'll see what the next few hours will bring forth."

Little did they dream of the surprising things the next few hours would bring forth.

# CHAPTER XVI.

## THE MAD INVENTOR.

Frank and Barney were strolling about the place when they came upon Professor Scudmore.

"Ha, young gentlemen!" cried the eccentric old fellow; "come with me. I am about to start upon my trial voyage. The Eagle is inflated and ready to soar. I wish you to witness my triumph."

He took them outside the town to a secluded glen, in which was an old cabin and a huge, odd-shaped arrangement of silk, fine wires, and wickerwork. It was, in fact, a balloon, shaped like an egg, and inflated with gas. To it was attached a large and comfortable car, and there were two huge fore and aft rudders, together with some fan-like arrangements that seemed to be sails. This strange contrivance was secured to the ground by strong ropes.

"There!" cried Scudmore; "you now behold the Eagle, a flying-machine that will fly, or, rather, sail. With the wind it will travel at wonderful speed, and it can beat to windward like a vessel. I have been at work upon it for years. Some time ago I perfected it, and I brought it here for my trial voyage. I have set it up and inflated it without attracting attention or advertising myself. I should not have called on Professor Scotch, but I was full of enthusiasm, and thought it would be a fine thing to have an eminent man like him accompany me on my first voyage."

The boys looked at each other.

"Phwat do yez think av it, Frankie?" asked Barney.

"Can't tell," was the reply. "Let's look her over."

"That's right, look her over," urged Professor Scudmore. "I am going to start at once, but I must first get aboard a few things that are in this hut."

So the boys examined the airship, while the inventor brought bundles from the hut and placed them in the car.

"Phwat do yez think now?" asked Barney, when they had looked it over quite thoroughly. "Will she sail?"

"She will rise in the air, like an ordinary balloon," said Frank; "but I am not satisfied that the rudders and sails will work."

"I will soon satisfy you on that point," said the professor, who happened to be near enough to overhear their words.

Immediately he set about explaining everything in connection with the handling of the singular craft, and it did not take him long to make it seem an assured thing that the Eagle could be steered in almost any direction, and that, with the aid of horizontal rudders, she could be brought to the ground or sent soaring into the air, without a change of ballast or the body of gas.

Frank was intensely interested.

"It is remarkable, professor!" he cried. "Scotch made a mistake when he refused to accompany you on your trial trip."

"Ha! You are a boy of sense! Saw it the first time my eye rested on you. I will make you famous."

Frank looked surprised.

"How?"

"You shall accompany me on my trial trip."

"How long will it be?"

"As long, or as short as we choose to make it. What do you say? Decide quickly. I am eager to be off."

"Can you take Barney along?"

"I can, but two is enough. I do not care for too many."

"Can you drop us in Blake by nightfall?"

"Yes."

"Well, if you will take us both, we'll go along, professor."

Scudmore considered, his right elbow resting in the hollow of his left hand, the long forefinger of his right hand touching his forehead.

"I will do it!" he cried, with a snap. "Get in. We'll lose no more time. In a few moments we shall be sailing away like a bird."

"Here goes, Frankie," grinned the Irish lad. "Av we're both killed, Oi want yez to tell me ould mither how Oi died."

They entered the car, and Scudmore prepared to cast off. He was full of anxiety and excitement.

At length but a single rope held the now swaying and surging air ship to the ground.

"Here goes the last strand that ties us to earth!" cried the professor, as, with the slash of a knife he severed the rope.

Up shot the air ship.

"Ha! ha! ha!" laughed the inventor. "Who said I would fail! We are off!"

"Thot's all right," muttered Barney; "but will we ivver come back?"

"Look!" cried Frank, pointing downward; "there is Professor Scotch! We are already passing over the town."

It was true; in a remarkably brief space of time the air ship had sailed out of the glen and was rising above the town. Looking downward, they saw Professor Scotch and a number of persons, including Walter Clyde and two rough-looking companions, staring up at the Eagle.

"Good-by, professor," shouted Frank, leaning out of the car and waving his hat. "We're off in search of the last of the Danites."

They saw the professor dance wildly around and beckon to them. Then his voice came faintly to their ears:

"Here, here, you rascals! come right back here this minute! If you don't, I shall have to——"

They could understand no more, for the swiftly rising air ship carried them beyond the reach of his voice.

Professor Scudmore was chuckling to himself, as he worked at the apparatus which controlled the sails and rudders.

"It is a success, and my fortune is made!" he was saying. "I shall become richer than Jay Gould ever was! Ha! ha! ha! I shall not only be rich, but I shall be honored!"

"Oi don't loike th' way he is actin', Frankie," whispered Barney. "Thot laugh does not sound natural at all, at all."

"You are right," admitted Frank. "Is it possible we have started out on this kind of a cruise with a man whose brain has been turned?"

"It may be thot."

"The situation will not be at all pleasant if it turns out that way."

"He is getting control av th' ship. See how he handles her now, me b'y."

It was true that the inventor was getting control of the Eagle, and he was beginning to "put her through her paces," as it were. He ran before the wind, then luffed and took first one tack and then the other. The remarkable craft behaved very well.

"Ha! ha! ha!" laughed the professor, wildly. "I am the king of the air! I am the first man to make a successful air ship. The world and all its countries are mine! I can destroy armies and change the destiny of nations! I am the greatest man who ever lived!"

"By Jove!" muttered Frank, in alarm; "I believe the man is going mad!"

"It looks loike thot," admitted the Irish boy.

"In which case, this will be the worst scrape we ever got into,

Barney. That is plain enough to see."

"Roight, me laddybuck! An' th' professor will soay it wur judgment on us fer runnin' away."

"He will. But we ought to be able to handle this man between us, if it comes to a struggle with him."

"We can; but can we handle th' ship afther thot, Oi dunno?"

"That is a question we cannot answer till we try the trick. But there may be no trouble at all with Scudmore if we do not anger him."

Below them lay a wild panorama of broken country, through which ran Green River to plunge deep into the winding mazes of Labyrinth Canyon, away to the southward.

Away to the west, beyond the San Rafael Swell, rose the Wasatch Mountains; being much nearer than the Rockies to the eastward, and, therefore, looking nearly as lofty.

To the north were Desolation Canyon and the Roan Cliffs, the latter rising brown and bleak at the southern boundary of the Ute Reservation.

To the south of mighty Colorado, rolling through the dark depths of canyons which seemed to sink deep into the bowels of the earth. Farther to the south, beyond the Fremont, which as yet could not be seen, Mount Pennell lifted its snow-capped summit eleven thousand feet in the air.

Mount Pennell was in the very heart of the mountain region in which the last of the Destroying Angels had found homes.

"Professor!" said Frank, speaking gently.

"Ha! ha!" muttered the inventor, as he threw over a lever and sent the Eagle scooting in a breathless sweep toward the earth. "She is like a bird! Up or down, to the right or left, she will sail in any direction."

"Professor!"

"Don't bother me now—don't bother me!" he almost snarled.

"I was a fool to take you along! I should have retained all the honor for myself. Now you will share it. It will be published all over the world that you accompanied Professor Scudmore on his trial trip in his wonderful air ship."

He glared at them a moment, as if he longed to cast them overboard, and then the handling of the craft claimed his entire attention.

"How do yez loike it, Frankie, me b'y?" asked Barney, with a sly nudge at his companion.

"It is decidedly uncomfortable."

"Phwat shall we do—jump th' son-av-a-goon at wance?"

"Nothing of the sort. We will keep still, as if we are quite satisfied and content. I will draw him into conversation when I think it proper, and he may be brought round all right."

So the boys remained silent and passive, one of them constantly watching Scudmore, so that they might not be taken by surprise, in case he took a fancy to attack them.

He continued to mutter and talk to himself, now and then laughing in a way that was not pleasant to hear.

The boys fell to wondering what the various bundles contained. Opening one of them, covertly, they found it was a supply of dried beef.

"Great shmoke!" gasped Barney. "He has laid in a supply av provisions to larrust a wake!"

Frank nodded.

"It looks that way; but these things are not all provisions. See there at his side—one of those bundles contains firearms, for you may see the muzzles of two rifles protruding. I fancy the bundle next to that contains ammunition."

"Whoy, thot's enoogh to shtock a small arumy, Frankie!"

"A man like Professor Scudmore has very little notion as to what he needs or desires, and so he is liable to obtain four or five times what is necessary."

"Are you talking of me?" harshly demanded the inventor. "Then speak up distinctly. I may think you are plotting against me—plotting to keep me from reaching the land beyond the ice."

"The land beyond the ice?" cried Frank.

"That is what I said."

"Well, what did you mean? Whither are we bound?"

"For the South Pole," was the answer. "Ha! ha! ha! We will pass over the ice floes and reach the land beyond them!"

# CHAPTER XVII.

## GONE.

All that day and far into the night the mad inventor held control of the flying-machine, refusing to listen to reason or argument, and keeping the boys at bay.

Some time in the night he fell asleep, and, when he awoke, he was enraged to find himself bound hands and feet, while the boys were trying to handle the Eagle.

"Let me go!" howled the mad professor. "You will send us to destruction! You will plunge us to ruin!"

"Keep still!" commanded Frank, sternly. "You are no longer master here."

"Villain!" screamed the helpless man; "I know your scheme! You mean to steal the Eagle! You mean to get rid of me, and then you will steal the work of my brain and hands!"

"Don't fool yourself. If I ever get to solid ground again, you may have your old air ship and sail away to the South Pole with it. I am figuring on getting back to Blake."

"Te, he!" laughed the madman, suddenly. "Is that all you ask? Why, it is very easy to fix that matter."

His voice was full of craft and deception.

"How would you fix it?" asked Frank.

"Set me at liberty, and I will take you back there."

"That sounds all right, but it is plain enough that you cannot be trusted. I prefer to experiment a little myself, before letting you have charge again."

"And you will bring us all to destruction!"

"Possibly I may. Keep still now, while I study out the working of these levers and wheels."

But Scudmore would not keep still. He shouted and talked, urging them to release him, begging and threatening by turns.

Meanwhile Frank and Barney were studying over the levers and wheels, and they finally discovered how to send the air ship down toward the earth, which lay asleep in the white moonlight.

They were directly over a mountainous region, having been soaring over the loftiest peaks. The boys were somewhat benumbed by the chilly air, but, as they came nearer to the earth, this numbness passed away.

"Are yez goin' ter land here, Frankie?" asked Barney, anxiously.

"I don't know," was the answer. "If we should happen to see a town——"

"Where do yez think we are?"

"That is another thing I don't know."

Down they went until Frank conceived a notion that they were near enough to the earth; but when he tried to reverse the lever and ascend again, it would not work.

"Ha! ha! ha!" laughed the inventor. "It is retribution! We shall be smashed into a thousand pieces when we strike. You will never steal the Eagle from me!"

Frank worked with all his energy, for they were sweeping toward the earth at an alarming rate of speed.

The laughter of the deranged professor rang out louder and wilder than ever.

"Oi think we're in fer it, me b'y!" gasped Barney.

"It looks like that," confessed Frank, as they barely cleared the crest of a mountain and went diving down into the unknown depths of a valley. "This confounded thing——"

Snap!—something broke, and their swift descent was suddenly checked, but they continued to settle gently.

"Ah!" breathed Frank, with relief. "If this keeps up, we'll come down all right."

"But it's nivver a bit can we tell where we'll land, me laddybuck."

"We'll have the satisfaction of getting on solid ground again, at least. I am yearning to feel it beneath my feet once more."

It was not long before the Eagle sank gently into the valley, settling to the ground as lightly as a bird.

Out leaped the boys, ropes in their hands, and they quickly made the air ship fast.

"Well, we are still living," said Frank.

"It's mesilf thot belaves we've much to be thankful fer," declared Barney.

"I wonder where we are, and how near we are to civilization. I am inclined to believe we cannot be far from the very region where the colony of Danites is said to be located."

"Suffering cats!" gasped the Irish boy. "If thot is the case, how are we ivver goin' to get out av here?"

"We'll have to trust to luck."

"Oi'll nivver thrust mesilf to thot air ship again."

"I do not care to do so, but we may have to do so whether we want to or not."

"Well, we have enough to ate, an' some guns to protict oursilves with. Oi am fer ixplorin' th' country before we do anything ilse."

"We can't do any exploring to-night."

"But we can early in th' marnin'."

So they provided themselves with two of the rifles, plenty of ammunition, and much of the provisions in the car.

In the shelter of the valley the night was no longer cool, but was warm and pleasant.

They found an overhanging shelf of rock where they could get close up under a bluff, and it made quite a satisfactory camp.

For some time the boys lay and talked over their adventure, wondering if they would get out of the predicament all right. At last they became drowsy, and finally fell asleep.

They slept soundly till morning. Frank was the first to awaken, and he shook Barney to rouse him.

"Come, you bit of the Old Sod," called Frank. "Turn out and pay for your lodging."

"Begobs! Oi fale loike th' bed had been shtuffed with bricks. Hurro! Oi must have fell out av bed in th' noight, an' dropped clane out av th' windy. It's a bit av a kink Oi have in th' small av me back."

Barney sat up, making a wry face, and staring about in a bewildered way.

"Phwat howtil is this, Oi dunno?" he cried. "Have Oi been slapin', or have Oi been in a thrance?"

"We came here in a flying-machine, you will remember."

"In a floying-machine? Oi thought Oi dramed it."

"It was no dream."

"Well, may Oi nivver live to see th' back av me neck!"

It took some time for the Irish boy to recover from his amazement.

"Where is thot floying-machine, Frankie?"

"It is just beyond this line of bushes, where we left it last night. Professor Scudmore is tied up in the car, and I fancy he must be a bit uncomfortable by this time. I did not mean to leave him that way so long. It was rather heartless."

"Ye can't be aisy wid his koind, me b'y. There's no tellin' phwat they'll do."

"That is true; but it is our duty to handle him as gently as possible. He is a most unfortunate man. His air ship seems an assured success, and yet he has lost his reason working over it."

The boys arose and passed round the bushes, Frank being in advance. A cry of wonder and amazement broke from Merriwell's lips.

"The air ship!" he gasped.

"Phwat's th' matter?" asked Barney, quickly.

"It's gone!"

# CHAPTER XVIII.

## MISKEL.

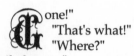one!"
"That's what!"
"Where?"

"Sailed away."

It was true that the Eagle was not where they had left it the night before, and, looking all around, they could find no trace of it.

"Thot bates me!"

The knees of the Irish boy seemed to weaken beneath him, and he sank in a limp heap on the ground.

"It beats the band!"

Frank was scarcely less broken up than his companion.

"How did it happen, Frankie? Th' ould thing didn't go off av itsilf, did it?"

"Not much!"

"Phwat thin?"

"Professor Scudmore must have succeeded in releasing himself."

"Roight, lad; an' thin he skipped."

"As soon as he was free, he sailed away in the Eagle, and we are left here in the heart of this mountainous region."

"Oi'm homesick! Oi wish Oi hadn't come!"

Frank laughed.

"This is not the worst scrape we have been in, by any means. We'll pull out of this, with our usual good luck."

But a feeling of loneliness and desolation did settle heavily upon them, for all that Frank made an effort to throw it off. The mountains lifted their heads on every hand like mighty sentries that hemmed them in, and they felt shut off from all the rest of the world.

When they fully realized that Professor Scudmore had released himself and escaped in the air ship, they walked round the place where the Eagle had been left the night before, but they discovered nothing beyond some severed bits of rope.

Then Frank became philosophical.

"We may as well take it easy," he said. "It is useless to make a fuss about it. Here we are, and——"

"Where we are Oi dunno!"

"You know quite as well as I do, old man."

"All roight. Phwat will we do?"

"Find some water to wash down our breakfast to start with. After we have eaten, we will feel better. Then we can settle on what we'll do next."

By rare good luck, they were near a spring of clear water, and it was found without trouble.

"It was fortunate we took the rifles and provisions out of the car last night," said Frank.

"Thot it wur," nodded Barney.

For all of their situation, they ate heartily, and, breakfast over, they felt better. Then they sat and talked the matter over a while, finally deciding to make an effort to get somewhere, and trust to fortune.

With the aid of the pieces of rope, they tied the provisions into bundles, which were easily carried, and before long they struck out.

Barney trusted everything to Frank who took the lead, and they headed for what seemed to be an outlet to the valley, away to the west.

During the next five days the boys passed through a few adventures, none of which, however, have any bearing on this story. They wandered round and round amid the mountains, finally coming back to the valley from which they had started.

This was discouraging, but they started over again, and they finally came to a narrow cut that seemed to lead into the very heart of the mountain that loomed before them.

"We will try it," said Frank, leading the way.

They passed through the cut, after traveling many miles, and came into a vast basin, with mountains looming on every hand.

"Pwhat do yez think, me b'y?" asked the Irish lad.

"It is not easy to tell what to think," was the reply. "However, I fear we are in Water Pocket Canyon."

"Phwat about Water Pocket Canyon?"

"It is said to be fifty miles in length to ten or fifteen in width, and to have no outlets."

"Well, this can't be th' place, me b'y, fer it has an outlet roight here."

"But one that would not be easy to find, and so it might go forth there were no outlets to the place."

"Begorra! it looks loike we naded Profissor Scudmore's floying-machane to git out av this scrape."

"It does look that way. We seem to be getting tangled more and more. All we can do is to make the attempt to get out."

"Av this is Warter Pocket Canyon, we may not be able to foind this pass if we lave it."

"We will mark the spot some way."

"How?"

"That is the question. Wait till I find a way."

It was not easy, but Frank finally decided that he could tell the mountain through the base of which the pass had seemed to wind.

Then they went into the wild and picturesque valley, while Frank continued to look back at intervals in order to impress the appearance of the mountain on his mind.

That night they camped beside a little stream that bubbled out from beneath the base of a cliff, and it was found that their stock of provisions was getting very low, even though they had preserved it as far as possible by shooting and cooking wild game.

"We have got to get out av here soon, Frankie," said the Irish boy, soberly.

Frank nodded.

"That is evident; but we are doing our best, and so we can do no better."

Frank was somewhat disheartened, but he did not wish Barney to know it, and so he pretended to be cheerful.

Darkness settled over the canyon, and the light of a tiny fire shone on the faces of the young adventurers.

Frank seemed to be dreaming, for, with a far-away stare, he was gazing straight into the flames, apparently quite unaware of his surroundings.

In the flaring fire he saw strange pictures of events in his own career—a career such as had never before fallen to the lot of a boy of his years.

He seemed to behold the scores of perils through which he had passed, and before him seemed to flit the faces of the many friends and foes he had made.

He saw the foes of his school days—Snell, Bascomb, Gage, and all the others—skulk past in procession. Snell had a sneaking, treacherous look on his face, Bascomb swaggered along in the old bullying manner, and Gage seemed to be driven along by the Evil One, who was constantly goading him to rash and desperate things. Then he saw the face of his most deadly enemy, his own cousin, Carlos Merriwell; but it no longer bore a look of malignant hatred, for it was white and cold in the last long sleep.

There were other enemies who had sprung up along his path, but they seemed like shadows in comparison to the ones of his school days.

Following these came others, and the dark look faded from his countenance. He saw Bart Hodge, who had once been his bitter enemy, but who had become his stanchest friend. Hodge held out a hand to him, as if longing to render aid in this hour of need.

Then came scores of others, the cadets at Fardale, the professors, and, last of all, the girls who had admired him and believed him noble and true.

Elsie Bellwood smiled at him sadly, and pointed to a mighty barrier that lay between them; Kate Kenyon tried to reach him, and then drew back, with a hopeless shake of her head; others came and flitted past, and last of all Inza Burrage was there, holding out her hands to him, her dark eyes full of trust.

"Inza!"

The name fell from his lips, and it aroused him. Barney had fallen asleep, and was snoring beside the fire.

But what was that? Did he still dream?

Just beyond the fire, within the outer circle of light, stood a girl! Frank rubbed his eyes and looked again.

She was still there, and she was pressing a finger to her lips, as if asking for silence.

"Great Scott!" muttered Frank, in a dazed way.

"Sh!" came back across the fire. "Do not wake him." She motioned toward the sleeping Irish lad.

Frank pinched himself.

"Yes, I am awake myself," he said, guardedly. "And it is a girl—a pretty girl at that! How in the name of all that is wonderful does it happen there is a girl here?"

"You have no time to ask questions," came back swiftly, in a low, musical voice. "You are in a bad snare, Frank Merriwell."

The boy started violently.

"How is it that you know my name?" he demanded, astonished beyond measure.

"I tell you you have no time to ask questions. Why did you come here?"

"You seem inclined to ask questions. I came because I could not help it."

"That is not true. You came to search for the hiding place of the last of the Danites. You may as well confess it."

"But I tell you I had no idea of coming here when I started."

"I know more than your name, Frank Merriwell; I know that you were eager to come in search of the place where Uric Dugan and a few of his former friends have hidden themselves from the world, hoping to remain there in peace to the end of their days."

Frank was filled with wonder unutterable.

"Are you a supernatural creature—a phantom?" he demanded. "If not, how do you know that I ever heard of Uric Dugan?"

"I am not the only one who knows. Uric Dugan and his companions know it. They are ready for you, and you have walked into their snare. You are meshed."

"What do you mean by that?"

"I mean that there is not one chance in ten thousand that you will ever be able to escape alive."

"By Jove! the prospect is pleasant!"

"I am in earnest. The pass by which you entered this basin is already guarded, and you cannot get out that way."

"Then we will have to get out some other way."

"There is but one other way, and that is also guarded. Do you see you are snared?"

"If you are not mistaken, it looks that way. What can I do?"

The girl made a despairing gesture.

"I don't know," she admitted. "I have begged them to spare you— to shed no more blood; but they say it is absolutely necessary in order that we may continue to live here in peace. The world at large must not know where to find the last of the Danites."

"If I give my pledge——"

"It will not be accepted. You are not the first to stray in here. Not one of them has ever gone away to tell the tale."

Frank shuddered a bit, beginning to realize that the situation was indeed a desperate one.

"If there is no chance for us to escape, why are you here to tell us?"

"I could not help warning you. I saw your fire twinkling, and I knew that you would sleep beside it. In the night death would come down upon you, and you would never awaken."

"Jupiter! That is interesting! I won't sleep for a week."

"Ah, but you cannot escape, even though you never again close your eyes in sleep. You can only avoid your doom for a little time. My heart is full of pity for you, but I am unable to do anything."

Her voice told him that she was sincere, and Frank thrilled with gratitude toward her.

"Who are you?" he asked.

"I am Miskel," she answered.

"Miskel! What an odd name! But you seem to be a most remarkable girl. How does it happen that you are here?"

"My father is one of the last of the Danites, and I live here with him."

"Your father—who is he?"

"Uric Dugan!"

"You must not linger here. * * * Even now the Destroying Ones may be moving to fall upon you."

# CHAPTER XIX.

## OLD SOLITARY.

**F**rank uttered a low cry, causing Barney to start up.

"Pwhat's th' matter?" asked the Irish boy, reaching for his rifle. "Is it Injuns, Oi dunno?"

"Easy, Barney!" cried Frank. "You will frighten her away from—Cæsar's ghost! She's gone!"

"Pwhat's thot? Who is she, me b'y? Is it dramin' ye wur, or have ye wheels in yer head?"

"Neither. She was here a moment ago, and I was talking with her."

"Who is she?"

"Miskel."

"An' a broth av a name thot is! It's wheels ye have in yer head, me b'y; Oi can hear thim goin' round."

Frank sprang up and passed round the fire.

"She disappeared like a phantom. I cannot understand how she came here, or how she went away so swiftly."

Not a trace of her could be seen.

All at once, Frank whirled about and kicked the burning brands in all directions.

"That fire shall provide no beacon for Uric Dugan and the Danites!" exclaimed the boy.

"Pwhat do yez mane by thot?" asked the puzzled Irish lad. "Is it daft ye have gone all at wance?"

Frank came swiftly to the side of his companion, a hand falling on Barney's shoulder, as he said:

"We must get out of this, for it is likely our fire has been seen by the Danites, who are somewhere near at hand."

"How do yez know thot, Frankie?"

"Know it? Why, she told me. She was here a minute ago, and you frightened her away when you awoke."

Barney looked at his friend in a doubting way.

"Be aisy now, Frankie, and if ye can't be aisy, whoy jist be aisy as ye can. This loife has affected yer brain, me b'y."

Frank saw Barney really thought he spoke the truth.

"You are wrong," he said. "I will explain what I mean, and I assure you that I am in my sober senses."

Whereupon, he told Barney everything, and the Irish lad listened with drooping jaw.

"Th' saints protict us!" he cried. "Pwhat are we goin' to do, Frankie?"

"Get out of this before Uric Dugan and his gang make us a call."

"They move swiftly as an arrow, and strike deep and sure. You have no time to spare."

The voice was hollow and blood-chilling, coming out of the darkness as from the depths of a mighty cavern, causing both lads to whirl, clutching their weapons, ready for an attack.

"Who is there?" challenged Frank, sharply.

"One who will do you no harm," was the answer. "And I alone am able to save you from Uric Dugan."

"Who are you?"

"I am known as Old Solitary."

Not far away could be seen the figure of a man, who seemed to be leaning on a stout staff. He made no menacing move.

Barney's teeth were chattering.

"Tin to wan it is th' Ould B'y himsilf!" gasped the Irish lad.

Barney was very superstitious. While he was not afraid of anything made of flesh and blood, whatever seemed supernatural filled him with the greatest terror.

"Steady," warned Frank. "It is a human being, and he seems to be alone. One man will not harm us."

"Not av he is a man."

"I am a man, and I mean you no harm," declared the same deep voice. "If you will trust me, I may be able to save you. Look—I will advance, and you may keep your weapons turned upon me."

The figure came forward through the gloom, and in a few moments he stood close at hand, so they could see he was a man whose head was bare, and whose white beard flowed over his chest. What seemed to be a staff at first glance, proved to be a long-barreled rifle.

Barney was intensely relieved.

"It must be Santy Claus himsilf!" exclaimed the Irish lad.

"You must not linger here," said the stranger. "Even now the Destroying Ones may be moving to fall upon you. They would wipe you from the face of the earth, as they have wiped away hundreds and thousands. They are terrible, and they are merciless. Their tongues are forked, and the poison of adders lies beneath their lips. For the Gentile they know not mercy. If the Mormon Church decrees that they destroy the babe at its mother's breast, they snatch it away and dash out its brains. On their knees innocent girls have pleaded in vain to be spared. Fathers and mothers have fallen before them. Old men with snowy hair have been slaughtered without pity. And chief among these inhuman monsters is Dugan of the dark face. I know him, and I know that his heart is made of adamant. But he shall not always escape the wrath to come. His days are numbered, and the days of his merciless comrades are numbered! All are doomed! Not one shall escape!"

"Easy, old man!" warned Frank. "Do you wish to bring them upon us? I shall think you are in league with them."

"Not I! Come; I will lead you to a place of safety."

The boys hesitated.

"Shall we thrust th' spalpane?" whispered Barney, doubtfully.

"I don't see as we can do better," returned Frank. "We must take chances."

"He may be wan av th' Danites, me b'y."

"He may be, but something tells me he is not."

"Thin how does it happen thot he is here?"

"That is something you can answer as well as I. Come, we will follow him. Keep your weapons ready for instant use."

So they followed, and, old man though he was, they found it no easy task, for he moved with a swinging cat-like step that carried him swiftly over the ground.

All at once, he turned, with a low hiss, motioned for them to follow, and, crouching low, crept behind some bowlders.

The boys followed, ready for a trap.

When they were behind the bowlders, the stranger whispered:

"They are coming—I hear their footsteps afar. They come swiftly, but they will not find their prey. They are the last of the Danites, and they are in hiding here amid these mountains, but they have not forgotten how to strike and destroy. Crouch low, keep still, and you shall see them pass."

It seemed that the old man's ears must be good, for it was quite a while before the boys heard a sound. At length, with a sudden rush of feet, six or eight dark figures flitted past and quickly disappeared.

"They come like shadows, and like shadows they go," softly breathed Old Solitary. "The day has passed forever when their power is felt and dreaded throughout Utah. Once they were far more dreadful than a pestilence. Started upon the trail of a man who had been doomed by the church, there was not one chance in ten thousand for him to escape. No man could seek his bed at night and be sure he would not become the victim of the Destroying Angels before dawn. No man could be sure he had not done something to offend Brigham Young. If by any means he became aware that 'the decree of death' had been made against him, it was no better than useless for him to take to flight. He might flee to the desert, but the Destroyers tracked him through shifting sands and across waterless wastes till he was run to earth and his body was left for the vultures and coyotes. If he plunged into the mountains, the canyons and ravines were not deep enough or dark enough to hide him from the keen eyes of the death-dealers on his track. Knowing his doom had been decreed, he might flee madly from his home and his loved ones, his heart alternating between hope and despair, knowing all the while that those deadly pursuers were on his track, hurrying on and on when he was in desperate need of rest, fearing to close his eyes in sleep, lest he open them to look upon his murderers, weak for want of food, his throat parched for a swallow of water, his blood pouring like melted lead through his veins, his brain on fire, and still all his struggles were unavailing. Relentless, unwearying, bloodthirsty and sure as death, the Destroying Ones tracked him down. He might begin to fancy that he had escaped, that he had thrown them off his trail. At last, overcome by his terrible exertions, he might sleep, feeling certain that in a few more hours he would be beyond their reach. They would come upon him like shadows, and they would leave him weltering in his gore. A curse they have been, and a curse they shall remain till the last one of them all is perished from the face of the fair earth which they have polluted."

The boys were spellbound by the intense language of the strange man. All fears that he might be one of the Danites departed from their minds.

"Begobs!" gasped Barney; "it's Satan's oun brewing they must be!"

"Come," said Old Solitary, "we must move on again. They will not find you, and the morning will see them on your trail."

"If what you say is true, it were better to be trailed by bloodhounds or wild Indians," said Frank.

"Far better. The Destroying Ones hastened to the slaughter with no more mercy in their hearts than is to be found in the heart of a fierce Apache. If they were instructed to kill, they believed it their duty—more than that, they would suffer the tortures of hell if they shirked or shrank from committing the deed."

"Oi'm not faling well at all, at all!" sighed Barney. "An' it's caught we are in a place where such craythurs be! Och, hone! Whoy didn't we shtay with th' profissor?"

Old Solitary again flitted away, and they hastened along at his heels. Now he was silent of lip and silent of foot. He seemed more like a shadow than anything else.

For more than an hour he led them forward with great swiftness, and then they came to a small stream.

"You must cover your trail," said the old man. "Follow me."

He stepped into the running water, walking along the bed of the stream.

They did not hesitate to follow in his footsteps.

Before long they came to where the stream fell splashing and tinkling down the mountain.

"Up," said Old Solitary.

It was a difficult climb, but the boys were young athletes, and they would have been ashamed to let the man with the white hair and beard climb where they could not go.

The stream was left, and, clinging to the points of rock with hands and feet, the old man still mounted higher and higher. He seemed to know every inch of the way, which became more and more difficult for the lads.

"Begorra!" gurgled Barney; "we'll nivver get down from here, Frankie, me jool."

"Well, we'll have no call to kick, if the Danites do not get up to us."

"Thot's right."

"But I cannot help thinking of Miskel's words. She declared that we were hopelessly snared."

"She may have troied to scare ye to death, lad."

"Well, what Old Solitary has said about the Destroying Angels has not made me feel any easier."

At last they came to a shelf of rock, along which they crept, inch by inch, clinging fast and feeling their way, with a blue void of night above and beneath them.

All at once a black opening in the face of the bluff yawned before them, and they saw the man of the white hair and beard standing in the mouth of a cave.

"This is my home," declared Old Solitary. "They have not dared attack me here, even though they know where to find me. They consider me harmless, but some day they shall know the difference. Uric Dugan shall know my power!"

He turned and entered the cave, and, still trusting all to him, they felt their way along after him.

# CHAPTER XX.

## MOUTH OF THE CAVE.

After a time, Old Solitary lighted a torch, and they were enabled to follow him with greater ease.

He led them into a circular chamber, where there was a bed of grass and some rude furniture of his own manufacture.

"This is my home," declared the strange man. "For the present, you are safe here; but there is no way of getting out of here without passing through territory where the Danites will be found."

"Then we are still in the meshes," said Frank.

"You are still in the very heart of Danite land."

"If what you say is true, then we cannot be safe here, for those human beasts know we are somewhere in the net, and they will find us, no matter what our hiding place may be."

"That is true, but it will take time, and they fear me. They will not rush hither. You may sleep without fear to-night."

"Surely we have need enough of sleep."

"Then do not hesitate to slumber, for I need little sleep, and I will see that no harm comes to you."

Frank would have questioned the man, but when he tried to do so in a manner that would not be offensive, Old Solitary suddenly became dumb, paying no heed to anything that was said.

Frank and Barney talked for a long time. They were impressed with the belief that they were in the gravest peril, and yet they could do nothing more to save themselves till the opportunity came. To a large extent, they were in the hands of fate.

Never before in all his life had Frank been utterly controlled by a feeling of utter inability to avert destruction by any effort of his own, even though his hands were free and he was armed. It seemed as if they had been doomed and were in a snare from which there could be no possible escape.

Everything must be trusted to Old Solitary, that was certain. Feeling thus, Frank flung himself down on the bed of grass, and was soon sleeping soundly.

It did not take Barney long to follow the example of his friend.

They slept for hours. When they awoke the torch had burned out, and the chilly darkness of the cave was dense around them.

"I wonder where Old Solitary is?" said Frank.

They called to him and their voices echoed hollowly along the passages.

No answer came.

"Begorra!" cried the Irish boy; "It looks loike he had left us to oursilves."

"It does seem that way," admitted Frank.

Our hero remembered seeing in a niche the night before a collection of sticks that he fancied were for torches, and so, lighting a match, he sought them. He had made no mistake, for one of them lighted readily.

"Our weapons are all right," he said, having made an examination. "It is probable that Old Solitary will soon return."

They waited an hour, but the strange man did not appear. Both grew restless, and finally started out to explore the cave.

With the aid of the torch, they picked their way along one of the passages. They were surprised at the distance traveled, and wondered when and where they would come out.

Finally, a gleam of light was seen ahead, and, as they came nearer, the torch was extinguished.

Climbing up a steep slope, they lay on their stomachs and peered out into the depths of a circular pocket that was inclosed by mountains on three sides.

An exclamation broke from the lips of both.

"A camp!" cried Frank.

"It's a town, me b'y!" Barney almost shouted. "We're all roight, afther all!"

"Easy!" cautioned Merriwell, quickly. "Keep your voice down. It is a town, but it is not the kind of a town we care to enter."

"Pwhat's th' matther wid it?"

"It is the town of the Danites. This is their retreat, where they have hidden themselves from the rest of the world."

Barney was soon convinced that Frank was right, and the boys drew back a bit, taking care not to be seen by anybody below them.

There was a collection of eight buildings upon which the morning sun was shining, six of which were dwelling houses, and two of which seemed to be stables. Taken all together, they made quite a little village.

The doors of many of the houses were open, and men were seen lounging about. Occasionally a woman could be seen, and there were a few children at play.

"Here live the last of the terrible organization that has shed the blood of hundreds of Gentiles," said Frank. "These men were known to be leaders, and the fate of John D. Lee was a warning to them. They saw the church could no longer protect them, and so they fled here. It is possible that some of those old men down there were concerned in the Mountain Meadow Massacre."

"It's the divvil's own set they are, to be sure."

"They have never hesitated to shed blood, and our lives will not be worth a pinch of snuff if we fall into their hands."

"Pwhat are we goin' to do?"

"That remains to be seen. For the present, we seem to be safe where we are. It is plain this cave extends through a spur of the mountain, and we are looking out on a side far from where we entered. It is also possible that, even now, some of these creatures may be climbing to the other entrance."

"Howly shmoke!"

"I said possible, not probable. I am trusting much to Old Solitary."

The boys lay there a long time, talking and peering down into the village of the Danites. They did not see a lithe, agile figure that was climbing in their direction. At length, having climbed as far as possible, this figure reached a stopping place, still below and at one side.

"Great shnakes!" gasped Barney, clutching Frank's arm. "Will yez take a look at thot!"

He pointed toward the figure.

"Cæsar's ghost! It is Miskel!"

"Pwhat is she doin' there, me b'y?"

"She seemed to be looking this way. I wonder if she has seen us here?"

"Oi dunno."

"She acts as if she has."

"Thot she does."

"She is hidden from the camp below by that mass of bowlders beside her, and she acts as if she were trying to keep out of sight of them down there."

"Pwhat's thot she has in her hand?"

"A bow. That is a perfect picture of the nymph Diana."

"Ay she ounly had some hounds an' a stag at hand."

"See—she has taken an arrow from a quiver at her back, and she seems to be attaching something to it. By the way she looks up here I should say she is measuring the distance with her eye, to see if she can make the arrow reach."

It certainly looked that way, and the boys watched her every movement with the keenest interest, still keeping as far concealed as possible.

Once Miskel lifted the bow and drew it taut, but something did not satisfy her, and she lowered it. After some moments the bow was lifted again, and then the arrow sailed upward through the air.

"It's coming!"

Both boys dodged.

Zip—click! The arrow cut through the air, sailed in at the opening of the cave, struck the face of the rock, and dropped to the ground.

Frank quickly picked it up.

"Ha!" he exclaimed. "Look, Barney—a bit of paper is attached here! There is writing on it! Ten to one it is a message!"

Eagerly he removed the bit of paper that was tied to the arrow, and he soon read aloud what was written on it.

"Frank Merriwell: It is known that you are there, but you are safe for the present, although still meshed and unable to escape. My father fears Old Solitary; but there are others who do not, and your refuge will not long continue a safe one. Your friends have arrived, and they are already in the snare, so it is not likely you will ever see either of them alive.

Miskel."

The last sentence filled both boys with the utmost wonder and perplexity.

"What does it mean?" asked Frank.

"Thot Oi'll nivver tell!" cried Barney.

"My friends? Whom can she mean? Who is it that is already within the snare?"

"Ax me something aisy!"

"And the Danites know where we are hidden!"

"Thot's pwhat she says, av ye read it roight."

"It is very comforting to know it! Uric Dugan fears Old Solitary, but there are others who do not."

"It's the others we nade to be afeared av, me lad."

"You are right. We must be constantly on our guard. Both of us must not sleep at the same time; we must take turns at sleeping. In that way we should be able to know when they try to come upon us, and we will sell our lives as dearly as possible."

"Av we've got to doie, Oi'd loike to wipe out the gang av spalpanes down there."

"Were they other than the murderous wretches they are, I should feel pity for them; but, as it is, there is no pity in my heart. It is a just retribution that they are outcast from their fellow-creatures, are forced to hide like hunted beasts, that they live in terror each day and each night of their lives."

"But this will nivver tell us who our friends are thot have entered th' snare, Frankie."

"No; nor do I know how we are to find out."

"Th' girrul——"

"Is descending."

It was true. Having accomplished her purpose in climbing up there, Miskel was descending. She was as sure-footed and agile as a mountain goat, and it was a pleasure to watch her.

"Frankie, she is a jool! An' do yez soay her fayther is ould Uric Dugan hissilf?"

"So she told me."

"It's a shame! Av it weren't fer thot, Oi'd thry me hand at makin' a mash on th' loikes av her."

Frank was silent; he seemed to be thinking.

"I have it!" he finally cried, striking his hands together.

"Kape it," advised Barney. "It's th' ounly thing ye're loikely to get around this place, my laddybuck."

"By my friends she must have meant Walter Clyde and his companions, Graves and Kerney. They have had time to cruise down the river, and they are here. I'll wager that I am right!"

"Ye may be. But soay! Look down there. So hilp me, there come some ay th' spalpanes, an' they have a prisoner!"

Barney was right. Several Danites were entering the pocket, conducting in their midst a captive. He was a small man, with red hair and whiskers.

"Heavens above!" gasped Frank, thunderstruck. "It's Professor Scotch!"

# CHAPTER XXI.

## HUMAN BEASTS.

It was indeed the little professor, who had, in some unaccountable manner, fallen captive to the Danites.

How it had happened the boys could not conceive.

"Be jabez! thot bates me!" gurgled Barney Mulloy, his eyes bulging. "It's hundreds av moiles from here Oi thought th' professor wur this minute."

"And I thought the same," said Frank. "How it comes that he is here I cannot understand."

"It's a moighty bad scrape he is in, me b'y."

"That is right. Now I know what Miskel meant when she said my friends had arrived and were already in the snare."

"The profissor makes but wan, an' she said 'friends.'"

"That is right. She must have meant Clyde and the others. That would make it appear that the professor came with them."

"Sure."

"In that case, where are Clyde and the two explorers, Graves and Kerney? Have they been killed already?"

"It moight seem thot way."

"It appears likely; but, if such is the case, I cannot understand why Professor Scotch was spared."

"No more can Oi, Frankie."

The boys were at their wits' end, and they were in an intensely agitated frame of mind.

Suddenly Frank clutched Barney's arm, pointing down into the pocket, and crying:

"Look! look! the professor has broken away! He is running for his life! But he cannot escape! They are hot after him."

It was true. The little man had made a desperate break for liberty, but it was folly to do so, as the Danites soon overtook him. One of them, a stout man, with a short white beard, held a revolver in his hand. He reversed the weapon, grasping it by the barrel, and struck the professor down with the butt.

The sight made Frank's blood boil.

"I will remember that wretch!" grated the boy, his eyes glowing. "If we do not get out of here, I may be able to square a score with him!"

Barney was scarcely less wrought up.

"Poor profissor!" he exclaimed. "It's loikely the divvils will finish him now."

The Danites stood over the man, who had fallen on his face, and lay in a huddled heap. They were talking loudly and making excited gestures. It was plain that they were discussing the advisability of dispatching Professor Scotch without delay, and, judging from his movements, the man with the short white beard was for finishing him without delay. Twice the man pointed his revolver at the prostrate figure, and twice a younger man seemed to urge him to spare the unlucky man's life.

"If he shoots, I'll try a shot at him from here!" cried Frank. "I may not be able to reach him, but I'll try it."

A third time the man pointed his revolver at the motionless form of the man who lay huddled on the ground. This time no one of the group interfered; all stood back, and the younger man, who had twice saved Scotch's life, turned away, plainly unwilling to witness the deed.

"He's going to shoot!" panted Frank, pulling forward his rifle, and bringing it to his shoulder. "I will——"

"Wait a bit, me b'y. Look there! Th' litthle girrul is thrying to save him."

"God bless her!"

Miskel had rushed into the midst of the men, and she was seen pleading with the man who seemed determined to kill the professor. At first, it seemed that she would fail, but she finally prevailed, and the man put up his weapon, with a gesture of angry impatience. Then he seemed to give some orders, and the unconscious captive was lifted and carried toward the camp.

"He is saved for the time," breathed Frank, with relief; "but it is simply a respite."

"Thot is betther than nothing, me b'y."

"Yes, it is better than nothing. Barney, I have a scheme."

"Spake out, Frankie. Me ears are woide open to-night."

"If they spare Professor Scotch till to-night, we will go down there and attempt his rescue."

"Oi'm wid yes, me b'y, to th' ind."

They watched the men bear the unfortunate professor into the camp, and noted carefully the building into which the man was taken.

"We must make no mistake to-night, Barney. It is our duty to do our best to save Professor Scotch."

"An' we'll do our duty av we nivver do anything ilse, begorra!"

"You are bold lads," said a voice behind them; "but you cannot save him from Uric Dugan."

They whirled swiftly, and found Old Solitary had come up behind them, without being heard.

"I found you had awakened," said the strange man; "and I wondered if you had come here."

"And we wondered where you had gone."

"I went forth to see what I should see," he said, in a peculiar manner. "Voices far away in empty space were calling to me— calling, calling, calling!"

The boys shot hasty glances at each other, the same thought flitting through the minds of both.

They had dealt with one maniac, and now was it possible that they were to encounter another?

It had been dark when Old Solitary came upon them the night before, and so they were unable to study his face; but now they saw that his eyes were restless and filled with a shifting light, while his general appearance was that of a man deranged.

Quickly leaning toward Barney, Frank whispered:

"He must be humored; don't anger him."

The man, although he could not have heard the words, noted that something was said, and he cried:

"Why do you whisper together. Would you betray me? Is there no one in the wide world I can trust?"

"Betray you?" said Frank. "To whom can we betray you? You have us in your power, and you can betray us to the Danites, if you choose. You need not fear that we shall betray you."

"Then it must be that you are afraid of me. All the world seems to fear me. Why is it so? What have I ever done to make men afraid of me?"

"Nothing evil, I am sure."

"And you are right. It cuts me to have men shrink from me; but they do, and I have become an outcast. There is something wrong about me—I feel it here."

His hand was lifted to his head, and his face wore a look of deep distress. He seemed to realize, in an uncertain way, that he was not quite right in his mind.

"You have lived so much by yourself that you have grown unsocial," said Frank. "That must be the trouble."

Old Solitary shook his head.

"That is not it. Listen, and I will tell you something. Uric Dugan hates and fears me. I do not care for that; it gives me satisfaction. Still I do not know why it gives me satisfaction, for it pains me when others shrink away in fear. Dugan would kill me if he could, and still he seems to regard me as one risen from death. Can you tell me why?"

He paused, looking at them in an inquiring way.

"You can't tell," came swiftly from his lips, as Frank was about to speak. "No one can tell. I do not know myself. My memory is broken into a thousand fragments. Some things I remember well; some things I do not remember at all. There was a time when I was young, and I had friends. Who were my friends? What has happened to rob me of my memory? I believe Uric Dugan can tell me. If I had not believed so, Dugan should have died long ago. Scores of times I have held his life in the hollow of my hand. I have longed to slay him—to kill him for some wrong he has done me. My hand has been held by a power I could not see. A voice has whispered in my ear, 'Wait.' I have waited. For what? I do not know."

He bowed his head on his breast, over which flowed his long white beard, and his attitude was one of intense dejection.

The boys were silent, wondering at the strange man who had befriended them.

Some moments passed.

"By going forth early I saw many things," the man finally declared, speaking quietly. "You are not the only ones who have strayed into the net of the Danites."

"We have been informed there are others," said Frank.

"Informed? How?"

Frank told how Miskel had shot the message into the mouth of the cave.

"I have seen her hundreds of times," slowly spoke Old Solitary. "She has a good face. It does not seem possible that she is his daughter—the daughter of Uric Dugan. I think the memory of her face has spared his life at times. But it will not be ever thus. The time will come when I shall steel my heart."

"We have just seen the Danites bear a captive into their village, and that captive is my guardian."

"A small man with reddish hair and beard?"

"Yes."

"I saw him captured. He had wandered from others. From a

height I saw them all."

"How many are there?"

"There were four, but two of them are Danites."

"What's that?"

"It is true. The man of the sandy beard and the boy came here with two of Uric Dugan's wretched satellites."

"Howly saints!" gasped Barney.

"He must mean the explorers, Graves and Kerney," said Frank.

"They were not explorers; if they said so, they lied. Caleb Kerney is one of the old band of Danites, as bloodthirsty and relentless as the worst of them. Colton Graves is the son of Pascal Graves, once a leader of the Destroying Angels—a man whose hands were dyed with innocent blood. They went forth, with others, to bring provisions from the settlements. All of the others have returned before them."

"And they led Walter Clyde and Professor Scotch into this snare!" said Frank. "They found out that Walter was coming this way to search for the retreat of the Danites, and they led him here, with the intention of destroying him."

"Thot's roight, me b'y," nodded Barney.

"Kerney slipped away, and hastened ahead to tell Uric Dugan who was coming," said Old Solitary, who seemed to know all that had taken place. "Graves remained to guide the victims to their doom."

"Is it possible such monsters can continue to live and carry on their murderous work?" exclaimed Frank.

"Some day Ko-pe-tah will find the way in here," laughed Old Solitary.

"Who is Ko-pe-tah?"

"A Navajo chief who hates Uric Dugan, and has tried to kill him. Twice within two years has Ko-pe-tah brought his braves into these mountains, searching for some access to this valley. The last time he was here, he found the passage by which you entered. Four of the Danites held the passage against a hundred warriors, and the Navajoes were repulsed. But Ko-pe-tah swore he would come again. If he ever gets in here, woe unto the Danites!"

"How did it happen that we came through that passage without being stopped?"

"You were alone, two boys. You were seen, and were allowed to enter, for they knew you could not escape. They made sure of you by letting you walk into the trap."

"But Ko-pe-tah was held out."

"Because he had a hundred warriors behind him, and he would

destroy the Danites if he got inside."

This was logical enough, and, at that moment Old Solitary scarcely seemed like a person deranged.

Frank spent some moments in thought, and then asked:

"Are Clyde and Graves still together?"

"They are."

"And Clyde has no knowledge that Graves is other than what he represented himself to be?"

"It is not likely that he has."

"He must be warned."

"It is too late.'

"Why?"

"Before you can reach him the Danites will have him in their power."

"That is not certain," cried Frank, starting up. "Come, we will try to save him. Lead us to him."

"You shall see that what I say is true," said Old Solitary.

He motioned for them to follow, and led the way back along the passage, the torch having been relighted.

Through the main chamber they passed, and came to another passage, which finally brought them out far from the mountain pocket in which was the home of the Danites.

"Look," directed Old Solitary, touching Frank's arm and pointing across the wide canyon. "Away there you see figures moving amid the rocks. They are human beings with hearts of beasts. They are Danites, and they are creeping like panthers upon their victim, the boy you call Walter Clyde."

# CHAPTER XXII.

## PROFESSOR SCUDMORE RETURNS.

e must aid him!" cried Frank.

"Thot's right," agreed Barney.

"It's too late," declared Old Solitary.

"Too late—why?"

"Long before we can get down into the valley the boy will be killed or captured."

"And must we remain idle and witness the butchery? It is terrible! I feel that I must do something."

"An' Oi fale th' soame, Frankie, me b'y."

"Look again," directed the strange man of the mountains. "The boy has discovered his enemies. See—he has leaped behind some rocks! Graves is with him. The man is playing his part still. It must be that the boy has called on his enemies to halt. They are hiding. See there! one of them is preparing to shoot at the boy. Watch! The boy will be killed! No, he has changed his position. The man fired too late."

Frank and Barney were intensely excited as they watched what was taking place in the canyon. Clyde, after leaping to the shelter of the rocks, had changed his position just in time to save himself from being shot. One of the Danites took careful aim, a puff of smoke shot from the muzzle of his rifle, and, some time later, the report of the weapon reached the ears of the trio at the mouth of the cave.

But Providence must have watched over Walter Clyde then, for the boy moved a moment before the rifle sent forth its dead messenger, and he escaped the bullet. Whirling swiftly, he brought the butt of his rifle to his shoulder, and fired straight into the midst of the puff of smoke.

"Hurro!" shouted Barney.

"He nailed the wretch!" cried Frank, with satisfaction.

It was true, Clyde's bullet knocked the man over in a twinkling, and he lay writhing amid the rocks.

"He is a brave boy," muttered Old Solitary. "It is a pity he cannot escape! He is but one of hundreds of brave hearts butchered by the Danites."

There was a lull far across the canyon.

"What is coming now?" speculated Frank. "The Danites seem dazed."

"Look, and you shall see what is coming," said Old Solitary, his fingers again closing on our hero's arm. "You can see Clyde's companion, the treacherous Graves. Watch; ah! I knew it!"

Graves was seen to rise behind Clyde, uplift some weapon in his hand, and strike the boy prostrate.

Then, with a yell that faintly reached the ears of the watching three, the Danites scrambled over the rocks.

"The tragedy is over," said Old Solitary, solemnly. "The deadly work is done. Poor boy!"

"Poor boy!" echoed Frank.

"It's dearly th' spalpanes will pay fer this noight!" grated Barney Mulloy. "It's nivver a bit will Oi hesitate about stoppin' wan av th' divvils from b'rathin' av Oi get a chance."

"I do not think my conscience will trouble me much if I am forced to finish one of them," said Frank, huskily.

"They are beasts—human beasts!" declared Old Solitary. "It is not a sin to place such where they can do no harm to the rest of the world."

"Sin!" exclaimed Barney. "It's a deed av charity!"

The Danites were seen leaning over their victim. In a few moments they lifted Clyde to his feet, and then it was evident that the boy had not been slain outright, but had been stunned long enough for them to make him their captive.

"It were better if they had killed him quickly," said Old Solitary.

"I don't know about that," panted Frank. "Where there is life there is hope."

"All who enter this canyon may leave hope behind."

"Av they let th' poor lad live till to-night, we'll do our bist fer him," said Barney.

"That we will," nodded Frank.

Clyde seemed to have recovered, and now he was marched along in the midst of his captors, who moved straight toward the pocket where the homes of the Danites were located.

For all of their situation, Frank Merriwell had not given up hope. He was young, and he still believed that all evil things come to an evil end, and all good things eventually triumph. He had not grown cynical and pessimistic.

Drawing back into the mouth of the cave, the trio watched the Danites march across the canyon with their captive.

Graves was with the men, and he no longer pretended to be friendly to the boy. At last Clyde knew him for what he actually was.

At length the entire party passed from view on their way to the pocket.

Then Old Solitary led the boys back into the cave, where they ate breakfast, such as it was, and attempted to lay plans for the coming night.

It was a long, dreary, wretched day they spent in the cave. Many times they went to the opening where they could look down into the Danite village. Once they saw Uric Dugan, and once they saw Miskel, his daughter.

But the day passed on, and, to their intense relief, they saw nothing to indicate that the captives were executed.

Night came at last.

The boys were eager to be astir. Their blood was throbbing hotly in their veins, and they felt capable of any deed of daring.

They looked to their weapons, making sure everything was ready for business, and then they followed Old Solitary from the cave.

The descent was slow and tedious, fraught with much peril, and long in the accomplishment. To the eager boys, it seemed that they would never get down.

The task was finally accomplished, and then they moved onward, with Old Solitary in the lead.

They had not gone far when a gasp of astonishment came from Frank's lips, and he clutched Barney, softly crying:

"Look up there! What do you make of that?"

Barney looked upward, as directed, and, high in the air, he saw a bright light that was swiftly settling toward the earth.

"It's a shooting shtar, begobs!" exclaimed the Irish lad.

"Not much!" broke from Frank. "That is no star. It looks like a light, with a reflector behind it."

"Well, who knows but thot's th' woay a shtar looks?"

"It is not a star," said Old Solitary; "but what it is I cannot say."

"I know!" cried Frank.

"What is it, then?"

"The Eagle."

"What is the Eagle?"

"An air ship."

Old Solitary gave a muttered exclamation of incredulity. "Impossible!"

"It is not impossible," asserted Frank. "It was in the Eagle that we came here from Blake."

"Thot's roight," agreed Barney.

Then in a few words Frank told the man of their trip from Blake, how Professor Scudmore had gone mad, and how they had captured the ship from the professor, who afterward escaped and got away with the Eagle in the night.

The boy's apparent sincerity convinced Old Solitary that he spoke the truth, and by the time Frank had finished, the air ship had settled close to the earth. They could see its outlines through the darkness, and could see a man in the car.

The Eagle came down gently, and the man stepped out.

"It was somewhere amid these mountains that I left those poor boys," he murmured. "There is not one chance in ten thousand that I shall ever find them again."

"You have stumbled on that one chance," said Frank, speaking distinctly, and advancing fearlessly toward the man.

"Eh!"

Professor Scudmore seemed on the point of leaping into the air ship and taking to flight, but he suddenly changed his mind.

"Can't get away quick enough to escape," he said. "Have let off enough gas so the ballast brought her down, and I could not throw out the rest of the ballast and get away. If enemies come, I am lost."

"We are not enemies," assured Frank. "We are the boys you left not many miles from here."

"It can't be possible!" cried the lank professor, in the greatest surprise and delight. "Then this is the work of Providence—it must be!"

His joy was almost boundless.

"I was mad at the time," he explained; "I must have been. Otherwise, I'd never done such a thing. I came to my sober senses after a time, and then I resolved to come back here, hoping to find you, but not expecting to."

"Begorra! ye done a great thrick thot toime!" put in Barney Mulloy. "Frankie, me b'y we'll get away in th' 'Agle, an' th' Danite thot catches us will have to have wings."

"That is right," said Frank. "This will provide a means of escape for us, if the professor will take us along."

"I am here to take you along," assured Scudmore.

"But we cannot go till we have done our best to rescue Professor

Scotch and Walter Clyde."

"Roight, me lad."

They then explained to Scudmore what had happened to the professor and the boy.

"If my gas generator is all right, so I can inflate the Eagle to its full extent, I shall be able to take four persons with me," said the tall professor. "While you are doing your best to rescue the captives, I will remain here and try to put the ship in condition to sail at short notice."

He seemed perfectly sane, and there was nothing to do but to trust him, and so this plan was agreed to by the boys.

Old Solitary kept in the background, saying nothing.

When everything was arranged, Frank and Barney left the professor, and once more followed the strange man of the canyon on their way to the village of the Danites.

They urged Old Solitary to lose no time, for they were eager to do their best in the effort to save Professor Scotch and Walter Clyde and get away from the canyon.

It was not long before they drew near the pocket, and they advanced with great caution, although it was not thought absolutely necessary, as there was not one chance in a hundred that the Danites would expect them to make such an audacious attempt.

Deep in the canyon the shadows lay thick, which was to their advantage. They succeeded in entering the pocket without being challenged.

Lights twinkled from two or three windows. Somewhere in the village a beautiful but untrained voice was singing the chorus of a love song.

"That is Miskel," whispered Frank.

They lay in the darkness, watching and waiting.

Of a sudden an unexpected thing happened. The door of the very building into which Professor Scotch had been carried was flung wide open, allowing a broad bar of light to shine out. Then, out of this lighted doorway streamed a dozen men, and a bell began to clang in a doleful manner.

"What does it mean?" whispered Frank, wonderingly.

"It means that the tribunal of death has pronounced doom upon the captives," answered Old Solitary. "The session has just broken up, and the captives will be executed without delay."

# CHAPTER XXIII.

## LAST OF THE DANITES.

ow do you know?"

"I have witnessed other executions here."

"Then no time is to be lost."

"What would you do?"

"I do not know—something, anything to save them!"

Old Solitary held Frank back.

"Do not throw your life away," he said. "Wait a while. See, they are lighting two bonfires, the piles of wood having been prepared in advance."

"What is that for?"

"That there may be plenty of light for the execution, which the entire camp will witness. See, a few moments ago the place seemed asleep, but now it is all astir with life."

"I see," groaned the wretched boy; "and it seems to me that there is very little chance for us to get in there and save Scotch and Clyde."

"Not one chance in a hundred. See those two posts in the full glare of light? Well, to those posts the captives are to be tied. It is plain that the tribunal have doomed them to death by shooting. What a farce!"

"That's right!" grated Frank; "it is a farce! As well might they have killed them in the first place. There was no chance for them to escape."

"Not the least."

"Look, Frankie," whispered Barney, "there comes th' poor profissor, an' Cloyde is clost behindt him."

The Danites were marching their captives out to execution!

In a very few moments the professor and the boy were tied to the death-posts.

Uric Dugan directed the movements of the Danites.

"Where is Miskel?" hoarsely breathed Frank. "Will she do nothing to prevent this?"

"She has done all she could," muttered Old Solitary. "It is probable she was not aware the tribunal was in progress. She will be prevented from interfering now."

And now six men, with rifles in their hands, formed a line in front of the prisoners.

Everything was done with startling swiftness.

Frank Merriwell was trembling with eagerness and excitement, and he appealed to Old Solitary:

"Are we to remain inactive and see this frightful deed? Are we to do nothing now that we are here?"

"We will do what we can," declared the strange man. "The time has come for Dugan's career to end! I feel that I must strike. He shall never give the fatal signal!"

The man lifted his old rifle, and the hammer clicked as he cocked it.

Dugan stepped forth to give the signal, and his harsh voice rang out distinctly:

"Ready!"

The firing squad lifted their rifles.

"Take aim!"

The fatal moment was at hand.

The butt of Old Solitary's rifle came to the man's shoulder. He was resting on one knee, and the weapon was held as steady as the hills. "One!" counted Dugan.

It was the last word he ever uttered, for a spout of flame leaped from the muzzle of Old Solitary's weapon, and the bullet sped on its fatal mission.

Without a cry or a groan, Dugan flung up his hands and plunged headlong upon his face.

There was a wild shriek, and the form of a girl rushed into the firelight. Down beside the fallen man she dropped, lifting his head and staring wildly into his face.

It was Miskel, but she could not save her wicked father, for the aim of Old Solitary had been accurate.

The Danites were thrown into the greatest confusion, and Frank Merriwell held back no longer.

"Come on, Barney!" he shouted.

"Oi'm wid yez!" assured the undaunted Irish lad.

Forward they rushed, each firing a shot as they did so, and adding to the dismay of the Danites.

Straight up to Professor Scotch ran Frank, and, with one slash of a sharp knife he had drawn, he released the man.

Barney did the same thing for Walter Clyde, and the two were set at liberty before the Danites realized what was happening. Then bullets began to whistle around them.

At that moment a wild, strange cry cut the night air, filling the hearts of the Danites with the utmost terror.

It was the war cry of the Navajoes!

A hundred dusky forms seemed to materialize from the darkness, and a hundred savage warriors, deadly enemies of the Danites, came charging into the camp.

Old Solitary had rushed to the side of Uric Dugan, into whose face he glared, as he cried:

"Look, Dugan, look! You robbed me of reason, of memory, of everything I held dear; but I have been avenged, for it was my hand that laid you low!"

"He is dead!" screamed Miskel, and she fainted on her father's body.

"Yes, he is dead!" said the avenger, in a half-regretful tone. "And he never knew who killed him."

Then he suddenly caught up the girl and rushed away into the darkness, with her flung over his shoulder.

How Frank and his companions escaped from that spot without falling before the Danites or the savages they scarcely knew. A dozen times they fancied all was lost. They emptied their weapons, they struck down every one who blocked their way, and they finally succeeded in getting out of the pocket.

That they did so at all was due to the fact that the Navajoes, who had surprised and overcome the guard in the pass, believed they held the only exit from the canyon, which made it impossible for any one to get away, even though they might escape temporarily. If two or three were to escape for the time, the Indians felt that it was impossible for them to get away entirely.

But Professor Septemas Scudmore, with his air ship, was in the canyon, and the boys, half lugging the exhausted Professor Scotch, found him waiting for them, greatly alarmed and excited by the sounds of the battle.

"What does it mean?" cried the lank professor, as the party rushed up. "What is all that shooting and yelling?"

"There is no time to explain now," said Frank. "Get in, everybody, and let's get out of this infernal place as soon as we can! There is not a moment to lose."

"I am bewildered," declared Scudmore. "A moment ago an old man with white hair and beard rushed up to me, bearing a girl in his arms. She had fainted, and he thrust her into the car, telling me to wait for you, and take her away with us."

"It was Old Solitary, and the girl must be Miskel. Is she in the car now?"

"Yes."

"And the man?"

"He is gone."

"It was Old Solitary, sure enough, and he will be able to hide from the savages. We cannot wait for him."

"The Eagle would not carry so many, even if we could wait. I have her inflated, and she is tied down. Get in, get in! We'll throw out every bit of ballast, and make the attempt to rise out of the canyon. It may be a failure, but I think it will succeed, if we can get high enough to strike the strong wind which is blowing above us. We can try."

They got into the car, and the bags of ballast were tossed overboard. Then the ropes were cut, and the air ship rose slowly with its heavy burden.

Four days later five persons were seated in a room in the town of Loa, which is located amid the mountains of Southern Utah. The five were Professors Scotch and Scudmore, and the three boys, Frank, Barney and Walter Clyde.

"Then you are determined to go back to Water Pocket Canyon and the place where the camp of the Danites was, are you, Clyde?" asked Frank.

"I shall not be satisfied till I do so," was the answer. "I must find Old Solitary, if he is living, for I believe he is my father."

"I have thought that such might be the case," said Frank. "In some way he has been wronged by Uric Dugan. He did not seem to know exactly how, but he was sure of it. It was only at times that he seemed deranged, but he did not remember much of his past."

"It would be most remarkable if he should turn out to be my father, whom I have believed dead all these years."

"It would be a miracle," declared Professor Scotch. "But do you know you can find Water Pocket Canyon again?"

"Yes, for I have Ben Barr to guide me. He will take me there."

"Well," said the little professor, "I wish you success, but I would not go back there for the worlds, and I absolutely refuse to let my boys go."

"I suppose we'll have to humor the professor in this instance," laughed Frank. "Our last escapade came near being fatal for all of us."

"You owe your salvation to Professor Septemas Scudmore," declared that individual, importantly. "But for his marvelous invention, the Eagle, you would have fallen victims to untamed savages."

"Begorra, thot's roight!" nodded Barney. "Th' 'Agle is a great birrud."

"It is bound to make me famous the world over, and send my name ringing down the corridors of time."

"But what of poor Miskel?" asked Frank. "She is heartbroken over the death of her father. She knows nothing of the world at large, and——"

"Under the circumstances," said Walter, "I feel that it is my duty to see that she does not come to harm. As long as she wants it, she shall have a home with my folks, if she will accept."

"Be aisy, me b'y!" chuckled Barney, roguishly. "It's a swate purty face she has, an' Oi'm thinkin' ye're a bit shtuck on her."

"Oh, come!" protested Walter, blushing. "I have known her but four days, and——"

"Ye've made good progress, me lad. Oi notice thot you have done firrust-rate comfortin' her. It's an invoite to th' weddin' Oi warnt, an' Oi think Frankie would look foine as th' bist man."

"If the wedding ever takes place, you shall be invited."

The mystery of Old Solitary remains still, for he was never found; although Walter and Ben Barr did make their way into Water Pocket Canyon once more. The ruins of the Danite village were found, also human bones, picked clean by wolves and vultures. No living thing seemed to remain in the vicinity, and the silence and shadow of death hung over the place.

Old Solitary's cave was deserted. It is possible that, after all, the strange man fell a victim to the savages; but it is more likely that, being deranged, he was spared by them, and they made him a great medicine man among them. Perchance he is living with them to-day on the Navajo reservation.

"I think we are well out of that," said Frank, when it was all over. "I want no more of the murderous Danites."

"Humph, I told you to keep off," grunted Professor Scotch. "But you'll soon run into equal peril, I'll warrant."

"No, professor—only sight-seeing in the future."

"And where?"

"Yellowstone Park, the great National reservation."

"Hurro!" cried Barney. "Just the sphot Oi've been wantin' to see."

"Yes, I'd like to see the park myself," said the professor. "We'll be safe there."

But were they? Let us wait and see.

# CHAPTER XXIV.

## YELLOWSTONE PARK.

**B**urro!"

"What is it, Barney?"

"Boofaloes, Frankie!"

"Buffalo?"

"Sure, me b'y!"

"Where?"

Frank scrambled eagerly to the crest of the ridge on which his friend was perched.

They were in the heart of that picturesque wonderland about the head waters of the Yellowstone River, known as the National Park.

Frank had a camera slung at his back, and for three days he had been trying to get a "shot" with it at a buffalo, having been told there was a small herd of the nearly extinct creatures somewhere in that region.

Neither of the boys had the least desire to kill one of the animals, and a "shot" with the camera at close range would have satisfied them.

And now, in the grassy valley below them, at a distance of half a mile, they could see five of the animals they sought. The creatures were grazing, with the exception of the largest of the herd, which seemed to be standing on guard, now and then snuffing the wind.

The moment Frank saw them he clutched his companion, drawing him backward and down behind some bowlders.

"Pwhat's th' matther wid yez?" spluttered Barney, in surprise.

"If we expect to get near enough to photograph those creatures, we must get out of this right away."

"Whoy?"

"Did you observe the old fellow who is standing on guard? Peer out and you can see him. He is headed this way."

"Pwhat av thot? He can't see us, me b'y."

"He might not see us, but he is liable to smell us."

"At this distance? Go on wid yer foolin', Frankie!"

"I am not fooling; I am in earnest when I say he is liable to smell us. We are on the wrong side of that herd, if so few may be called a herd."

"Whoy on th' wrong soide?"

"We are to windward."

"Not doirectly."

"No, not directly. If we had been, those creatures would be scampering off already. Their sense of scent is remarkable."

"Is it a jolly ye're givin' us?"

"Not a bit of it, Barney; I am in earnest. Their power of sight is not particularly acute, but it is said that they 'can smell a man a mile.'"

"Thin how can we ivver induce th' bastes to sit fer their photygrafs?"

"We'll have to get on the other side of them, and creep up behind that small clump of timber."

"It will take an hour to get round there, me b'y."

"All of that; but I shall be well repaid if I can obtain a picture of some real wild buffalo. What a sight it must have been to behold one of those immense herds which once covered the plains 'from horizon to horizon,' as we are told. Now it is a known fact that there are less than fifty wild buffaloes in existence. A little more than fifteen years ago it was said that about three hundred thousand Indians subsisted almost entirely on the flesh of the buffalo."

"An' is thot roight?"

"It is right, Barney. The hide-hunter has destroyed the buffalo. The creatures were slaughtered by thousands, stripped of their hides, and their carcasses left to rot and make food for wolves and vultures."

"An' wur there no law to stop th' killin' av thim?"

"No. If there had been, it could not have been enforced on the great plains. The railroad, civilization, and the white man's lust for killing, which he calls sport, doomed the buffalo.

"But this is not getting a picture of 'real wild buffalo.' I have pictures of Golden Gate Pass, Fire Hole Basin, Union Geysers, and almost everything else but wild buffalo, and I have vowed I would not leave the park till I had one of the latter. Come on."

He backed from the crest of the ridge and down the slope, Barney following. In a few moments the boys could rise to their feet and make their way along.

Both were armed, for it was not known what danger they might encounter, and wild animals of all kinds were plentiful enough, from the beaver to the grizzly bear, thanks to the very effective policing of the park by two troops of United States Cavalry. Two regiments could not entirely prevent poaching, but two troops were very successful, and the boys had found sections of the American Wonderland exactly as primitive as when the lonely trapper Coulter made his famous journey through it.

Frank and Barney had taken care not to slaughter any of the game they saw, although they had been tempted by wild geese, which were so tame they would hardly get out of the way, and by deer and bears innumerable.

The lads believed in the laws which protected these creatures, and knew that this great game preserve and breeding-ground, if not disturbed, must always give an overflow into Montana, Wyoming, and Idaho, which will make big game shooting there for years to come.

Frank led the way at a swift pace, keeping the ridge between them and the buffalo for a time, and then making use of other shelter.

It was nearly an hour before they came round to the windward side of the herd and began working in upon it.

All at once, with a low exclamation, Frank stopped, shifted his position quickly, and hissed:

"Down, Barney!"

"Pwhat is it, Frankie?"

"Be careful! Look there by the base of that bluff. Can you see them?"

"Oi see something moving. Pwhat is it?"

"Hunters, I reckon."

"Afther th' boofalo?"

"Yes. They are nearer than we are, and they will be taking a shot at the creatures in a minute. It's a shame! If the soldier-police were only here!"

"Nivver a bit do Oi loike th' oidea av seein' thim boofalo shot onliss Oi can do th' shootin'."

"No more do I, and I am not going to stand it! Come on, Barney. We'll get after those fellows. We may be able to stop them before they shoot, and then get a picture of the buffalo afterward. Lively now."

The boys sprang to their feet and went running toward the spot near the base of the bluff, where they had seen men moving. As they ran, they crouched low, holding their rifles at their sides, and taking great pains not to be seen by the buffalo. In fact, they paid so much attention to this that they did not note how near they were to the bluff, till they almost ran upon the very men they had seen moving there.

Then there was a shock and a surprise, for they found themselves face to face with a dozen Blackfeet Indians!

"Howly shmoke!" gurgled Barney, as he came to a sudden halt.

"Jupiter!" muttered Frank, also stopping quickly.

The Indians stared at them, and grunted:

"How, how! Ugh!"

One of them, a villainous-looking half-blood, spoke up:

"What white boys do? shoot buffalo?"

"No," answered Frank, promptly, "we are not here to shoot them, but we want to get a picture of them."

"Pic'ter? Hugah! No good!"

The half-blood was doubtful; he believed they had intended to shoot the buffalo, and his eyes glittered with greed as he noted the handsome rifles carried by the lads.

"Lemme looker gun," he said, stepping toward Frank, and holding out a hand, nearly one-half of which had been torn away by some accident.

Now Frank knew there would not be one chance in a thousand of getting back his rifle if he let the fellow have it, and so he decisively said:

"No, I will not let you look at it. Keep off! The soldiers will have you for killing game in this park if you do not make tracks back to your reservation."

"Ha! Soldiers fools! Half Hand not afraid of soldier. He watch up. They be way off there to north, ten, twenty, thirty mile. No soldiers round—nobody round. White boy lemme looker gun."

Again he advanced, his manner aggressive, and the boys realized they were in a decidedly perilous situation.

# CHAPTER XXV.

## FAY.

h' spalpane manes ter kape it av he gits his hand on it," whispered Barney. "It's murther he has in his oies."

Frank knew well enough that Barney was right, and he had no intention of relinquishing his hold on his rifle for a moment. He fell back a step, lifting the weapon in a suggestive manner, and Half Hand halted, scowling blackly and smiling craftily by turns.

"Hold up!" came sharply from the lips of the boy. "Keep your distance, or you will get damaged."

"Ha! White boy threaten Half Hand! Be careful! Half Hand good when him not threatened; heap bad when him threatened. White boys two; Injuns big lot more. White boys make Injuns mad, then where um be?"

"I have no desire to make you mad, but this is my rifle, and I mean to keep it."

"Half Hand want to look."

"You may look at a distance, but you can't lay a hand on it."

"White boy heap 'fraid. Give gun back pretty quick bimeby."

"I fancy it would be bimeby. No, you cannot take it, and that settles it."

"Mebbe Half Hand trade with boy."

"I do not wish to trade."

"Mebbe Half Hand give um heap good trade."

"Possibly, but that makes no difference."

"White boy fool!" snarled the half-blood. "If um don't lemme take gun, Half Hand take it anyhow, and then white boy no git a thing for it."

This was quite enough to startle Frank, and he sharply declared:

"If you attempt to take this rifle, you will get a pill out of it in advance! That is straight business, Mr. Half Hand."

"Hurro!" cried Barney, his fighting blood beginning to rise. "Av it's foight ye want, ye red nagurs, jist wade roight inter us! We'll give ye all th' foight ye want, begobs!"

The Blackfeet jabbered among themselves a minute, and it was plain that they were not all of one mind. Some seemed to be for attacking the boys, while others opposed it. Half Hand hotly urged them on.

"Fall back," said Frank, speaking softly to the Irish lad. "Be ready for a rush. If they come, give it to them. I will take Half Hand myself. You take the fellow with the red feather. If they kill us, we'll have the satisfaction of getting two or three of them in advance."

The boy's voice was cool and steady, and his nerves seemed of iron. He glanced over his shoulder in search of some place of shelter, but could discover none near by, much to his disappointment.

Barney was also cool enough, although the hot blood was rushing swiftly through his veins. He was holding himself in check, in imitation of his friend and comrade.

In truth, the two lads were in a tight corner. It was plain that the Indian poachers were made up of rebellious Blackfeet, who could not be kept on the reservation, and their faces showed they were the very worst sort. Having been caught almost in the act of killing game within the park, and believing the two lads had no friends near by, the dusky villains might not hesitate at outright murder spurred on by their greed for plunder, lust for blood, and a desire to keep the boys from notifying the soldiers of the presence of Indians on forbidden ground.

Frank fully understood their peril, and he felt that they would be lucky indeed if they escaped with their lives.

He blamed himself for running into the trap in such a blind manner, and still he felt that he was not to blame. He had seen moving figures at a distance, and, as the Indians were keeping under cover, in order to creep upon the buffalo, he had no more than caught a glimpse of them. They were dressed in clothes they had obtained by trade or plunder from white men, and so, at a distance and under such circumstances, it was not remarkable that Frank had not noted they were savages.

In a few moments Half Hand seemed to bring the most of the Indians to his way of thinking, and he again turned on the boys.

"Good white boys," he croaked, craftily. "Don't be 'fraid of Injuns. Injuns won't hurt um."

"We are not afraid of you," returned Frank; "but you want to keep your distance, or you will get hurt by us."

"Thot's roight, begorra!" cried Barney, fingering his Winchester. "It's stoofed to th' muzzle, this ould shootin' iron is, wid grapeshot an' canister, an' av Oi leggo wid it, there won't be a red nagur av yez left on his pins."

"Injuns want to talk with white boys," said the half-blood, edging nearer, inch by inch. "Injuns want to hold powwow."

"We are not at all anxious to hold a powwow with you. Stand where you are!"

Up came Frank's rifle a bit.

It was plain that the red ruffians meant to make an assault, and the moment was at hand. They were handling their weapons in a way that told how eager some of them were to shed the blood of the boys.

Barney, in his characteristic, devil-may-care manner, began to hum, "My Funeral's To-morrow." He seemed utterly unable to take matters seriously, however great the danger.

A moment before the rush and encounter must have taken place, all were startled to hear a merry, childish laugh, and a voice saying:

"I knowed I'd find tomebody tomewhere. I wants to tome down. Tate me down, please."

On the top of the bluff, forty feet above the heads of the Indians, stood a little girl, dressed in white. She had golden hair and blue eyes, and, on her lofty perch, she looked like a laughing fairy.

"Mother av Mowses!" gurgled Barney.

"A child!" exclaimed Frank, astonished. "Here!"

The Indians muttered and hesitated. Half Hand still urged them on, but it was plain that they believed there was a party of white persons near at hand, and they feared to attack the boys. The urging of the half-blood was in vain, and he was forced to give it up.

Then he turned fiercely on the boys, snarling:

"Good thing for you your friends come! They no come, we kill you and take your guns! Mebbe we see you 'gain some time bimeby."

Then the Indians turned and quickly scudded away, soon disappearing from view amid some pines.

Frank drew a breath of relief.

"That was a close shave," he muttered.

"Begorra! It was thot," nodded Barney. "Av it hadn't been fer th' litthle girrul, we'd lost our scoolps Oi belave."

"The little girl!" exclaimed Frank. "She appeared like a good fairy, and——"

"Dat's my name. Mamma talls me Fairy Fay."

She was still standing on the bluff, and she had heard Frank's words. Now she held out her arms to him, crying:

"Tome tate me down. I wants to tome down."

"Get back from the edge, dear," Frank quickly called. "You may fall. We will come up to you as soon as possible."

"Tome wight away."

"Yes, we will come right away."

"I's tired playing all alone—an' I's hundry," said the sweet little voice. "I's awsul hundry. You dot somet'ing dood to eat?"

"You shall have something to eat very soon, if you will keep back from the edge, so you'll not fall down," assured Frank.

He then directed Barney to remain there and watch her, cautioning her to keep back, while he found a way to reach the top of the bluff.

Frank hastened away, looking for some mode of getting there. In a short time, he found a place to ascend, and lost no time in doing so.

When he came panting to the top of the bluff, the little girl was waiting, having seated herself contentedly on a stone, where she could call down to Barney.

Seeing Frank, she held out her arms, crying:

"I's awsul glad you tome! I'll be your Fairy now."

"You have been my good fairy to-day, little one," he earnestly said, as he lifted her in his arms and kissed her cheek. "Without doubt you saved my life."

"Mamma says I's pritty dood Fairy all the time."

"I haven't a doubt of it."

"But I's awsul hundry now. I touldn't find mamma, and I walked and walked, and I falled down and tored my dress, and I dot tired and awsul hundry, and I cwyed some, and nen I 'membered mamma told me it wasn't nice to cwy, and I walked again, and I heard somebody talkin', and I looked down and it was you."

She ended with a happy laugh, clasping her arms about his neck.

"Where is your mamma?"

"Oh, I don't know now," she answered, a little cloud coming to her face. "I touldn't find her. You tate me to her."

"You do not live near here?"

"We live in New Yort."

"New York?"

"Yeth, thir. Dat's a dreat bid place wif lots and lots of houses."

"Then you must be traveling with your mamma?"

"I's trafeling wizout her now. We has had jes' the longest wides on the cars. And we stopped in lots of places, but we didn't find papa."

"Then your papa is not with you?"

"Papa goed away long time ago, and that made mamma cwy. I seed her weadin' a letter and cwyin' awsul hard, and papa didn't tome bat some more. You know where to find my papa?"

"No, little one, I do not; but I will help you find your mother. What did you say your name is?"

"Fay. Tometimes mamma talls me Fairy."

"What is all your name—the rest of it besides Fay?"

"Why, jes' Fairy. I's awsul hundry. Dot a tookie?"

Finding himself unable to learn her full name from her lips, Frank started for the foot of the bluff, bearing her in his arms.

# CHAPTER XXVI.

## OLD ROCKS.

arney was waiting, and he drew a breath of relief when Frank appeared with the child.

"Oi wur afraid th' litthle darlint would tumble off bafore ye could rache her," he said.

"But I tept wight away from the edge, same as you toldt me to," chirped Fay, cheerfully. "If I did tumbled, you tould catch me."

"Begorra! Oi wur ready to thry it, me swate."

"You never wanted to see me fall and hurt myself bad, did you?"

"Nivver a bit."

Frank told Barney how much he had been able to learn from her lips, and they were not long in deciding it would be folly for them to attempt to find Fay's mother.

"The guide is the one to do that," said Frank.

"Roight, me b'y. Ould Rocks knows ivery inch av th' parruk."

"Then we had better return to camp at once."

"Sure."

"But the buffalo—I had forgotten them. We have not obtained that picture."

"An' nivver a bit we will this doay, Frankie."

"Why not?"

"Th' boofalo have shkipped."

"Gone?"

"Thot's roight."

"Too bad!"

Frank felt that he must satisfy himself with his own eyes, and so he hastened to a spot that commanded a view of the place where the creatures had been feeding.

Sure enough, they were gone.

"That's hard luck!" he muttered. "Here we have been hanging a whole week in the park just to enable me to get a snap at some of the creatures, and we lost our only opportunity. Well, I suppose we should be satisfied to get off with our lives."

He knew this was true, and so there was reason to be thankful, instead of grumbling.

He returned to where Barney was talking to Fay. The child was anxiously watching Frank's movements.

"You ain't doin' away and leave me, is you?" she asked.

"No, dear."

"I was 'fraid so, and I's awsul hundry."

"An' wouldn't ye go wid me av Oi'd take ye where ye'd get plinty to ate?" asked the Irish lad.

"Him tome, too?" She held out her hands to Frank.

"An' wouldn't ye go av he didn't come?"

"I dess not," she said. "I like you pitty well; but I kinder like him better. Him goin' to find my mamma. I dess him dit me somefin to eat."

Frank caught her up in his arms.

"Yes, dear," he laughed, his heart swelling with a feeling that convinced him he would lay down his life in defense of her, if needs be. "I will find you something to eat as soon as possible, and I will take you to your mother."

"Dat's all wight. I ain't doin' to cwy. You don't like little dirls we'en they cwy, does you?"

"In your case, I do not think crying would change my feelings. Little girls have to cry sometimes."

"I dess dat's wight," said Fay, very soberly.

Frank surrendered his rifle to Barney, who insisted on taking the camera also, and then, with the child in his arms, followed the Irish lad on the return tramp to camp.

It proved to be a long, tiresome trudge, and the sun was setting when the boys came in sight of a white tent that was pitched near a spring of cool water and a growth of pines down in a pretty valley.

Once or twice Fay had murmured that she was "so hundry," but when the camp was sighted, she was asleep in Frank's arms, her head of tangled golden curls lying on his shoulder.

A fire was blazing in front of the tent, sending a thin column of smoke straight up into the still air.

Near the fire, with a pipe in his mouth, was sitting a grizzled old man, whose appearance indicated that he was a veteran of the mountains and plains.

This was Roxy Jules, generally known as "Old Rocks." He was one of the professional guides who make a business of taking parties of tourists through the park and showing them its wonders.

Between two trees a hammock was strung, and another man, a

little fellow with fiery-red hair and whiskers, was reclining. Gold-bowed spectacles were perched on his nose, and he was studying a book.

All at once Old Rocks gave a queer kind of a grunt. As it did not arouse the man in the hammock, he grunted again. That not proving effectual, he growled:

"Wa-al, I wonders whut kind o' game them yar kids hev struck now?"

"Eh?" exclaimed the little man. "Did you speak to me? My name is Scotch, as you very well know—Professor Horace Scotch."

"Wa-al," drawled Old Rocks, with a sly grin, "I reckons I has heard them yar boys call yer Hot Scotch enough to know whut yer handle is."

"Those boys are very disrespectful—very! They should be called to account. I object to such familiarity from others, sir—I distinctly object."

Old Rocks grunted derisively, having come to regard the timid little man with contempt, which was natural with him, as he looked with disfavor on all "tenderfeet."

That grunt stirred the blood of the quick-tempered little man, who sat up, snapping:

"I should think there was a pig somewhere round, by the sounds I hear!"

The guide grunted again.

"I detest pigs!" fumed Scotch. "They're always grunting."

"Thar's only one thing I dislike wuss'n pigs," observed Old Rocks, lazily.

"What is that, sir; what is that?"

"Hawgs," answered the guide, with his small, keen eyes fixed on the professor. "Of course, I don't mean to be personal, nor nawthing, an' I don't call no names; but ef you want ter know who I mean, you kin see whar I'm lookin'."

"This in an insult!" squealed the little man, snapping himself out of the hammock. "I'll discharge you at once, sir—at once!"

"All right. Just you pay me whut you owe me, an' I'll leave ye ter git out o' ther park ther best way ye derned kin. You'll hev a heap o' fun doin' it."

The professor blustered about, while Old Rocks sat and smoked, a patronizing smile on his leathery face.

Suddenly Scotch observed the approaching boys, and saw the child Frank carried in his arms.

"Goodness!" gurgled the little man, staring. "What does that mean?"

"Oh, you have jest woke up!" said the guide, continuing to pull at his black pipe. "I wuz tryin' to call your 'tention to thet thar. Whut has ther boy found? An' whar did he find it?"

"You know quite as well as I. It is surprising—very much so!"

Frank and Barney came up, and explanations followed. Old Rocks pricked up his ears when Frank told of the Blackfeet, and how near they came to having a fight with the Indians.

"Is thet onery skunk in hyar again?" exclaimed the guide. "Why, he's wuss'n sin, is ole Half Hand. He'd ruther cut a throat than do anything else, an' ye're derned lucky ter git away. It wuzn't by yer own nerve ye done it, howsomever. Ef ther gal hedn't 'peared jest as she did, you'd both be food fer coyotes now."

"Two or three Indians, at least, would have kept us company," declared Frank.

Old Rocks grunted.

"Yah! I'll bet a hawse you wuz so derned scat ye shivered clean down ter yer toes. Ef ther red skunks hed made a run fer ye, ye'd drapped right down on yer marrerbones an' squealed."

A bit of warm color came to Frank's face, and he said:

"It is plain you have a very poor opinion of my courage."

Barney was angry, and he roared:

"Oi'd loike ter punch yer head fer yez, ye ould haythen! It's me-silf thot's got nerve enough fer thot!"

This awakened Fay, who looked about in a wondering manner with her big, blue eyes, and then half sobbed:

"Where is my mamma? I was jes' finkin' I was wiz her, and she was divin' me somefin' dood to eat. I's awful hundry!"

In the twinkling of an eye, Old Rocks changed his manner. His pipe disappeared, and he was on his feet, saying, softly:

"Don't you go to cryin', leetle gal. You shell have something to eat in abaout two shakes, an' I'll see thet you finds yer mother all right. Ye're a little angel, an' thet yar's jest what ye are!"

Straightway there was a bustle in the camp. Frank sat on the ground and entertained Fay, while Old Rocks prepared supper. The child was given some bread, and she proved that she was "awsul hundry" by the way she ate it.

There was not a person in the camp who was not hungry, and that supper was well relished.

Fay was questioned closely, but no one succeeded in obtaining much more information than Frank had already received.

When she had eaten till she was satisfied, Old Rocks tried to coax her to him, but she crept into Frank's arms and cuddled close to him, whispering:

"I likes you the bestest."

So Frank held her, and sang lullaby songs in a beautiful baritone voice, while the blue shadows settled over the valley and night came on. Long after she was sound asleep he held her and sang on, while the others listened.

Beyond the limits of the camp was a man who seemed enraptured by the songs, whose eyes were wet with tears, and whose heart was torn by the emotions which surged upward from his lonely soul.

# CHAPTER XXVII.

## THE HERMIT.

t last little Fay was placed within the tent on the soft-
est bed that could be prepared for her.

"In ther mornin'," said Old Rocks, "I'll hunt up her
mamma."

The fire glowed pleasantly, being replenished now and then by
Barney.

Professor Scotch occupied the hammock, Frank stretched himself at full length on the ground, and the guide sat with his back
against a tree, still pulling away at the black pipe, his constant
companion. He had smoked so much that his flesh seemed cured,
like that of a ham.

At heart Old Rocks was tender as a child, but he had a way of
spluttering and growling that made him seem grouty and cross-
grained. He seemed to take real satisfaction in picking a quarrel
with any one.

Professor Scotch was alarmed by the story Frank had told of the
encounter with the Blackfeet, and he was for leaving that vicinity
as soon as possible.

"Not till I get a photograph of real wild buffalo," said the boy,
stiffly.

Old Rocks grunted derisively.

"I reckon you came as nigh it ter-day as ye will at all," he said.
"You've clicked yer old machine at everything from one end o'
ther park to t'other, an' I ain't seen nary picter yit."

"They have not been developed."

"Woosh! Whatever is thet?"

Frank explained, and the guide listened, with an expression of
derision on his face.

"I'll allow you don't know northin' abaout takin' picters,"
drawled the man. "I hed my picter took up at Billings last winter,
an' ther man as took it didn't hev ter go through no such fussin'

as thet."

"How do you know?"

"Wa-al, I know."

"But how do you know?"

"I jest know, thet's how!"

Frank laughed.

"You are like some other people who know everything about anything they don't know anything about."

That was quite enough to start the old fellow, and he seemed ready to fight at the drop of the hat; but, at this moment, something happened to divert his attention.

Out of the darkness stalked a man, who calmly and deliberately advanced toward the party.

"Halt thar!" cried Old Rocks, catching up a rifle and covering the stranger.

The man did not pay the least attention to the command, but continued to advance.

"Halt, or I'll shoot!" shouted the guide.

Still the unknown refused to obey, and, to the bewilderment of Old Rocks, he walked straight up to the muzzle of the weapon, where he stopped, saying:

"I knew you wouldn't shoot. If you had, you could not have killed me. Nothing can kill me, because I have sought death everywhere, and I have not been able to find it. It is he who flees from death who finds it first."

Then he sat down.

"Wa-al, dern me!" gasped Old Rocks. "I dunno why I didn't soak yer; but thar wuz somethin' held me back."

"It was the hand of fate."

The man was dressed roughly, but he carried a handsome rifle. His wide-brimmed hat was slouched over his eyes, so the expression of his face could not have been seen very well, even if it had not been covered by a full brown beard. His hair was long and unkempt.

Having seated himself on the ground, he sat and stared into the fire for some moments before speaking again. Finally he turned a bit, saying:

"Who was singing here a short time ago?"

Frank explained that he had been singing, and the stranger said:

"I don't know why I should wish to take a look at you, for you caused me more misery than I have known for a year."

"Thot's a compliment fer ye're singing, Frankie!" chuckled Barney.

"I tried not to listen," said the stranger; "but I could not tear myself away. What right has a man without a home to listen to songs that fill his soul with memories of home and little ones!"

He bowed his face on his hands, and his body shook a bit, betraying that he was struggling to suppress his emotions.

After a moment, Old Rocks said:

"I reckons I knows yer now. You're the hermit."

The man did not stir or speak.

"Ain't yer the hermit?" asked the guide.

"Yes," was the bitter reply, "I am a man without a home or a name. Some have said that there is trouble with my brain, but they are wrong. I am not deranged. This is the first time in a year that I have sought the society of human beings, unless it was to trade for such things as I need to sustain life. It was those songs that brought me here. They seemed to act like a magnet, and I could not keep away."

Then he turned to Frank, and asked him to sing one of the lullabys over again.

For all of his peculiar manner, the man seemed sane enough, and the boy decided to humor him.

Frank sang, and the man sat and listened, his face still bowed on his hands. When the song was ended, and the last echo had died out along a distant line of bluffs, the man still sat thus.

Those who saw him were impressed. Beyond a doubt, this man had suffered some great affliction that had caused him to shun his fellows and become one "without a home or a name."

All at once, with a deep sigh, he rose. He was finely built, and, properly dressed and shaved, he must have been handsome.

"Thank you," he said, addressing Frank. "I will not trouble you longer. I am going now."

"Look yar," broke in Old Rocks, in his harsh way; "I wants ter warn you ag'in comin' round yere ther way you done a short time ago. It ain't healthy none whatever."

"What do you mean?"

"Jest this: I might take a fancy ter shoot fust an' talk it over arterward. I don't want ter shoot yer."

A strange, sad smile came to the man's face.

"You need not fear," he said. "If you were to shoot at me, you would not hit me."

The guide gave a snort.

"Whut's thet?" he cried. "I allow you hain't seen me shoot any to speak of, pard. I ain't in ther habit of missin'."

"That makes no difference. A man who seeks death cannot die.

Fate would turn your bullet aside."

"Wa-al, I don't allow thet I wants ter try it, fer Fate might not be quick enough. Jest you keep away, 'less you hollers out ter let us know when ye're comin'."

As the hermit turned away he happened to glance into the tent, the front of which was still open. The firelight shone in and fell on the face of the tired child, who was sleeping sweetly.

The man paused, staring at the face revealed by the flickering light. His hand was lifted to his head, and he swayed unsteadily on his feet, his face marked by a look of astonishment and pain.

Old Rocks, Professor Scotch, and the boys watched the hermit's every movement with breathless wonderment. They were impressed, they were held spellbound, they scarcely breathed.

For some moments the strange man stood there, and then, inch by inch, step by step, he advanced toward the tent. He seemed trying to hold back, yet there appeared to be some power dragging him toward the sleeping child.

Frank's first thought was that the man might harm Fay, but the look on the face of the hermit told that he had no such intention. Into the tent he crept, and he knelt beside the bed on which little Fay was sleeping, gazing longingly into her pretty face. A sob came from the depths of his broad breast, and, finally, he stooped and lightly kissed the child's cheek. As he did so, the little girl murmured in her dreams:

"Papa!"

The hermit sprang up, leaped away, and, with a low cry of intense pain, fled into the darkness.

# CHAPTER XXVIII.

## VANISHING OF LITTLE FAY.

For some moments after the strange man had disappeared the guide, the professor, and the boys sat staring into the darkness in the direction he had taken.

"Wa-al, dog my cats!"

The exclamation came from Old Rocks, who had ceased to pull at the black pipe for the time being.

"Thot bates th' band!"

Barney Mulloy could not express the astonishment he felt.

"What can that mean?"

Professor Scotch rose from the hammock, asking the question in a bewildered manner.

"I can tell you what it means," said Frank, also rising to his feet. "It seems to me there is but one explanation. Fay told me her father was not with her mother, that she had not seen him for a long time, and that her mamma cried when he went away. I believe there was some kind of trouble between the child's parents, and that the one who is known as the hermit, who calls himself 'the man without a name or a home,' is the father of that child."

"Wa-al," drawled Old Rocks, "you may be a tenderfoot an' a kid, but yer has a little hawse sense. Ef you ain't right, I'll chaw my boots fer terbacker!"

"It certainly seems that you are right, Frank," nodded the little professor. "The man was drawn into the camp by your songs, he was fascinated when he saw the sleeping child, and he fled, with a cry of pain, when she murmured 'papa.' Yes, it seems quite certain that the hermit is the child's father."

"Ef thet is right, things is comin' round sing'ler," said the guide. "Ef you kids hedn't seen ther Injuns crawlin' up on ther bufferler you wouldn't got inter ther scrape ye did; ef ye hedn't got inter thet scrape ye wouldn't found ther babby; if yer hedn't found ther babby it's likely she might hev starved ur bin eaten by wild critters; ef Frank hedn't sung them songs ther hermit w'u'dn't come inter camp; ef he hedn't come inter camp he w'u'dn't seen ther leetle gal; an' ef he hedn't seen ther leetle gal we'd never suspected he wuz her father."

This was an unusually long speech for Old Rocks, who was given to short, crusty sentences.

"Do you know where this man lives?" asked Scotch.

"Wa-al, I dunno prezactly, but I reckon I kin find him ag'in."

"That is important; he must be found. The mother of this child must be taken to him. In that way a reunion may be brought about. Probably the unfortunate woman is quite distracted to-night. In the morning we will lose no time in finding her and restoring the child to her arms."

For some time they sat about the fire, discussing the strange events of the day. Finally, all became sleepy, and it was decided that they had better "turn in."

As Old Rocks seemed to sleep "with one eye open," they had not found it necessary to have any one stand guard since he had been with them. No wild animal could come prowling about the camp without arousing the old fellow in a moment.

The fire was replenished, the flap of the tent left open, so the warmth might enter, as the nights were rather cool, and the party retired.

In a short time all were sleeping soundly.

Frank's slumber was dreamless, but he was finally aroused by being shaken fiercely.

"Git up hyar!" commanded a snarling voice.

In the twinkling of an eye he was wide awake and sitting up.

"What is the matter?" was the question that came from his lips, as, by the dim light that came from the dying fire, he recognized Old Rocks bending over him.

"Ther dickens is ter pay!" grated the guide. "She's gone!"

"She? Who?"

"Ther leetle gal."

"Fay?"

"Yep."

"Gone?"

Frank was dazed. He looked around and saw Barney and the professor sitting up near at hand, but, sure enough, he could see nothing of the child.

"Yep," nodded Old Rocks. "She ain't in this yar tent."

"But—but how——"

"Dunno how she done it 'thout wakin' me, but she's gone."

"It must be that the Hermit crept in here and kidnaped her."

"Begorro!" cried Barney; "Oi belave thot is roight!"

"It seems reasonable," said the professor.

"Whut d'yer think!" snarled Old Rocks; "fancy I'd snooze right along an' let anything like thet happen? Wa-al, I guess not! Dog my cats ef I know how it kem about, but there gal jest vanished."

"She appeared like a fairy, and like a fairy she has disappeared," said Frank. "But she may be near the camp. We must lose no time in making a search for her."

"Right ye are!" cried Old Rocks, as he led the way from the tent.

Hastening outside, they called to the child, but received no answer.

"Wait a little," advised the guide, as he replenished the fire. "Don't go ter trompin' round yar too much. I wants ter look fer sign."

In this emergency they knew it was best to rely on his judgment, and so they remained quiet, watching his movements.

Having started up the fire, the guide began looking for "sign." His eyes were keen, and it did not take him long to find what he sought.

"Hyar's whar she left ther tent," he declared.

The others looked, but the ground told them nothing.

"That's foolishness," said Professor Scotch, sharply. "You don't mean to say you can see anything here?"

"Wa-al, thet's whut I mean. You're a tenderfut, an' so yer can't see anything. She wuzn't carried off."

"It is not likely she went away alone."

"Likely or not, thet's whut she done."

Bending low, Old Rocks followed the trail as far as the light of the fire reached.

"I reckon I kin torch her," he muttered.

"What do you mean by torching her?" asked Scotch.

Old Rocks made no answer, but returned to the little pile of fuel he had accumulated. This he quickly pulled over, selecting several sticks. He thrust the end of one into the flames, and, in a few moments, had a lighted torch.

"Git yer guns," he directed, "an' come erlong with me."

They did so, with the exception of the professor, who never touched a weapon if he could avoid it. However, he followed the others, and Old Rocks quickly took up the trail once more.

Frank was filled with anxiety for the safety of little Fay. He wondered greatly that the child should arise and creep from the tent without disturbing any one, and then flee into the darkness, but he did not doubt that Rocks had read the sign correctly.

It almost seemed that the guide was able to follow the trail by scent, for he moved swiftly, bending low, and holding the torch close to the ground.

In vain Frank looked for a footprint. The ground did not seem soft enough to yield such a mark, and still Old Rocks seldom hesitated a moment.

Along the valley they went, stringing out one after the other, their hearts throbbing with anxiety.

In this manner they proceeded at least half a mile, and then they came to a stretch of timber. The trail led straight into the woods.

Old Rocks growled and shook his head, and it was plain that he was quite as anxious as any of them.

For a moment they paused on the border of the strip of woods, while the guide got down on his hands and knees and closely inspected the trail.

"Was she alone when she reached this spot?" asked Frank.

Old Rocks nodded.

"It's ther dernedest thing I ever heerd of!" he grumbled. "How a little babby like thet should git up o' her own accord and go prowlin' off inter ther night gits me."

"It is ridiculous," said Professor Scotch. "Such a thing never happened before, and I can't believe it happened on this occasion. Why, she would have been frightened out of her senses. Somebody must have lured her away. That man you call the Hermit must have done it, and I will wager something she joined him as soon as she left the tent."

The guide gave a snort.

"Thet's enough to say I'm a derned fool! Ef ther babby left a trail, you will allow ther man must hev done ther same."

"Of course he did."

"Wa-al, looker yere. Hyar's a bit o' soft ground, an' you kin see whar she crossed over, but I'll be derned ef you kin see any track but ther ones she made."

He held the torch for them to examine the ground, and the tracks left by the child were plainly visible. It was true that she had passed into the timber alone.

"There's a mystery about this that I cannot understand," murmured Frank.

"It looks loike she wur a sure enough fairy," said Barney. "Av not thot, thin this is th' Ould Nick's oun worruk!"

At this moment all were startled by a cry that came from the timber—the cry of a child, broken and smothered.

139

Old Rocks straightened up, and the light of the torch fell on four pale, startled faces.

"Something has happened to her!" panted Frank. "Forward, man, forward! She may have been attacked by a wild beast!"

In another instant the guide was striding swiftly along the trail, making it necessary for the others to run in order to keep up with him.

They penetrated the timber for a considerable distance, and then, of a sudden, Old Rocks stopped short, stooping low to stare at the ground, grinding an exclamation of dismay through his teeth.

"What is it?" demanded Frank fearing the worst.

After a hasty survey of the ground, the guide replied:

"Injuns! Ther leetle gal has been ketched by ther p'izen varmints, sure as shootin'!"

# CHAPTER XXIX.

## FACE TO FACE.

h' saints defind her!" cried Barney.

"Indians?" panted Frank. "Are you sure?"

"Wa-al, I reckon! Hyar's ther marks. See them hoof prints thar. Notice they toe in. Thet is Injun sign."

"I—I think we had better return to the camp at once," fluttered Professor Scotch.

"Not much!" exclaimed Frank, fiercely. "If she has fallen into the hands of those red wretches, we must follow them and rescue her."

Old Rocks nodded.

"You talk all right, youngster; but I reckon yer sand would ooze out on a pinch. All ther same, we must foller ther skunks."

"Go on!" came from Barney. "Begobs! we'll show yez av we've got sand!"

"But I am not feeling well," protested the professor.

"Then ye'd better go back," snarled Old Rocks. "You'll be more bother then good, anyhow."

"I—I can't go back through the darkness. I should lose my way. You must accompany me to the camp."

"An' waste all thet time? Wa-al, I ruther guess not! Time is too valuable just now."

"This is a terrible scrape!" fluttered Scotch. "I expect we'll all be killed before we get out of it!"

The guide seemed to hesitate, casting a sidelong look at the professor, as if he longed to get rid of the man in some way, but did not know how.

"I kin do as much erlone as I kin with ther hull o' yer," he finally said. "I reckons ye'd best all go back."

"I guess not!" cried Frank. "I am with you through thick and thin! You will remember that I found the child, and she called herself my fairy. It is my duty to help rescue her."

"Wa-al, I 'lows ye'll stick ter thet," growled Old Rocks; "an' so I'll hev ter take yer erlong."

"An' Oi'm wid him, begobs!"

But the guide would not agree to that.

"Somebody's got ter go back ter camp an' look out fer things," he said. "I reckons you an' ther professor is ther ones."

Barney groaned.

"Profissor, can't yez go alone?" he asked. "It's nivver a chance have Oi had ter take a hand in a bit av a ruction loately, av ye will except th' chance Oi had th' doay."

But Professor Scotch had no fancy to return through the darkness to the camp, and he insisted that Barney should accompany him. The Irish boy was forced to succumb, and he parted from Frank with the utmost reluctance and regret.

"We have fought an' bled togither," he said, "an' it's harrud to be parruted loike this."

In a short time Barney and the professor were returning to the camp, while, with Frank Merriwell at his heels, Old Rocks again took up the trail.

Frank marveled at the swiftness with which Old Rocks swung over the ground.

Through the timber they made their way, and then through a narrow ravine, and four or five miles had been covered before the guide paused to speak.

"They're makin' straight fer ther lake," he said. "I don't like that."

"Why not?"

"Ef ther p'izen varmints has canoes—wa-al, we won't be liable ter foller 'em farther than ther lake."

"That is true. We will hope they have no canoes."

Onward they went once more, Old Rocks having lighted a fresh torch, which left but one remaining.

The night was on the wane. Already the sounds of the middle night were hushed. The owls had stopped their hooting, and now, on noiseless wing, were making their last hunting rounds before day should come.

Afar on the side of a mountain a wolf was howling like a dog baying to the moon. The stars which filled the sky seemed to prophesy of dawn.

Bending low, now and then swinging his torch to fan it into a stronger flame, Old Rocks almost raced along the trail, while the boy at his heels kept close.

They were like two tongueless hounds upon a hot scent.

And thus they came, at last, to the lake.

Not a word did Old Rocks say for several minutes, but he moved up and down the shore, reading the "sign," while his companion waited with the greatest anxiety.

At length, with a grated exclamation of rage and dismay, the man flung himself on the ground.

"It's jest as I feared," he growled. "Ther onery varmints hed canoes hid hyar, an' we kin trail 'em no farther."

"Then what can we do?" fluttered the discomfited boy.

"Northin' but wait fer daylight."

Now on the still air very faintly was heard a distant tone of music; a sweet whistle, at first low, rising and falling, and then gradually becoming more distinct. It came nearer and nearer till it seemed to fill the air all about, and then, looking upward, they saw dark forms flitting between them and the stars.

The wild ducks were flying.

The musical note passed on, receded, grew fainter and fainter, till, at last, it died out in the distance.

From the lake came a far-off trumpet call, and then another—the mellow note of the wild geese.

The world was awakening; the day was near.

The stars were growing paler now. In the eastern sky was a bit of gray, which slowly broadened, pushing upward and blotting out the stars.

Where all before was dark, the morning twilight began to show the black forms of things.

The outlines of tree trunks could be seen, and they seemed to stand like ghosts, reaching out shadowy arms, as if feeling their way through the dimness.

The birds which through the long night had slept in the low bushes were beginning to chirp and flutter.

All at once, Old Rocks started and clutched Frank's arm.

"Listen!" he whispered.

The sound of footsteps told them some one was approaching.

"Back!" whispered the guide, leading the way. "We must see who ther critter is, an' he musn't see us."

Hastily they drew into the deep shadows, holding their rifles ready for use in case they should need them.

Nearer and nearer came the footsteps, and then the dark figure of a man appeared, advancing through the dusky darkness.

The man was alone, and he halted on the shore of the lake, within a short distance of the crouching man and boy. They saw him bow his head on his breast and stand there in silence.

Several minutes passed. At last, the unknown lifted his head, stretched out his arms, and uttered a long, mournful cry that seemed to come from a breaking heart.

Old Rocks rose and glided swiftly and silently toward the stranger, who did not hear him approach. The guide's hand dropped on the man's shoulder, and he said:

"Hello, Hermit. Whatever be yer doin' hyar?"

The strange man turned, and Frank saw that it was indeed the Hermit of the Yellowstone.

"Doing?" he said, hoarsely. "I am seeking rest—seeking rest! I'll never find it till I rest in the grave!"

"You must hev a derned bad liver, or somethin' o' ther sort," sneered Old Rocks. "I don't understand a critter like you none whatever."

"I do not expect you to understand me. You do not know my story. If I were to tell you——"

"We ain't got time ter listen; but I'll tell you a leetle story. You know ther babby-gal whut yer saw at our camp?"

The hermit bowed, and then, as if a suspicion of the truth had flashed over him, he fiercely grasped the guide with both hands, hoarsely demanding:

"Has anything happened to her? Tell me—tell me quick!"

With a few well-chosen words, Old Rocks told exactly what had happened. The hermit seemed overcome with horror and dismay.

"She must be saved!"

"You're right; but how wuz we ter foller ther red varmints 'thout a canoe. Now they hev got clean away."

"I will find her!" cried the hermit, with one hand uplifted, as if registering a vow. "I will find her and restore her to—hold! How did she happen to be with you?"

A further explanation was in order. Frank told how Fay had appeared in time to save himself and Barney from being attacked by Half Hand and the Blackfeet, what she had told them, how they had taken her to the camp, and how Old Rocks had agreed to find her mother with the coming of another day.

The guide and the boy believed the Hermit must be little Fay's father, and they watched him closely as he listened. When Frank had finished, the strange man eagerly asked:

"Her name—her full name—did you learn it?"

"No. She told us her name was Fay, and that her mother sometimes called her Fairy Fay; but we were unable to learn her last name."

"From whut we saw in ther camp, we allowed as how it wuz likely you hed seen ther babby afore, an' you knowed her proper name," insinuated Old Rocks.

The Hermit did not answer the implied question.

"Come," he said, "follow me. I have a canoe."

"I s'pose we can't do any wuss," mumbled Old Rocks; "though I don't prezactly know how we're goin' ter trail them critters through ther warter."

The Hermit moved along at a swinging stride, and they followed him through the morning twilight.

Less than half a mile had been covered when the man in advance suddenly paused, uttering an exclamation of surprise.

Straight ahead, amid the trees of a little grove on the shore, they beheld the snowy outlines of a tent.

In a little park beyond the camp could be seen the dusky outlines of horses feeding. Close to the open flap of the tent two dogs were curled, both sleeping soundly, so silent had been the approach of the trio.

The light in the eastern sky was getting a pink tinge, and, with each passing moment, objects could be seen more distinctly.

A tiny column of blue smoke rose from the white ashes of the camp-fire, telling that a brand still smoldered there.

There was a stir within the tent. There were muffled grunts, a yawn or two, the rustle of clothing, faint sounds of footsteps, and then the flap of the tent was flung wide open, and a man came out into the morning air. He paused and stretched his limbs, standing so the trio obtained a fair view of him.

With a sudden, hoarse cry, the Hermit rushed forward and confronted the man.

"Foster Fairfax!" he shouted, with savage joy; "at last we are face to face!"

# CHAPTER XXX.

## SEARCH FOR THE TRAIL.

reston March!"

The man who had just stepped out of the tent fell back, a look of astonishment, not unmingled with fear, on his face.

"Yes, Preston March!" cried the Hermit. "You know me, and I know you, treacherous friend, base scoundrel that you are!"

The man called Foster Fairfax lifted his hands, as if to ward off a blow.

"Preston, it was a mistake—a fearful mistake."

"For you—yes! I have sworn by the heavens above to have your life if fate ever threw you across my path. I shall keep that oath!"

"I expect it."

"Then draw your weapon, and defend yourself! I shall not murder you in cold blood. Draw, draw!"

"No! Shoot, if you will! I'll never lift a hand against you."

"Coward?"

The Hermit was quivering with fury, while the face of the other man was still ghastly white.

Other men came from the tent, rubbing their eyes, all of them very much surprised. One of them attempted to intervene.

"Here!" he cried, addressing the Hermit; "what do you mean by coming into this camp and raising such a row? Are you insane? You are not going to do any shooting here!"

Old Rocks strode forward, Frank Merriwell at his heels.

"I'll allow as how the Hermit has fair play," said the guide, grimly. "He ain't alone in this yar deal."

"Who are you?" demanded the man, haughtily. "Are we to be assailed by a band of desperadoes?"

"None whatever. I'm hyar ter see fair play. I'll allow thar's some deeficulty atwixt these yere gents, an' ther Hermit feels like settlin' right now an' yere."

"It is an outrage! You have no right to come here and make trouble. Fairfax, if that ruffian touches you——"

Foster Fairfax motioned the speaker to be silent.

"This man is not a ruffian," he declared, speaking as calmly as possible. "There is a misunderstanding between us. I have wronged him, and he has a right to seek satisfaction."

The man's companions were astonished by his words. They looked at him in a dazed way.

Even the Hermit seemed a trifle surprised, but he said:

"It is true, and I demand satisfaction. Draw and defend yourself, Fairfax!"

"No; you have not wronged me. Here, March—here is my heart! Shoot! You cannot miss it at this distance."

Preston March, the Hermit of Yellowstone Park, half lifted the weapon which he had drawn. Then he fell back a step, hoarsely saying:

"Would you put a curse upon me by making me a murderer? You have a weapon. Draw it, and we will play fair and even. It shall be a duel to the death at twenty paces. One of us shall die! The other can go back to——"

"Hold! Speak not the name here! I tell you, Preston, there was a blunder—a frightful blunder. If you will listen——"

"You will tell me a mess of lies. A man who would deceive his best friend as you deceived me would not hesitate to lie with his last breath!"

"You shall judge if I lie. If you demand that I meet you, I demand that you first listen to my explanation."

"If I must——"

"On no other condition will I meet you."

"But there are others to hear. Will you speak before them?"

"No. Come aside where no one but ourselves may hear."

The Hermit bowed, and they walked away, keeping several feet apart.

"Wa-al," drawled Old Rocks, "we don't seem ter be in thet none whatever, an' so we'd best make ourselves easy."

He flung himself down upon the ground, produced his black pipe and a plug of tobacco, and began preparing for a smoke, whittling off the tobacco with his bowie-knife.

The campers drew aside and talked among themselves, regarding their uninvited visitors with suspicion, which did not disturb the guide at all.

Frank was restless. He walked up and down, keeping his eyes on Fairfax and the Hermit, who had halted at a distance and were talking earnestly.

In the east the streaky clouds had flushed to a deep red and paled again to richest gold. To the west the mighty mountains which rose beyond the lake were wrapped in garments of rose. The light of day had spread itself over all the heavens, and the sun was shooting glittering glances above the horizon.

The campers began to move about. Wood was piled upon the ashes where the last embers of the old fire still smoldered, and the crackling of a match was followed by a blaze.

Some of the campers prepared breakfast, while one of them approached Old Rocks, whom he questioned concerning the Hermit.

"Yer know purty derned nigh ez much 'bout him ez I do," grunted the guide. "All I know is thet he's bin hyar in ther park fer ther last y'ar ur so. Some galoots has said as how he wuz cracked in ther upper story, but I'll allow thet's a mistake. Yer heard t'other gent admit thet he'd done the Hermit a crooked turn, an' I reckons thet's whut makes ther Hermit whut he is. Now I've tol' yer whutever I know 'bout ther Hermit, mebbe ye'll give me a few p'ints 'bout t'other gent?"

"We know nothing in particular of him, save that he seems to be a man of leisure and means, rather melancholy, given to fits of despondency, followed by spells of wild hilarity."

A queer look came into the guide's eye, and he asked:

"How much o' it does he drink a day?"

"How much what?"

"Hilarity. Does he kerry it in quart bottles, or by ther gallon?"

"He does drink at times," admitted the camper; "but he declares that he hates liquor, and I believe him. He seems to take it to drown memory."

"Wa-al, he may drown memory fer an hour ur so, but he'll find it comes back a derned sight harder when he lets up on drinkin'."

Rocks lighted his pipe, settled himself into a comfortable position, and began to smoke.

The fire was burning brightly, and a blackened coffee-pot was brought forth. As soon as there were some coals, the pot was placed upon them, and it soon began to simmer and send forth a delightful odor, making Frank ravenously hungry.

Old Rocks was hungry, but he showed no symptom of it, smoking on indifferently, all the while keeping an eye on the Hermit and Fairfax.

Frank offered to pay for something to eat and a cup of coffee; but the campers declined to take anything, telling him he was welcome. They then offered Old Rocks something, and the guide accepted gracefully.

For nearly an hour the Hermit and Foster Fairfax talked. The manner of both became subdued, and the strange man of the park seemed to have lost his desire to meet Fairfax in a deadly encounter.

All at once they parted, and the Hermit hurried away, while Fairfax walked back toward the camp.

Old Rocks shouted to the Hermit, but the man paid no heed to the call.

"Come, youngster," said the guide, getting on his feet and picking up his rifle. "We'd best foller thet critter. He said he hed a chance, an' thet wuz whut we wuz arter."

Frank thanked the campers for their hospitality, and then hastened after Old Rocks, who was striding away after the Hermit, who had already vanished from view.

"Whatever's got inter ther man?" growled the guide. "He seems ter hev clean fergot we're on earth."

For at least a mile Old Rocks followed on the trail of the Hermit, and it finally ended at the shore of the lake, where it was seen that the man had taken a canoe.

And far out on the lake he was paddling swiftly away.

Putting his hands to his mouth, the guide sent a call across the water:

"Oh, Hermit!"

The man paddled on without looking back. Rocks repeated the cry several times, but without apparent effect, and then gave up in disgust.

"I'll allow this is onery!" he growled, as he sat down and lighted his pipe once more. "Dog my cats ef it ain't!"

Frank was disheartened.

"Poor little Fay!" he murmured, sadly. "What will become of her?"

"We'll find her," declared Old Rocks, grimly. "We'll find her ef we hev ter tramp clean round this yar lake ter strike ther trail o' them p'izen Blackfeet!"

"Do you think we can ever find their trail?"

"Wa-al, I'll allow! Ain't we got ter find 'em? Ain't they got ter come ter shore somewhar? You bet yer boots! Old Rocks is on ther warpath, an' ther measly varmints want ter look out!"

The guide seemed very much in earnest, which gave Frank fresh hope. The boy was ready to spend any length of time in the search for the missing child.

Having smoked and meditated a short time, Old Rocks arose.

"Come," he said, and he struck out once more.

Along the shore they went, the eyes of the guide always search-ing for the trail. Sometimes they were forced back from the water by steep bluffs and precipices, but the guide missed no places where the Indians could have landed.

It was about midway in the forenoon that the trail was struck. The canoes were found craftily concealed, and in the soft ground near the lake were the imprints of tiny feet.

"Thar!" cried Old Rocks, looking at the marks; "thet shows we ain't on a wild-goose chase. Now we don't hold up none what-ever till we overtakes ther p'izen skunks an' rescues ther gal. You hear me!"

"The grizzly folded Frank in his embrace, crushing the lad against his shaggy breast."

# CHAPTER XXXI.

## A FIGHT WITH GRIZZLIES.

Frank found Old Rocks a hard man to follow, and the guide was amazed by the endurance of the boy.

It was long past midday when Rocks sat down on a fallen tree, and filled his pipe.

"Say," he drawled, surveying his companion, "you beat all ther tenderfut kids I've ever seen, dog my cats ef you don't!"

"How is that?" asked Frank, who was glad to have a few moments' respite. "What do you mean?"

"Wa-al, I hev bin expectin' all along as how you'd peg out, but I'm derned ef you don't seem fresh as a daisy now!"

"Oh, I am good for a few miles more," said the boy, smiling.

Rocks nodded.

"Thet's whatever. You've got buckram; but I know yer ain't got sand. Tenderfeet never has any."

"I don't suppose you have ever found any exceptions?"

"Derned few! Now I've got somethin' ter say."

"Say it."

"It's plain these yar red varmints are makin' a run fer it, kinder thinkin' they might be follered. It's liable ter be several days afore they're overtook."

"Well?"

"Wa-al, we ain't fitted fer such a tramp."

"What's that?" cried the boy in dismay. "You do not think of giving it up, do you?"

"Nary bit; but I kinder 'lowed you might feel thet way."

"I guess not!"

"Stiddy! Don't be too quick. Wait till I tells yer whut yer may expect."

"Go ahead."

"Jest ez long ez I'm on this yar trail I shell keep up ther pace I hev bin makin' this day su fur."

"That is good."

"Huah! Think yer kin stan' it, eh? Wa-al, thet ain't all."

"Give us the rest of it."

"It'll be a case o' sleepin' in ther open, 'throut kiver, eatin' w'en yer kin, an' gittin' anything we kin shoot an' havin' it hafe cooked ur not cooked at all, an' lots o' other inconveniences thet'll make yer long fer ther comforts o' home."

"And you fancy I'll not be able to stand it?"

"I kinder 'lowed it'd be hard on a tender kid like you be."

Frank had flung himself on the ground, but now he arose and faced the guide, speaking firmly and calmly:

"Rocks, you heard the child say she'd be my fairy, you saw that she took to me, I sung her to sleep, and she clung to me. I will tell you now that I am ready to go through anything for Fairy Fay. She is in terrible danger. If she is not rescued, her fate is frightful to contemplate. I shall never rest till she is saved! I want to go along with you; but I shall continue the hunt alone, if you will not have me."

The old fellow grunted sourly, and puffed away at the black pipe for some moments. At last, he got upon his feet and held out his hand to Frank.

"Put ther thar!" he cried. "You talk all right; we'll see how yer pan out. You kin go erlong."

They shook hands, and Frank was well satisfied.

"You stay right yere by ther trail," directed the guide. "I'm goin' over yon a piece ter see ef thar is some mud geysers down thar. It's been some time sence I wuz in this yar part o' ther park, an' I wants ter git my bearin's. I'll be back yere directly, an' you kin be restin' meantime."

Frank felt like demurring, but he believed it best to do exactly as the guide directed, and so he nodded and sat down again, while Old Rocks strode away and soon disappeared.

Nearly thirty minutes passed, and then, of a sudden, the boy was startled by the report of a rifle, the sound of the shot coming from the direction in which the guide had disappeared.

"I wonder what it can mean?" speculated Frank.

He was uneasy. He knew the guide might have fired at some kind of small game, but for some reason he fancied such was not the case.

Was Old Rocks in trouble?

Catching up his rifle, Frank started on a run in the direction taken by the guide.

Down into the valley he went, his eyes wide open. Suddenly, a short distance before him, there was a hissing, rushing roar, and a column of mud and water shot into the air.

There were the mud geysers Old Rocks had started out to look for.

Toward the geyser hurried Frank, still looking for his companion.

Before the column of mud and water had ceased shooting into the air, Frank came upon a startling spectacle.

Not far from the geysers Old Rocks was engaged in a hand-to-hand encounter with a huge grizzly bear!

On the ground near by lay the body of another bear, telling how accurate had been the guide's first shot.

The guide was using his bowie knife, which was already stained with blood to the hilt.

Frank did not hesitate about rushing straight toward the battling man and beast, and Old Rocks saw him coming.

"Keerful, boy!" panted the man; "keerful with thet thar rifle! Don't shoot yere, fer yer might bore me."

"I won't hit you," promised Frank. "I will shoot the bear."

"You don't know whar ter put yer lead, an' yer might fire a dozen bullets inter this varmint 'thout finishin' him."

It was evident that the old man was badly winded.

Thus far he had avoided the bear's hug, but he could not hold out long. Barely had he uttered the last words when, with a sudden blow of one paw, the grizzly struck him to the ground.

Frank rushed in, seeing the monster settle on all fours over Old Rocks.

"I'll fix him!" grated the boy, as he thrust the muzzle of his rifle almost against bruin's head and pulled the trigger.

For the first time on record the weapon missed fire.

With a fierce growl, the bear whirled and knocked the rifle out of Frank's grasp.

In a dazed manner, Old Rocks saw everything.

"Ther kid's a goner!" thought the guide. "We're both done fer!"

Out Frank snapped a revolver, and then, taking a step toward the bear, he fired five bullets into the creature in marvelously rapid succession.

A roar came from the bear's throat, and the beast reared on its hind feet, its jaws dripping blood and foam, and rushed upon the dauntless boy.

Frank flung aside the revolver, just as Rocks struggled to a sitting posture, thickly crying:

"Run, kid! run fer yer life!"

"Not much!" came through Frank's set teeth. "Think I'd run and leave you to the bear! I guess not!"

"Dog my cats!" murmured the guide, weakly.

The bear, dripping blood from its many wounds, still fierce as a raging tiger, came at Frank. The boy dodged, managed to avoid the rush, and gave the beast a wicked stab with the knife.

"Dog my cats!" murmured the dazed guide once more.

Frank Merriwell's face bore a look of fearless determination, and he was ready for the bear to charge again.

It came.

Frank tried to repeat the trick, slipped a bit, saw he could not escape, and then met the formidable beast.

"Now he is a goner!" gurgled Old Rocks, faintly.

With outstretched paws the bear closed in.

Frank saw he was not going to be able to escape the hug, and he placed the haft of the knife against his own breast, with the point directed toward the bear.

The grizzly folded Frank in his embrace, crushing the lad against his shaggy breast, and, in this way, the creature drove the knife home to its own heart.

Uttering a great groan, it relaxed its hold, dropped on all fours, hung its head, and then sunk in a heap upon the ground, dying.

Frank felt as if his ribs had been crushed, and he was covered with blood, but he had conquered.

Old Rocks was so dazed that he sat on the ground, staring at the "tenderfoot kid," and faintly gasping:

"Dog my cats!"

Frank flung the knife to the ground, and then sat down, panting, in a desperate endeavor to get a full breath.

Old Rocks got up very slowly, stood looking at the dead bear some moments, and then looked at the boy.

"This beats me!" he grunted. "Whoever heard o' a tenderfut doin' sech a thing! An' he didn't seem ter be scart a tall!"

Then he came nearer Frank, at whom he still stared.

"It ain't a mistake, none whatever. This yar kid done it, and he done it in great shape! Say, youngster."

"What?"

"I wants ter 'polergize."

"What for?"

"Fer sayin' tenderfeet never has sand. I'll take it all back. You've got sand enough fer anything, you hev! Do you know whut you done? Wa-al, a grizzly is harder ter kill then a hull tribe o' Injuns! I wuz dead lucky ter kill t'other one by a chance shot, an' I'd never done it ef I hedn't been so nigh ther muzzle o' my rifle wuz right up ag'in' ther varmint. You worked an old hunter's trick on him. Thet fust jab you gave ther whelp kinder spruced him up, an' he wuz ready ter crush ther stuffin' outer yer. By holdin' ther knife ez yer did, yer made him kill hisself. Guv us yer hand! I'll swar by you through thick and thin!"

So they shook hands again.

# CHAPTER XXXII.

## TRAILED DOWN.

her trail's gittin' derned hot, boy!" said Old Rocks, near sunset. "Ther p'izen varmints can't be fur ahead." They were passing through one of the wildest sections of the park. Mountains, capped with eternal snow, were on every hand. Their sides were seamed with mighty chasms and strewn with huge bowlders, many of which, it seemed, the weight of a hand would send crashing and thundering into the dark depths below.

Some of the mountains bore traces of vegetation, pine and cedar showing darkly on many a jagged cliff. Some were bleak and barren, but none the less grand, impressive, and awe-inspiring.

Amid these mountains were desolate canyons, which seemed to hold some dreadful secret locked fast in their silent bosoms.

Since the encounter with the grizzlies Old Rocks and Frank had paused to eat a square meal of bear-steak, and it had braced them for the tramp, so they were able to cover ground swiftly without fatigue or discomfort.

They had passed through a region of boiling geysers, where the water shot more than a hundred feet into the air, and came down in a rain, across which a beautiful rainbow formed, the roaring sound which accompanied this exhibition being as loud as the exhaust of a thousand locomotives.

In one marshy valley they had passed pools of water, sulphur yellow, bright green, pink, crimson, and nearly all colors of the rainbow, the pools being from twenty to fifty feet apart.

They had seen other things which were not given a second glance by Old Rocks, but which Frank longed to stop and examine.

But it was no time for sight-seeing, as the boy well knew, and he held close to the heels of the unwearying guide.

And now, near nightfall, Old Rocks declared that the trail was getting hot.

"Shall we be able to overtake them before dark?" asked Frank, with the greatest anxiety.

"I dunno," was the answer. "But it's derned certun thet we ain't goin' ter come fur from it."

"Oh, for two hours more of daylight!" sighed the boy.

"We'd run ther critters down dead sure in thet time. But I don't want yer ter git ther idee thet they're goin' ter give up ther gal 'thout a murmur."

"But they will have to give her up."

"Thet's whatever. All ther same, we may hev ter fight, an' ole Half Hand is a mighty bad critter ter buck agin'; you hear me shout!"

"I am ready to fight, if necessary."

"Ef I'd heerd yer say so this mornin', I w'u'dn't putt no dependence on it; but now I'll allow thet yer means whut yer says, an' yer've got sand ter give erway. Boy, you're a holy terror on trucks, an' you may quote me ez sayin' so."

Frank did not smile.

"Wait," he said. "I may not show up so well in the encounter with the Blackfeet. I was lucky in the bear fight."

"Wa-al, dog my cats ef you ain't ther fust tenderfut I ever saw thet wouldn't hev bragged his head off ef he'd killed a grizzly! Why, boy, you don't seem ter know whut ye've done! You've made a record. Ary other tenderfut I ever saw'd go back East an' publish ther story in all ther papers. He'd be hailed ez a mighty chief an' a tin god on wheels."

"Tenderfeet are not all braggarts, any more than Westerners are all brave men."

"Thet's whatever," nodded Rocks; "but it's took me a gaul derned long time ter find it out."

The sun was low behind the western mountains, and darkness was filling the great canyons.

The guide swung onward at a steady pace, following the trail with the same readiness and ease that had proved a source of wonder all along to his companion.

It was evident the Blackfeet had not anticipated hot pursuit, and so they had made little or no effort to hide their trail after passing across an arm of the lake.

The trail grew hotter and hotter, but night came on swiftly, and Old Rocks was forced to bend low and keep his eyes on the ground.

"Watch out ahead, boy," he directed. "I've got all I kin' tend ter in follerin' ther trail. Don't let us run plump onter ther varmints, fer they might take a notion ter wipe us out."

So Frank followed the guide, keeping his eyes to the front, and watching for danger.

Darker and darker it became. Rocks was forced to proceed more slowly, as there was danger of losing the trail entirely.

Finally he found it necessary to stop now and then and examine the ground thoroughly.

"We shall not overtake them before dark, shall we?" asked Frank, anxiously.

"Hard tellin'. Watch out. May run onter 'em any time."

When they halted again, Frank suddenly uttered a low cry of warning, caught hold of the man, and exclaimed:

"Look there!"

Through the darkness they saw the twinkle of a camp-fire.

"Thet settles it!" breathed Old Rocks, exultantly. "The skunks are thar! We've run 'em down!"

He gave no further attention to the trail, but straightway made sure that every weapon he possessed was ready for use.

"Now, boy," he whispered, "keep yer nerve. Thar'll be need enough o' it afore long."

"I am with you," assured Frank. "I do not think I shall lose my nerves in this case."

"Wa-al, I don't," confessed the man. "I've got heaps o' conferdence in yer now. We'll creep up."

Then followed something that sorely tried the patience of the boy, for Old Rocks seemed to crawl forward like a snail, taking advantage of every cover that would shield them from the sight of any one in front.

The guide warned Frank to "hug ther ground," and made him creep, and skulk, and wiggle along when there seemed no need of it.

In this way they slowly drew near to the fire, about which figures moved now and then.

"It's ther onery Blackfeet," the guide finally announced. "We hev done a good job so fur ter-day, an' now we wants ter finish it right, you bet!"

"What do you mean to do?" asked Frank.

"Make a bluff," was the answer.

"What kind of a bluff?"

They had reached a point where they could look into the camp and see the savages feasting on some kind of game they had killed and cooked by the fire.

"I'm goin' in thar an' demand ther gal," said the guide.

"Won't that put us in their power?"

"You won't go with me."

"No?"

"No. You'll keep in ther background."

"What for?"

"As a reserve force. You must keep yer peepers open, an' ef you see ther skunks is goin' ter do fer me, jest open up on 'em. I reckon you kin shoot some?"

"Yes."

"Take good keer not ter bore me."

"I will."

"But, ef yer start, pump ther lead ter ther critters ter beat ther Ole Nick."

"I will do it."

"Make sure whar ye're puttin' yer bullets, fer ye don't want ter kill ther leetle gal."

"You may depend on me."

"While you're slingin' lead I'll try ter git ther gal an' git erway with her."

"Won't we get into trouble if I should kill one of these Indians?"

"How?"

"Why, the Blackfeet are peaceable, and it may create a disturbance. We may be hauled over the coals."

"Haul an' be derned! Ther onery varmints hev kidnaped a white gal, an' they're poachin' on forbidden territory, besides bein' off ther reservation. Ef they try ter kill me, it will be a case o' self-defence. I'll allow as how we kin defend ourselves. You do ez I say, an we'll come out all right, dog my cats ef we don't!"

"All right."

"But don't shoot 'less yer hev ter, remember thet."

"I will remember it."

"Ef I hedn't seen ther b'ar, an' seen hwar yer putt five bullets inter him inside ther space uv a silver dollar, I might be skerry 'bout lettin' yer shoot inter thet camp while I wuz thar; but I'll admit ez how I reckon ye kin shoot."

They now crept forward till they were within easy shooting distance of the camp, and then Rocks paused once more, putting his lips close to Frank's ear, and whispering:

"See them rocks down thar?"

The boy nodded.

"Wa-al, jest you creep down behind them an' take yer position ready ter sling lead."

"What are you going to do?"

"Git inter ther camp. I'm goin' ter walk in from t'other side, so they'll be lookin' fer any further danger frum thet quarter. Don't git impatient, fer it'll take me some time ter git round thar. Wait easy."

"I'll wait."

Then the old man crept away into the darkness, and Frank began working his way down to the rocks.

He finally reached the position, and there he waited, being able to look into the camp and see every figure revealed by the flaring fire.

The little girl was there, exhausted by the day of hardships, sleeping soundly. One of the Indians had thrown a greasy blanket over her, so she was protected from the night air, which is always chilly in Yellowstone Park.

Frank's heart throbbed with sympathy as he gazed down on her.

"Poor little Fairy!" he thought. "How she did cling to me! I am ready to wade through fire and water for her. We will save her to-night if we live!"

He found it difficult to restrain his impatience as the time crept slowly away and Old Rocks failed to appear. Some of the Indians rolled themselves in their blankets and prepared to sleep. Others sat and smoked in grim silence.

Frank had spotted Half Hand, and he felt that it would be some satisfaction to send a bullet after the villainous half-blood.

"He is at the bottom of this business," thought the boy. "He would not hesitate at murder."

Nearly an hour passed after Old Rocks crept away before the guide appeared. At last, to the astonishment of Frank and the utter consternation of the Indians, the man seemed to rise up in the very midst of the camp, as if he had suddenly sprouted from the ground.

# CHAPTER XXXIII.

## THE RESCUE.

A yell of astonishment broke from the throats of the Indians who were awake, and it brought the sleepers out of their blankets in a moment.

With the utmost coolness, Old Rocks stepped toward the fire, sat down on a log near the sleeping child, and took out his black pipe.

"Any o' you fellers got any good smokin' terbacker?" he asked, coolly. "I ain't got northin' left but chawin', an thet's derned pore stuff ter burn."

"Ugh!" grunted the Blackfeet, staring at him in unutterable amazement.

"Hey?" questioned the guide. "Whut did yer say?"

"Where white man come from?" demanded Half Hand, harshly.

"Over yon," was the answer, and Rocks made a sweep of his hand that took in half the horizon.

"What white man want here?"

"Terbacker."

The Indians looked at each other, and then looked at the cool visitor, their amazement not a whit abated.

"Ugh!" they grunted in chorus.

"Wa-al, I'll allow thet you fellers know whut thet means all right," drawled Old Rocks, whimsically; "but dog my cats ef I do! Do I git ther terbacker? ur do I hev ter pull my liver out tryin' ter make chawin' terbacker burn?"

"Ain't got no 'backer," declared Half Hand, sullenly.

"Thet may be so," admitted the guide, "an' may be 't'sn't. Howsomever, I don't s'pose I've got any license ter search ye."

He then appealed to the other Indians, but they all affirmed that they did not have a morsel of tobacco in their possession.

"Blamed ef I ever saw sech a pore crowd," grunted Old Rocks. "Wa-al, I'm goin' ter smoke."

He pretended to search round in his pockets, and, after a time, he drew forth a small bit of tobacco, uttering an exclamation of satisfaction.

"Dog my cats ef I ain't got a leetle mite o' smokin' terbacker left, an I 'lowed I wuz all out! I kin git erlong with this yere comfortable like."

He drew his knife, and began whittling at the tobacco, seeming to pay not the least attention to the Indians around him.

The Blackfeet were troubled, for they did not know what to make of the old fellow. Some of them put their heads together and spoke in their own language, but Rocks had sharp ears, and he understood them well enough to get the drift of what they said.

They were wondering if he had come there alone, or if he had companions near.

"Where come from?" Half Hand again asked.

"Over yon," the guide once more replied, with a sweep that was fully as wide as before.

"Ugh! Where others?"

"What others?"

"Others that be with you?"

"Over yon."

Again that wide and baffling sweep of the hand.

Half Hand scowled blackly.

"What white man here for?"

"Terbacker."

Old Rocks was most aggravating in his answers. He calmly filled his pipe, and then lighted it with a coal from the fire.

"Thar," he said, flinging one knee over the other and settling into an easy position, "now I kin enjoy a good squar' smoke."

Up behind the rocks the boy saw Rocks had not taken his rifle into the camp, and Frank knew well enough that was so he might not be incumbered with it if forced to take to flight suddenly and make an attempt to get away with the child.

The little girl heard his voice, and sat up, rubbing her eyes. She stared at him in wonderment, but he still pretended that he did not see her, puffing on.

One of the Indians attempted to grasp the child and draw her back, but she saw him, avoided his hands, and ran to Rocks, crying:

"Oh, I's awsul dlad you've tome! Tate me to my mamma! I don't lite dese dreful mans!"

The Indian made a jump for her, but Old Rocks caught her and swung her beyond the Indian's grasp, exclaiming:

"Hello! hello! Whatever is this yar? Dog my cats ef it ain't a bab-by—an' a white babby, at thet!"

"Don't you 'member me?" asked Fay, innocently. "I 'members you."

"See hyar, Half Hand," said Old Rocks, grimly; "this yar looks kinder queer. How did you come by this white babby?"

"Found her," sullenly answered the half-blood.

"Is thet so?"

"Ugh."

"Wa-al, whar wuz yer takin' her?"

"Nowhere."

"Seems ter me it didn't look thet way."

The half-blood said nothing, but he and his companions were beginning to finger their weapons.

"You may hev found her all right," admitted Old Rocks; "but yer made a mistake in keepin' her. I'll take her now."

"Dunno 'bout that," muttered Half Hand.

"Whut?" roared the old man, suddenly aroused, having thrust his pipe into his pocket. "You dunno? Wa-al, I will allow thet I know! Look yar, you'll be gittin' inter one o' ther derndest scrapes you ever did ef you tries ter kerry off this yere gal. It'll be report-ed, an' ther United States soldiers will take an' hang yer all!"

"Bah!" sneered the half-breed. "Who care for soldiers! We find gal; she b'long to us."

"Not much!"

"What white man do?"

"Take her."

"Him can't."

"Dog my cats ef I don't!"

"Him can't git erway."

The Blackfeet had formed a circle about Old Rocks.

"Stiddy, critters!" he warned. "Don't try ter stop me, fer ef yer does, som' o' yer will bite ther dust."

"White man give up gal, we let um go 'thout hurtin'."

"Thet's kind; but I reckons I'll hev ter be hurt, fer I'll never give her up."

"Then white man dies!"

One of the Indians slipped up behind Old Rocks and lifted a hatchet to split open the head of the guide.

Crack! the report of a rifle rang out.

A yell of agony broke from the lips of the Indian, and the hatchet dropped from his hand. A bullet had shattered his forearm.

Frank's aim had been true, and he had saved the life of Old

Rocks.

At that instant, just as the guide stooped to lift the child, a man broke through the circle of savages and snatched up the child, tearing it from the fingers of the guide, to whom he cried:

"Hold them off, and I will get away with her!"

It was the Hermit.

Out came a brace of revolvers in the hands of the weather-tanned guide, and the yells which broke from his lips awoke a hundred echoes. He began shooting to the right and left.

Over the top of the rocks, behind which he had been concealed, Frank was sending a shower of bullets whistling. After the first two shots, he aimed high, counting on demoralizing the savages by terror, instead of taking chances of hitting Old Rocks or the child.

The trick worked long enough for the guide to get away, and he followed close at the heels of the Hermit.

By chance the man with the child passed near Frank, and then Old Rocks came along, shouting:

"Up an' dig, boy! Ther trick is did!"

In a moment Frank dashed after the old man.

The Blackfeet recovered quickly, and they leaped in pursuit, uttering fierce cries.

Old Rocks was surprised by Frank's fleetness on foot.

"Derned ef you can't run, ez well ez do other things!" he muttered, as the lad forged along by his side. "You're a holy wonder, boy. It's twice you saved my life this day. I trusted everything ter you this last time, an' yer didn't fail me."

"I broke the Indian's arm as he was on the point of striking."

"Thet wuz ther only mistake yer made. You oughter broke his head, an' thar'd bin one less. They're arter us hot foot, an' it's a race fer life now."

# CHAPTER XXXIV.

## IN SAND CAVE.

ehind them the enraged Blackfeet began shooting, and the bullets whistled over the heads of the fugitives.

"I pray none of those hits little Fairy," panted Frank.

"Ef we could strike some kind o' cover an' hed a minute to spar', we'd be able ter stan' ther varmints off," came from Old Rocks.

"My rifle is empty."

"I ain't got mine, an' I'll allow my small guns are empty; but I kin load 'em as we run."

"We may have to fight anyhow."

"Right, boy. Ef we do, dog my cats ef we don't make some o' them onery skunks gaul derned sick!"

Still running, Old Rocks snapped the empty shells from his revolvers, and replaced them with fresh cartridges.

At times it was not easy to keep track of the Hermit, who ran through the night with the speed of a deer and the tirelessness of a hound.

Now and then the frightened child cried out, and this aided Frank and the old guide in following.

Rocks soon replenished his revolvers, and said:

"Thar, I kinder 'lows we kin make it interestin' fer them varmints ef they press us too hard. Dunno ez I kin find ther place whar I hid my rifle, but I reckons I oughter."

"If we escape."

"Ef we escape! Whut's ther matter with you, boy? Think we can't dodge them red whelps in ther dark?"

"We might alone; but the man ahead of us may make no attempt to do so, and we must stand by him. It would not do to let the child fall into the hands of those wretches again. They would surely murder her."

"They'd be likely ter, an' that's facts. Oh, we'll back up ther Hermit, an' thar won't be no trouble 'bout gittin' erway, 'less them varmints behind manages ter hit one o' us with a lead pill."

The flight and pursuit continued, the Blackfeet seeming to have the eyes of owls or the scent of hounds. They pressed the fugitives hard, and Old Rocks feared that some of the flying bullets which whistled around them would find a mark.

At length the guide gave an exclamation of satisfaction.

"Reckon I knows whar ther Hermit is headin' fer," he said.

"Where?" asked Frank.

"Straight fer Sand Cave."

"Where is Sand Cave?"

"Not very fur ahead. Thar is some bowlders at ther mouth o' ther cave, and we oughter be able ter stand ther red niggers off thar."

"Are you sure the Hermit is going there?"

"I ain't sure, but it looks thet way. It ain't likely he kin keep up this pace much farther, an' kerry ther child."

However, Old Rocks feared the man ahead might not be making for Sand Cave, and so he called to the Hermit, asking him if he knew where to find the cave. The Hermit replied that he did, and Rocks urged him to go there.

"Git in with ther gal—git in out o' ther way o' bullets," advised the old guide. "Ther boy an' me will stand ther red dogs off all right."

To this the Hermit agreed.

A short time later, as they were rushing along the base of a bluff, the Hermit was seen to disappear.

"Hyar's ther cave!" panted Old Rocks, catching hold of the boy. "Right yar behind these boulders. In with yer!"

Frank saw the dark mouth of the cave behind the bowlders, over which he vaulted.

The cry of the child came out of the darkness of the cave.

The Hermit and little Fay were there.

"Reddy!" hissed Old Rocks, crouching behind the bowlders—"reddy ter repel invaders!"

The Blackfeet were coming on, and their dusky forms suddenly appeared near at hand in the darkness.

On his knees behind a bowlder, Frank had drawn a revolver, and he began firing with Old Rocks.

The flash of the weapons blinded the boy for the moment, and he stopped shooting when he had fired three times.

Old Rocks stopped at the same moment, growling:

"Thet's ther way with ther onery skunks! They'll never come up and be shot down ther way they oughter!"

The Indians had disappeared.

"Where are they?" asked Frank, wonderingly.

"Right near yere, you kin bet yer dust," answered the guide. "They drapped down ther instant we begun slingin' lead, an' they're huggin' ther yearth, you bet!"

"Did we kill any?"

"Wa-al, I dunno; but I'll allow thet I didn't do any shootin' fer fun. I don't b'lieve in thet under such circumstances."

"This affair may bring on an Indian war."

"Let'er bring! It'll be er good thing ef it does, an' ther hull Injun nation is wiped out. But ther chances are thet it'll never be heard of by anybody except them we tell it to. Ther varmints will make tracks outer ther park, fer they're on forbidden ground."

"If the soldiers should turn up——"

"It'd be a mighty good thing fer us. Still, I kinder reckon we'll be able ter hold Half Hand an' his gang off till they git weary."

They took care that their revolvers were replenished with cartridges, and then Frank loaded his rifle.

A sudden silence seemed to brood over the whole world.

Old Rocks stirred uneasily.

"I don't like it," he muttered, speaking to himself.

"Don't like what?" asked Frank, who felt a foreboding of some coming catastrophe.

"This yare stillness. Why, thar ain't even an owl hootin'."

"What do you think it means?"

"Dunno; but it means somethin'. Keep yer eyes an' ears open, an' be ready fer what may come."

Little Fay had ceased her sobbing, and the silence was finally broken by her voice:

"Who's doin' to tate me to my mamma?"

Then the Hermit was heard trying to comfort and reassure her.

"Dog my cats ef I wouldn't like ter smoke!" muttered Old Rocks; "but I'll allow thet it w'u'dn't do ter light a match hyar."

"No; it might be fatal. The light——"

The sharp report of a rifle rang out, and Frank fell backward behind the bowlder.

With a grated exclamation, Old Rocks flung up his revolver, and took a snap shot at the spot where he had seen the red flash of the weapon as it was discharged.

"Did you get him?" asked Frank, as he sat up.

"Dunno," was the answer; "but I wuz afeared he'd got you."

"The bullet whistled so close to my head that I felt the wind of it. It must have penetrated the cave."

To their ears came the sound of a deep groan, and then the voice of the Hermit reached them:

"The bullet came in here. I am shot!"

"Holy cats!" gasped Old Rocks.

"The child!" panted Frank. "What if the red wretches fire again, and their bullets reach her? She must be placed where she will be safe."

"Right."

"Can you hold the mouth of the cave?"

"I kin try it."

"I will go in there and see how badly the Hermit is injured, and will see if both cannot be placed beyond the reach of bullets."

"Thet's easy. Ther cave is a big one, but this hyar is ther only entrance ter it."

Frank crept back into the cave, softly calling to the Hermit. The man was groaning, and, as Frank crept near, a pair of soft arms suddenly closed about the boy's neck, while a sweet voice sounded in his ear:

"I knows you w'en I hears you speak. You singed me to sleep. I tolt you I'd be your Fairy."

"So you did, dear," said the boy, giving her a tender embrace; "and I have done my best in the work of saving you from the Indians."

"Bad Injuns!" exclaimed Fay. "Dey tarry me off fwom my mamma. You tate me to my mamma?"

"We will, dear."

Frank's hands found the wounded man, and he asked:

"Where did the bullet strike you, Hermit?"

"Here in the side," was the faint answer. "I think I am done for! I have found death at last!"

The boy shivered, for the words were uttered exultantly, as if the man actually rejoiced.

"Are you able to creep back farther into the cave?" Frank asked.

"I don't know. Why should I do so? It is too much exertion."

"If not for your own sake, you should do so for the child. Another bullet may reach her."

The man stirred and sat up.

"That is true," he panted. "She must be returned uninjured, and Foster Fairfax must know that I did my best to save her."

"Foster Fairfax! He is the man you saw this morning?"

"Yes."

"What is he to this child?"

"He is her father."

168

"And you—what are you to her?"

"Nothing."

Frank was somewhat dazed, for he had felt sure that the Hermit was Fay's father.

"We were friends," explained the wounded man. "I can't tell all the story. We both loved Marian Dale. Our rivalry was fair and square, and we swore that the one who won her should still retain the friendship of the other. At last, she promised to be mine at the end of six months. Business took me into the Southwest, and there I met Fairfax, who had rushed away as soon as he learned of my success. He was somewhat bitter toward me, and accused me of using unfair means to win Marian. We parted, and the very next day I was in a railroad collision, being injured about the head, so I did not know my own name. I recovered, but I was still unable to tell my name or remember anything of my past. In this condition, I wandered over the country four years. I was able to make a living, and seemed all right, with the exception that I could not remember anything back of the accident. One night in Omaha I was in a hotel fire, and I jumped from the window to escape. They took me up in an unconscious condition, and carried me to a hospital. I recovered, and my memory came back to me. Then I hurried East to Marian, and I found her married to Foster Fairfax, who had told her that I was dead, and that he had seen my dead body. This little girl is their child."

"While you are talking, you are losing blood," said Frank. "Move back, and let me see if I cannot stop the flow."

He induced the Hermit to move back into the cave, where he was able to light some matches and examine the wound. Not being a physician, Frank could not tell how severe it was; but, with considerable difficulty, he finally succeeded in stanching the flow of blood to a certain extent.

"It is useless," declared the Hermit. "I am booked, and I am glad of that. I have nothing to live for."

"Yes, you has!" cried little Fay, creeping close to him. "I dess you is pretty dood man. One time I had a birdie that die, and it was all tovered up in the dround. You don't want to be all tovered up like dat. I don't want you to be."

"God bless you!" murmured the Hermit, thickly. "You are a dear, sweet child, and I shall not live to make more trouble for your father and mother."

All was quiet at the mouth of the cave. Frank was longing to hear more of the Hermit's story, and so he questioned the man.

"How does it happen that Foster Fairfax and his wife are not living together?"

"I separated them."

"How?"

"I appeared like one risen from the dead, and Marian was pros-trated by the sight of me. I denounced Foster, called him a false friend and a dastardly traitor. I was insane at the moment, and it is remarkable that I did not kill him. However, I swore to have his life if we ever met again. Then I left them."

"And you did not see Fairfax again till you met him here in the park?"

"No."

"How did it happen he left his wife?"

"When I met him I did not know they were not living together. He forced me to listen, and he told me how he had taken a man-gled corpse from the wreck and buried it as me—how he had firmly believed me dead. Then he bore the news to Marian, and she was prostrated.

"He loved her, but it was long before she consented to marry him. At last, she did so, and they married, both believing me in my grave."

Frank was fascinated by the story.

"Go on," he urged.

"When I appeared both were horrified. When I left them, Marian accused Foster of treachery. She was unreasonable and would listen to nothing he could say. She bade him leave her and never return. He departed, and they have not seen each other since. He does not know she is somewhere in the park, as she must be, else the child would not be here. I did not tell him of the peril of his child, but I resolved to save her and restore her to his arms. I have saved her, but I shall be unable to take her to him. I shall not live to see the light of another day."

"Oh, you may not be so badly injured as all that."

"I am. I am sure of it. I will leave the child in your care. Take her to him, and tell him that I forgive everything. Never again will I rise like one from the dead to come between Foster and Marian."

Frank remained with the man a while longer, and then, telling Fay to stay there that she might keep beyond the reach of bullets, he returned to the mouth of the cave.

"I'm glad ye've come, boy," said Old Rocks. "Ef them pesky var-mints ain't gone away entirely, they're up ter mischief, an' I needs yer hyar."

They crouched behind the bowlders and waited, while the min-utes slipped away, and the same silence reigned.

At least an hour passed, and then came a sudden sound that filled both with surprise and alarm.

Behind them there was a faint dropping in the cave, a movement, a rush, and a roar. Then a cloud of dust swirled out and nearly smothered them.

"What is the meaning of that?" said Frank, bewildered.

"A cave-in!" shouted Old Rocks, making a hasty examination. "By ther livin' gods! ther hull derned cave is blocked, an' ther Hermit an' ther leetle gal is both buried beneath ur beyond thet fall!"

Frank was horrified beyond measure.

"It is terrible!" he gasped. "Poor little Fay!"

"What you want?" asked the familiar voice of the child, near at hand. "It was lonetome in dere. The mans goed to sleep, an' I tomed out to see you."

"Thank God!" came fervently from Frank's lips, as he caught her up in his arms and covered her face with kisses.

"Wa-al, thet's whut I call luck!" gurgled the guide.

"Luck!" cried Frank, rebukingly. "It was the hand of Providence! Can you doubt the wisdom and goodness of an Overruling Power after this?"

"Dunno ez I kin," admitted the old man. "It duz look like something a' ther kind took her out o' thar jest at ther right time."

A complete examination showed that the whole roof of the cave had apparently fallen in, and the passage was blocked with tons upon tons of earth and sand.

"This yar's ther end o' Sand Cave," said Old Rocks.

They kept the child with them and waited behind the rocks for the attack of the Blackfeet, but no attack came. Thus the long night passed, and another day came round.

Then it was found that the Indians had departed.

"They didn't dar' stay hayer longer," said Old Rocks. "Ther whelps wuz afeared o' ther soldiers. I'd like ter run onter ther soldiers an' set 'em arter Half Hand an' ther gang."

Led by the guide, they left the spot. Frank carried Fay in his arms.

Old Rocks first proceeded to the spot where he had hidden his rifle, and, with that again in his possession, he expressed himself as feeling ready to "chaw up ther hull Blackfeet tribe."

They found some game for breakfast and dinner, and before nightfall they reached the camp on the shore of the lake, where Preston March and Foster Fairfax had met.

A large party of tourists had gathered there, and the appearance of the man and boy, the latter bearing Fay in his arms, created the greatest excitement. Several persons rushed into the tent and drew forth a man and woman, the latter white and grief-stricken, and pointed out the child, who was sitting on Frank's shoulder and waving her hand, as she laughingly called:

"I dess my mamma is dere! I knowed you'd tate me bat to my mamma!"

The man and woman were Foster Fairfax and his wife, who had met by accident there in the Wonderland of America. She had told him how little Fay had wandered away and become lost, and both had feared that they would never see their child again.

Their unutterable joy cannot be depicted in words. Frank and Old Rocks were the heroes of the occasion.

"Yer don't want ter give me too much credit fer this yar," said the guide. "I done ther trailin', but this yar tenderfut saved me frum bein' killed twice, an' he's got nerves o' steel. It ain't often I take ter a tenderfut, but I will allow thet this yar chap is a boy ter tie to. Ther babby sticks by him; he has won her heart. Dog my cats ef I blame her either!"

Then the old man told how Frank had saved him from the grizzly, how the boy had been tireless on the trail, how he had not murmured at any hardship, and how he had broken the arm of the Blackfoot Indian who was about to brain the guide.

As a result, Frank found himself regarded with unspeakable admiration by all the tourists, while Foster Fairfax and his wife could not say or do enough to express their feelings.

Frank told them of the death of Preston March, and, later, when Professor Scotch and Barney had been found by Rocks and brought into the party, all visited the spot where the Hermit of Yellowstone Park lay buried beneath tons of earth.

At the mouth of the cave Foster Fairfax caused a cross to be erected, bearing the name of the unfortunate man, the date of his birth and of his death.

Frank remained in the park till he succeeded in photographing some "real wild buffalo," and then he was well satisfied to move on to other fields of adventure.

Half Hand was shot while trying to get away with a stolen horse about a year later.

When the time came to part from Frank, little Fay was almost heart-broken. She clung to him, sobbing:

"Is you doin' to leave me? I don't want you to! You know I is your Fairy."

"You will ever be my Fairy," said the boy, with deep feeling. "Your mamma has promised me your picture, and I shall keep it with me ever. Some time by and by, dear, I will come back to you again."

And he kissed her farewell.

# CHAPTER XXXV.

## A PECULIAR GIRL.

The remainder of the stop in Yellowstone Park proved a delightful time.

"I wish I could sthay wid ye, Frankie, me b'y," said Barney, one day.

"Stay with me? What do you mean?" asked Frank.

"Oi have news from home. Oi must go back to Fardale to rasume me studies."

"I'll be sorry to lose you Barney." And Frank spoke the truth, for he loved his Irish chum a good deal.

Just then Professor Scotch burst in on the pair, telegram in hand.

"I must return East at once," he cried. "A relative of mine has died and I must settle up his affairs."

"Two at once!" ejaculated Frank. "Then I'll be left to continue my travels alone."

"Not for long, my boy," answered the professor. "I will soon return to see that you fall into no more danger."

Two days later found Frank alone, the professor and Barney have taken the eastbound train the evening before. Frank proceeded to Ogden, Utah, where he spent three days in sight-seeing.

But he was anxious to go farther West, and one fine day found him a passenger on the Pacific Express, bound for San Francisco.

Every seat in the parlor cars was taken, as Frank discovered, on endeavoring to obtain one. Then he decided that any kind of a seat would do, but nearly every one was occupied.

As he passed through the train, he noticed a girl of seventeen or eighteen who seemed to be sitting alone. She was reading, and, as Frank came along, she dropped the book in her lap, looked up, and smiled.

Frank touched his hat, paused, and asked:

"Is this seat taken, miss?"

"No, sir."

"Would you object——"

He paused significantly, smiling back at her.

"Not at all," was her immediate reply, as she drew a bit nearer the window, and he sat down.

The book in the girl's lap was a noted one of detective tales. Frank caught his breath in astonishment as he noted this.

"Queer literature for such a girl to be perusing," was his mental observation.

He cast a sly glance at her. She was looking out of the window, but the side of her face was toward him. Frank noted that she had a beautiful profile, and that there was a most innocent and winsome expression about her mouth. Her hair was golden and her eyes were blue.

There was a refinement and delicacy about the girl which impressed Frank favorably.

Still, he wondered that a girl like her should be reading a book of detective tales. She was the sort of a girl he would have expected to see perusing love stories of the "Bertha M. Clay" class.

He longed to get into conversation with her, and yet, for all of the smile with which she had seemed to greet him, something held him back and told him it was not wise to be too forward.

At last she resumed reading again. She did not read long. With a faint, scornful laugh, she dropped the book in her lap.

Frank fancied he saw an opportunity to "break the ice."

"You do not seem to like those stories," he observed.

"They are very amusing, and utterly improbable and impossible," she said.

The boy laughed.

"Then you fancy the author overdrew his hero?" he asked.

"To be sure he did. There is no detective living who can do such astonishing things as this one is credited with. No such detective ever lived."

"Possibly not."

"Surely not. You cannot make me believe that a detective could come in here, look me over, and then tell everything about me almost to my name and the hour of my birth. Rubbish!"

Frank's wonder at the girl was on the increase. She did not talk much like the ordinary girl of seventeen.

"If you dislike the stories so much how does it happen you are reading them?"

"Oh, I do not dislike them. I confess that I found them very amusing, but I am beginning to weary of them."

"I consider it remarkable that you attempted reading them."

"Why?"

"Young ladies like you seldom care for this kind of literature."

"Oh, I see. I presume not. They are too sentimental—soft, some call it. Well, I am not sentimental."

"Perhaps not."

She lifted her eyebrows and pursed her lips a bit.

"You say that as if you do not believe me. Never mind. It makes no difference whether you believe me or not."

She did not seem offended, and still she gave him to understand that what he thought was of little consequence to her.

"Well," laughed Frank, "I have never yet met a girl who did not declare she was bound to be an old maid, and those are the very ones who get married first."

"And you think, because of that, that I must be sentimental, as I have said that I am not, do you?"

"Oh, well—you see—I—I——"

She interrupted him with a merry laugh.

"Do not be afraid to answer. I don't mind. We are strangers, and why should I be offended?"

"It is true we are strangers," said Frank; "and, as we may be seat-mates for some time to come, I will offer my card."

He drew out a cardcase and gave her a delicate bit of cardboard, with his name engraved upon it.

"Frank Merriwell," she read. "Why, that is a splendid name, and it seems to fit you so well! I like you all the better for your name."

"Whew!" thought Frank. "That is point-blank, and still she says she is not sentimental. She may not be, but she is decidedly complimentary on short acquaintance."

Aloud, he said:

"I am happy there is something about me that you admire, if it is no more than my name."

She smiled, looking at him in a big-eyed, innocent way.

"Why, I didn't say that was all. I have not known you long enough to tell. I am no gifted detective, and I cannot read your character at a glance."

"Well, supposing we say the detective was a freak or a myth, and relegate him to the background."

"That goes," she said.

Then she clapped her hand over her mouth, with a little exclamation of dismay, quickly exclaiming:

"That is dreadful! I completely forgot myself! You see, I have been away to school, and I caught on to some slang there, and I find I can't shake it, although mamma doesn't like to have me make such breaks."

She paused, a look of the utmost dismay coming to her face, as if she just realized what she had been saying.

It was with the utmost difficulty Frank restrained his laughter. At the same time he felt his liking and admiration for the strange girl growing swiftly. The little slip into slang seemed to add to her innocence, especially when followed by such utter dismay.

"I am bound to do it occasionally," she said, after a few moments. "I can't seem to get out of the habit, although I have tried. I trust you will pardon me."

"Certainly."

"Thank you. I'll keep this card. I have none of my own with me. My name is Isa Isban."

Somehow, that name was a shock to Frank. He could not have told why, to save his life, but there was something unpleasant about it. It did not seem to fit the girl at all.

However, this feeling soon passed, and they were chatting freely in a short time. Their conversation drifted from topic to topic, and Frank was delighted to find his fair companion wondrously well informed on subjects such as are given little attention by most young girls. She could even talk politics rationally, and she rather worsted Frank on a tariff discussion.

"You are beyond my comprehension," he declared, admiringly. "Where you ever learned so much is more than I can understand."

"Do you fancy that young men are the only ones who know things? If you do, you are sure to find there are others—— Oh, dear! there I go again."

Having become so well acquainted, Frank asked if she were bound for San Francisco, and, to his disappointment, she informed him that Carson City was her destination.

The conductor came through the train for tickets. Frank had his ready, and the girl began searching for hers, but had not found it when the conductor came along.

"Oh, dear!" she exclaimed, and Frank was about to offer to aid her, if she needed a loan, when she opened her purse and took out several bills, every one of them new and crisp, and of large denominations.

"The smallest I have is fifty dollars," she said. "Papa gave me large bills, as he said they would not be so bulky."

"I can't change a bill of that size," said the conductor.

"I can," put in Frank, immediately producing his pocketbook. "I will break it for you."

So he took the new bank-note, and gave her two twenties, a five and five ones for it, enabling her to pay her fare without difficulty.

The conductor gave the girl a rebate ticket and passed on.

"Thank you so much!" she said to Frank. "I believe I may have trouble in getting those large bills broken. Would you mind giving me small bills for another fifty?"

Frank did not mind, and he gave them.

Thereby hangs a tale.

# CHAPTER XXXVI.

## FRIENDS AND FOES.

The Pacific Express drew into Reno on time, and Frank Merriwell was about to bid adieu to the beautiful girl whom he had first met the day before.

"I shall not soon forget this pleasant journey," he said, sincerely. "Your company has made it very agreeable, Miss—Isban."

Somehow, he stumbled over that name, to which he had taken such a strong dislike.

"Thank you," she said, and he half fancied her lip quivered a bit. "You have been very kind, Mr. Merriwell."

Frank's heart fluttered a bit; the train was drawing into the station; the boy leaned toward her, his eyes shining, a flush in his cheeks.

"And now we are to say good-by, without the least probability of ever seeing each other again," he said, his voice not quite steady.

She turned away for a moment, and then, as she turned back, she swiftly said:

"It is possible we may never see each other again, but you have given me your home address, and you say any letter I may send will be forwarded to you. You may hear from me—some time."

"I may—but if you would promise to write——"

"I have told you I cannot promise that."

"And you will not give me your address?"

"I cannot for reasons known to myself. Do not ask me."

"Miss Isban, I believe you are in trouble—some things you have told me have led me to believe so. If you need a friend at any time, let me hear from you."

She gave him her hand, looked straight into his eyes, and said: "I will."

The brakeman thrust open the door and shouted:

"Reno. Change here for Carson, Virginia City, Candelaria and Keeler."

The train came to a dead stop.

Frank escorted Isa from the car, carrying her traveling bag, which he gave to her when the station platform was reached.

"Remember!" he breathed in her ear.

Her hand touched his, she smiled into his eyes, whispering:

"I will! Good-by."

He lifted his hat, as she turned away.

At that moment a youth came hurrying forward, lifted his hat, his face radiant, and accosted Isa:

"Vida," he said, "I am here. You did not come when you said, but I have been watching for you."

Frank staggered back.

"Cæsar's ghost!" he palpitated. "Is it possible, or do my eyes deceive me? Can that be Bart Hodge, my schoolmate, chum, and comrade of Fardale? As I live, I believe it is! And he knows Miss Isban! What's the matter? She does not seem to know him!"

The girl had drawn back, with an expression of alarm.

"I think you have made a mistake, sir," she said, rather haughtily.

"A mistake!" gasped the handsome youth, astonished and dismayed. "Why, you know me! There is no mistake."

"But there is. I do not know you."

"Vida, you say that? Why, I am——"

"An impertinent young scoundrel!"

Smack!—an open hand struck Bart Hodge on the cheek, sending him reeling. The blow was delivered by a large man, with a heavy black mustache and the manner and appearance of a "gentleman rowdy." His clothes were flashy, and he "sported" several large diamonds.

Frank was not the boy to stand idle and see a friend struck. Without a word he made a leap for the big man. His fist was clinched, his arm shot out, and his knuckles took the fellow under the left ear.

It was a beautiful knock-down blow. The man measured his length on the platform in an instant.

"All aboard!"

The train was about to start, the conductor was giving the signal.

"Let it go," said Frank, quietly. "It is possible I had better stay here and see this matter through. Bart may need me."

The train began to move.

With a cry of dismay, the girl had knelt beside the fallen man.

A bit dazed, Bart Hodge had faced around in time to see Frank strike that telling blow. Bart stared, almost doubting the evidence of his eyes.

"Great guns!" he gasped.

Then he sprang forward, his hand outstretched, shouting:

"Frank Merriwell!"

"Bart Hodge!"

They shook hands, both laughing forth their delight.

"You are a sight for sore eyes, old man!" cried Bart.

"You're another!" flung back Frank.

The man with the black mustache pushed away the girl and sat up, staring, in a dazed way, at the two boys.

"Who struck me?" he asked.

"I believe I had that pleasure," smiled Frank.

"You? Did you knock me down? Why, you're a kid! I can kill you with one blow!"

He got upon his feet, his face dark as a thundercloud.

The girl caught him by the arm, crying, in distress:

"Don't Paul—don't harm him! He has been kind to me on the train. I beg you not to hurt him!"

This seemed to anger the man still more.

"Kind to you, eh?" he snarled. "And the other one tried to flirt with you. I will——"

His hand went round to his hip, and there was a mad, deadly gleam in his eyes. He looked murderous.

Neither of the boys made a move to draw a weapon.

"I wouldn't do it," said Frank, coolly. "I know this section of the country is called 'the wild and woolly West,' but it is not sufficiently wild and woolly to overlook a cold-blooded murder. If you take a fancy to shoot two boys you will be pretty sure to get yourself beautifully hanged."

"Oh, I won't shoot!" growled the man, his hand dropping away from his hip. "But I will——"

"Easy, there!" came sharply from the lips of a police officer. "Somebody is going to get yanked here."

He forced his way through the crowd that had formed a circle about the principal actors on the scene.

"Who is talking about shooting here?" he demanded. "Where is the man who carries concealed weapons?"

"Come away, Paul," whispered the girl, pulling at the man's arm.

"All right," he muttered—"all right, but there are other days. Those young whelps had better keep out of my way."

"Disperse, here!" ordered the officer, commandingly, flourishing his stick. "Be lively about it, too."

The crowd began to disperse.

The big man turned away, and the girl took his arm. Bart Hodge took a step after them, but Frank caught hold of his arm, saying, sharply:

"Easy, old boy! Let her go."

"But——"

"Are you looking for further trouble right here?"

"No, but——"

"Then mind me."

"I suppose I'll have to, as you always were the boss. But I know that girl, and she refused to recognize me."

"Well, what do you think you can do about it?"

"I was going to demand an explanation, and——"

"You would have received it—from the man who accompanies her."

Frank drew Bart away, but the latter still grumbled.

"If you understood it—if you knew, Frank. Why, I have chased across the continent to meet her, and then to have her cut me dead! It is terrible!"

Frank smiled.

"I should fancy it would seem a bit hard," he confessed. "But you may have made a mistake."

"Not much!"

"Still, it is possible you did, Bart—it is probable."

"Probable! Get out! I——"

"Wait a minute. It happens that I am slightly acquainted with the young lady."

"You? She never mentioned you to me."

"Still, I am slightly acquainted with her," smiled Frank, who knew well enough why she had never mentioned him. "I heard you call her Vida, and——"

"That is her name—Vida Melburn."

"It's just as I thought—you have mistaken this girl for some one else. The name of this young lady is Isa Isban."

"Impossible!"

"It is the truth. I traveled with her from Ogden, and she left me a moment before you observed her. Now, I know what I am talking about, and you are twisted, old boy."

Bart smote his hands together, his dark eyes glowing.

"I will not believe it yet; but, if it is true, there are two girls in the world who look exactly alike."

"Come away from here," said Frank. "Where can we obtain something to eat? We can talk it over——"

"Hold on, Frank. I believe those people are going to take the next train south, which leaves immediately."

"That is right. Miss Isban is on her way to Carson."

"Then I shall take that train."

Frank looked his friend over from head to foot.

"Say," he chuckled, "you are hard hit! I will confess that I was a bit stuck on the girl, but I did not have it this way."

"She is in trouble," asserted Bart. "I mean to be on hand to help her, if she needs assistance."

"All right; we'll take the next train south."

# CHAPTER XXXVII.

## BOY SHADOWERS.

nd so they took the next train for Carson City.

Isa Isban and her companion of the dark mustache were on the same train, as they learned without difficulty.

The girl and the man were in the same car with the boys, but neither of them seemed to pay the least attention to the latter.

"Look here, Frank," said Bart, "tell me how you happened to get acquainted with her."

Frank did so, and Bart's face clouded as he listened.

"I know you are great at catching on with the girls," Bart observed; "but I swear I did not believe Vida Melburn was the sort to take up with a chance acquaintance, under any circumstances."

Frank laughed.

"Now, you are jealous, old man," he said. "It came about naturally enough, and she acted like a lady."

"But not like the Vida Melburn I know."

"I do not believe she is the Vida Melburn you know. You have been deceived by a resemblance, my boy."

Bart shook his head.

"Not much! Don't take me for a fool, Frank! I am not such a dunderhead as that—oh, no!"

"Then she lied to one of us."

Bart's face lighted a bit.

"Possibly she did not care to give you her right name, having made your acquaintance in such a manner. That must be the real explanation."

"Look here, Bart, that girl is too unsophisticated, too innocent to work that kind of a game. She has the most innocent face I ever saw."

"You are right," the dark-haired lad confessed, "Vida would not be likely to do such a thing. She is frank and open as the day."

"Well, what do you make of it?"

"I don't know what to make of it."

"Tell me how you came to know her."

"She was visiting at Fardale, and I became acquainted with her. She liked me and—I liked her. We were together a great deal. She did not tell me much about herself, but, still, I learned a few things. Her home is in Sacramento, but she has relatives in Carson City. I found out that there had been trouble between her father and mother, and they had separated. That is how her father happened to send her East. Her relatives at Fardale did not regard me with favor for some reason, and they ordered me to have nothing more to say to her. Still, we met occasionally, and—to tell the truth, old boy—I fell in love with her. They found out we were seeing each other secretly, and they made a rumpus about it. Then they wrote to her father, and they sent for her to return to the West. She was shipped off in a hurry, so we would see no more of each other; but she wrote me a short note, telling me to address her at Austin, Nevada. I did so, and, as I happen to have a rich old uncle in California, I proposed to come out here. She answered, saying she would be in Reno just three days ago, and for me to meet her at the railway station, if possible. It looked impossible then, but I was hard hit, and I made a big hustle to get away from school and come out here. I worked all kinds of schemes on the governor, and he finally agreed to let me come West to visit Uncle Hiram. I came, and I was in Reno on the date set, but she did not appear. I have been there every day since, and to-day she came. You know the rest."

Frank regarded his friend steadfastly for some moments, smiling covertly.

"You are a queer fellow, Bart," he said. "You go to extremes in everything. Now, stop and think of chasing away out here after a girl. It is——"

Bart interrupted him with a sharp gesture.

"Oh, I know—I don't deny that I am a fool! At the same time I can't help it. I never saw a girl before this one that I cared a snap for. She seems to be my affinity."

Frank's laugh rang out merrily.

"Affinity is good!" he exclaimed. "You are hard hit. And the girl threw you down when you appeared on the scene. What do you make of that?"

Bart scowled.

"I am sure of one thing."

"And that is—what?"

"She is in trouble."

"Who is the man with her?"

"That is what I'd like to know. I am sure she fears him. She must have seen him, and she must have feared to recognize me. There can be no other explanation."

"He is not her father, is he?"

"That creature the father of that girl? Well, not much!"

"No, he is not. If I remember right, she called him Paul. Can he be her brother?"

"Never!"

"Then, what is he?"

"You tell."

"I can't."

"More than ever am I sure she is in trouble—great trouble. I am determined to know the truth. I will learn it from her own lips."

"How?"

"By following her till I get an opportunity to speak with her."

"Well, Bart, you are so badly struck that all I can do is hang by you and see you through. We will solve the mystery of this girl, if we are capable of doing so."

"Right you are, Frank."

Then they spoke of other matters, old friends at Fardale, and how things were moving there. Bart told all about the events that had taken place at the academy since Frank left, how they had missed him as a leader in sports of all kinds, how often he was spoken of with admiration and affection by his old comrades, and how even the professors held him up as a model to be emulated.

"They seem to have forgotten the pranks you were up to and the larks you were in," said Bart; "but they remember that you stood at the head in everything you undertook."

Then Frank told of his own adventures in knocking about, and Bart regarded him with still greater admiration.

"You are the luckiest fellow alive!" declared the dark-haired lad. "I wish I had a rich and eccentric old uncle to kick the bucket and leave me a big fortune on condition that I would 'travel over the world to advance my education and broaden my ideas.' Say, that uncle of yours was a good thing!"

"Uncle Asher was original in everything."

"I should guess yes. When are you going abroad?"

"Very soon. Professor Scotch will make arrangements for such a move while he is in the East."

"You are the envy of Fardale. Hans Dunnerwust returned with a stock of tales of astounding adventures, which he managed to bungle badly in the telling. And now I suppose Barney Mulloy will take his turn. Between them they will make you out one of the most remarkable heroes of modern times."

Thus the boys chatted till Carson City was reached.

All the while Bart was watching the girl closely, and he saw that she really intended to get off at Carson.

The boys slipped out of the car, and were on the platform as soon as the pair they were following reached it. It happened that the station platform was crowded, and they were swallowed by the throng, so they found it easy to keep out of sight of the man and girl.

The man seemed to watch to see if the boys left the car, while the girl tried to draw him away. After some moments he submitted, and they entered a closed carriage.

"Here!" exclaimed Frank, catching hold of a sleepy driver and giving him a whirl; "see that carriage?"

"Yep."

"Don't lose sight of it for a moment, but do not seem to follow it. Understand?"

"I reckon."

"Good! If you do the trick well, you get a tenner."

"Got it?"

"See."

Frank showed his roll, on the outside of which were the bright new fifty-dollar bills.

"Get in."

The boys sprang in lively, the door closed on them, the driver leaped to his seat, the whip cracked, and away they went.

"This is the first time I ever played the detective," said Bart.

"But it is not the first time for me," declared Frank. "I have found it necessary, several times, in New York, Chicago, New Orleans and elsewhere."

"I noticed how ready you were to do the proper thing. You did not give them the start."

"Not a bit of it."

"You are the same old, self-reliant, hustling, go-ahead Frank Merriwell. The only changes I can see in you are for the better."

"Thank you."

The driver in advance was a hustling fellow, and he had two good horses. He sent them right along. Now, it was fortunate that, although, the driver behind was a sleepyhead, he, also, had some fine horses, and he did not make any great effort to keep them at a clipping pace.

It is probable that the man with the black mustache regarded the boys with no little contempt, for he surely made no effort to give them the slip. It is likely he did not fancy they would follow him so hotly.

At length the carriage in advance stopped before a certain house, and the driver got down to open the door.

The driver who was carrying the boys continued past, turned the first corner, stopped short, jumped down, opened the door, and said:

"Got 'em? They're just round the corner back yon."

"And you have earned your X," said Frank, springing out.

# CHAPTER XXXVIII.

## "QUEER" MONEY.

his is counterfeit!"

It was in the First National Bank of Carson, between nine and ten o'clock of the day following Frank's arrival in the city.

Frank had found it difficult to get either of the new fifty-dollar bills changed, and so he stepped into the bank and asked if he could be favored there.

The bill had been scrutinized closely, the cashier had examined it beneath a magnifying glass, after which he questioned the boy concerning his manner of obtaining the paper, and Frank had told the truth fully and without hesitation. Then the boy had been called into a private room, and the cashier had declared the bill counterfeit.

Frank had been prepared for such an assertion by what went before it, and he immediately opened his pocketbook and produced the other bill which he had received of Isa Isban.

"Please look at this, and see if it is also counterfeit," he asked, with remarkable coolness.

In a moment the cashier said:

"It is a mate for the first one. Both are 'queer.' My boy, this is bad stuff to be carrying around. It is liable to bring you into no end of trouble."

As he said this he was regarding Frank's face with a searching stare, as if seeking to discover if the lad were honest or crooked.

Frank knew he was under suspicion, and he bore himself as quietly as possible.

"This is the first intimation I have received that the bills are bad," declared the lad. "I received them as I have explained, and I have tried in several places, this morning, to get one of them broken, but did not succeed. I finally came here."

The cashier's brows lowered. He partially closed his eyes, and regarded the boy steadily. Then he began once more to ask questions.

Frank knew he was in an unfortunate situation, and he decided the best thing he could do was to answer every question truthfully, which he did.

It happened there was not much business going on in the bank. The paying teller and the receiving teller listened to the questions and answers. The receiving teller was a young man, and his face wore a sneering look of incredulity. He regarded Frank with open doubt, and, once or twice, muttered, "Ridiculous!" "Nonsense!" "A clever lie!" or something of the sort.

The face of the paying teller was calm and unexpressive. It seemed that he had not determined in his own mind if the boy were telling the truth. He was listening to hear everything before he decided.

Frank explained how he came to be in Carson City, having given his name, age, his guardian's name, told where his home was, and answered more than a score of other questions.

The sneers of the receiving teller angered the boy; but he held his feelings in check, and did not seem to hear the man when he proposed that Merriwell be handed over to the special policeman in front of the bank.

"Mr. Merriwell," said the cashier, "I shall have to take possession of these bills."

"Why is that?"

"It is my duty. I have such instructions. You are getting off easy at that."

"But I shall not recover my hundred dollars."

"No; that is lost. Let me tell you something: There is a band of queer-makers somewhere in this vicinity. They do not attempt to run their stuff into circulation around here; the most of it is put out in Chicago. But they have been traced to this part of the country. Detectives are at work on the case—Secret Service men, in the employ of the government. Who these detectives are no one can say, although it has been reported that Dan Drake is in it. Up to this time they have been putting out tens and twenties. This fifty must be a new bit of work. And I have something more to tell you. It is said that the queen of this gang of counterfeiters is a beautiful young girl, who does not look to be more than seventeen years of age. It is possible——"

But he made a gesture of anger, because such a thing should be thought for a moment.

"It is not possible!" he said, sharply. "She is innocent of such a thing as that! You cannot make me believe——"

He stopped, noting that the look of scorn on the face of the receiving teller was deepening. Then, slowly and surely, the thought that the girl had deceived him, that she was not as innocent as she looked, came upon him. The mystery that surrounded her deepened, and a sudden longing to know the truth grasped him.

The receiving teller laughed shortly, as he saw the changes which flitted across the lad's face.

"There's guilt for you!" he muttered.

Frank stiffened up, giving the man a cutting look.

"What became of this girl for whom you changed two fifty-dollar bills?" asked the cashier.

"I do not remember what became of her," declared Frank. "She was a passenger on the Pacific Express. I left the express at Reno."

"And she went on? Bound for 'Frisco, it is likely."

Frank had not said she went on. He explained that he met a friend at Reno, and that was how he happened to leave the express; that friend was coming to Carson, and that was how he happened to come to Carson.

He did not tell that they had followed the girl to Carson, had shadowed her to the house where she had stopped, and that his companion or himself had watched that house constantly, ever since.

"Bart is watching it now," he told himself. "She can't get away. She must explain to me how that bogus money came into her possession. I believe I know! The man with the black mustache must have given it to her!"

That the man with the sinister mustache was a villain he did not doubt, but he still doubted that the girl was anything but what she seemed—young, innocent, incapable of crime.

The cashier spoke a low word to one of his companions, and a sudden fear came upon Frank. Was the man ordering his arrest? He could not afford to be detained and bothered at that time. How would he solve the mystery if they placed him under arrest?

But Frank had nerve, and he would not take to his heels, knowing such an act would make it seem certain that he was guilty.

The receiving teller spoke sharply to the cashier, seemingly urging him to some action; but the boy heard the cashier reply:

"It will spoil the whole thing to be too hasty."

"The boy can be made to peach on the gang," said the teller, in a guarded tone.

"That's folly!" declared the cashier, shortly. "The boy is not connected with the gang. Think they would send him here—to a bank—if he were! Have a little sense, Burton!"

The teller mumbled, looking sullen and rebuffed, while Frank felt relieved.

Then the cashier once more questioned Frank, as a lawyer might question a witness. He tried, in various ways, to entrap the boy, but Frank made no blunders.

After a time, the cashier seemed satisfied.

"I am sorry for you," he said. "You have lost a hundred dollars, but you are fortunate to escape arrest and imprisonment."

"I suppose I am," admitted Frank; "and I will tell you something, now; I propose to solve the mystery of this money. I am going to find that girl, I am going to find out how she came to have the bogus stuff, and I am going to bring this band of queer-makers to book, if possible."

The receiving teller laughed scornfully.

"A fine bluff!" he muttered.

The cashier gave him a crushing glance.

"You have undertaken a big job, my boy," said the latter. "I hardly think you will be able to carry it out when government detectives are bothered."

"I'll do my best."

"And you'll be pretty sure to get into further trouble."

"I may, but I am lucky about getting out of trouble."

"Yes, you are dead lucky," muttered the receiving teller.

The cashier gave Frank some outspoken advice, and then told the boy he might go.

Frank left the private office and walked out of the bank. There was a look of determination on his face.

"I don't fancy being beaten out of a hundred dollars," he said to himself. "It's not the money so much; but if that girl knew—if she played me——"

He stopped short, anger and disgust expressed on his face. His pride was touched. He did not like to think that he had been thus deceived.

"I am going to know!" he vowed. "I am going to know the truth!"

He walked away, his head down, thinking. He was trying to form a plan of action. Within a short time the mystery that surrounded the beautiful girl with two names had deepened. He must find a way to learn the truth; he would not be satisfied till he knew the truth.

For some time he walked along, paying little heed to his surroundings, and then, all at once, a thought came to him:

"I am followed!"

He was confident of it. He did not look back, but he seemed to see the shadower on his trail. They were determined to know at the bank if he had told the truth, and a detective had been detailed to keep watch of him.

Frank loitered along, looking into windows. He betrayed no uneasiness. At last he came to a restaurant. Into this he wandered, proceeding to a table at the farther end. Here he sat and gave his order.

The boy had taken a seat where he could watch the front door. In a short time a small man entered quietly, walked straight to a table, sat down, without glancing round, having hung his hat close at hand, and looked over the bill of fare.

"You are the shadower," decided Frank. "I wonder how I can give you the slip?"

# CHAPTER XXXIX.

## PURSUED.

**F**ortune gave the boy the opportunity he desired.

Along the street came two runaway horses, attached to a carriage. In front of the restaurant they crashed into another team, and there was a rush to see how much damage had been done. The attention of every one seemed diverted toward the front.

Frank had observed an open door at the back of the room, and through this he quickly sprang, ran along a narrow passage, and burst into the kitchen.

"Hello, here!" cried the cook, in astonishment. "What's the matter?"

"Terrible smashup, out in front," replied the boy. "Don't know how many have been killed. It is awful!"

"That so?" came stupidly from the bewildered man in white. "How did it—— Well, he was in a hurry!"

But Frank had sprung out by an open door and was gone.

The boy reached a side street, sprinted round a corner, doubled and turned at every opportunity, and settled to a swift walk.

He soon discovered which direction he should take without having asked to be directed toward any particular point.

"This is an unpleasant scrape," muttered the boy; "and it came about through my readiness to exchange my good money for bad. If I remain in this town I am liable to be arrested at any moment."

He wondered what Bart would say when he was told. What could Bart think about a girl who carried two bright new counterfeit fifty-dollar bills in her purse?

Frank began to doubt. He was forced to confess to himself that such a thing was remarkable. If the girl had had but one bad bill in her possession, it would have seemed that she had obtained it unwittingly; but two—and exactly alike——

"Can it be possible she is, in some way, connected with a gang of counterfeiters?" Frank asked himself. "I will not believe it! Her face is too innocent."

Then he remembered how, in the city of Chicago, he had encountered a beautiful girl who was connected with counterfeiters; but he also remembered that she was an unwilling tool, and had embraced the first opportunity to get clear of the meshes of the net into which she had fallen.

"If Isa Isban is connected with such a gang, I am certain it is against her will."

Then he thought how, when she had discovered that he had plenty of money, she had hastened to get him to change two fifty-dollar bills, and his faith was shaken.

"It looks bad," he confessed.

As he approached the place where he had left Bart on guard over the house in which the girl was believed to be, he passed a livery stable. He was hurrying on when some one ran out of the stable and clutched him by the arm.

"Just in time!" palpitated the voice of Bart Hodge.

"Hello!" exclaimed Frank, surprised. "Just in time for what?"

"They're gone!"

"Who?"

"Vida Melburn and that man."

"Gone where?"

"Taken the lake road. Something has caused them to hustle out on the jump. I do not believe they are coming back here."

"Then we must follow."

"Sure."

"How——"

"Here—in the stable. I have ordered a horse. We'll have two. They'll not slip us easily."

"How did they travel?"

"Horseback."

"How much of a start?"

"Twenty minutes."

Together the boys ran back into the stable, and another horse was ordered saddled.

"Look here," cried Frank, displaying his money. "We wish to overtake some people who have a start on us. Give us the best animal in the stable."

The proprietor of the stable was on hand, and he looked the boys over doubtfully.

"How do I know I'll ever see my critters again?" he asked.

"We'll make a deposit," declared Frank. "We'll stick up a hundred dollars apiece on 'em. If they are worth more you can afford to take chances. If we're horse thieves you won't have much trouble in tracing us. Besides that, horse thieves do not work in this way. If they did they'd get the worst end most of the time, for they'd have to chance it on the horses being worth a hundred each."

The proprietor was rather bewildered. He believed something was wrong, but still he did not wish to refuse to let the boys have the horses.

The money was counted out and thrust into his hands.

"Hustle!" cried Merriwell. "We can't afford to lose a moment."

The stable-keeper roared out an order to his assistants. The horse that Bart had ordered was quickly brought out, ready for mounting, and then he was followed by another, onto which a saddle was flung. Frank looked the animals over with a critical eye.

"They'll do," he said, approvingly.

In a few seconds the lads were mounted and dashing away from the stable. The proprietor stood looking after them, doubt written on his face.

"Gee whiz!" he muttered. "I never thought of that! Bet I've made a derned fool of myself! Well, I reckon I'll git the critters back."

"What is it you did not think of?" he was asked.

"Why, it's remarkable kids like them should be so flush with money. And they looked scared. They're runnin' away. I reckon they've been stealin' an' they wuz hustlin' to get away before they wus arrested."

The boys disappeared down the street.

Frank allowed Bart to take the lead.

"I suppose you know the shortest cut to the lake road?" he asked.

"I do," said Bart. "You follow close, that's all."

As they rode, Frank related his adventure in the bank.

Bart whistled in astonishment.

"Bogus money?" he cried. "And you received it of the girl? That is strange."

"It looks bad," said Frank.

"I don't understand it. How do you suppose she happened to have it? It's not at all probable she knew what it was."

"I am not so sure of that."

The dark-eyed boy gave his companion a reproving look.

"She is as innocent as a flower! I will not believe she could do such a thing! But she is in trouble."

They were regarded with some surprise as they dashed along the streets. The citizens wondered why two boys were riding at such speed. A sleepy policeman shouted at them, but they gave him no heed.

Soon they came to the outskirts of the city. Before them lay the lake road.

"This is the way they came?" questioned Frank.

"Sure," nodded Bart. "They are somewhere ahead."

"What makes you think they are skipping the city? It strikes me they may be simply out for a canter. Perhaps they are going to take a look at Tahoe up there among the mountains."

"They did not buy horses for a canter of a few hours."

"They bought horses?"

"Yes."

"Then it is pretty certain they have no notion of coming back to Carson. You have a level head, my boy. Forward!"

The road became rugged and steep. They were looking for a mounted man and girl in advance, and they constantly urged forward their sweating horses.

"I do not see anything of them."

"The road crooks away up yonder, so they would be hidden. They have quite a start, and they are in a hurry."

A cloud of dust rose behind the galloping horses, drifting away to the left. The road was rough, but the boys did not mind that.

"Tahoe must be on the top of a mountain," grumbled Bart, after a time.

"It is six thousand, two hundred and eight feet above the level of the sea," said Frank. "That is elevated somewhat."

"I should say so. It must be the highest body of water in this country, if not in the world."

"It is higher than the peaks of many lofty mountains."

"And this so-called 'lake road' is hardly better than an ordinary trail. We are in for a hard pull of it."

"But the ones we are pursuing are in for just as hard a pull."

"That's right, and one of them is a girl."

The mountains loomed formidably before them. The bleak heights seemed to block their way. But the road wound onward and upward, and they followed it.

"What was that?" questioned Frank.

"What? I did not hear anything."

"It sounded like a cry. There it is again."

"I heard it that time. It did not seem to be ahead of us, and so it—— Great Scott! Look back!"

Frank looked back down the road. Far away, several horsemen were riding toward them. They were urging forward their animals, and the sunlight glinted on polished weapons.

"We are pursued, partner!" said Frank, grimly. "We are in for a hot chase."

# CHAPTER XL.

## ELUDED.

ho are our pursuers?" asked Bart, angrily. "What do they want? They are shouting and waving their hands."

"They are shouting for us to stop. They want me."

"For what?"

"Have you forgotten, as soon as this, what I told you about the queer money I tried to get changed at the bank?"

"Think that is why they are after you, eh?"

"Without a doubt?"

"Then they must be officers."

"It is certain that at least one of them is an officer. The others he may have called to his aid hastily."

"It will not do for them to overtake us."

"Surely not. I would be arrested and taken back into Carson. Even if I were sure of proving my innocence, the man and girl would get away."

"And you cannot be sure you could prove your innocence. The working of the law is sometimes strange and erratic. That money has placed you in great danger, Frank."

"You are right. I wish I had kept my money in my pocket, and had not been so ready to break fifty-dollar bills for a pretty girl."

Frank said this laughingly, but Bart's dark face wore a very serious look. He was not at all inclined to regard serious matters in a humorous light, while Frank had faced deadly dangers many times, and had come to laugh in the face of the gravest peril.

"We'll have trouble in escaping those men," came soberly from Bart's lips. "It is still rather wild up around Tahoe, I fancy, and this road must end at the lake."

"Well, we'll leave the road and ride over the mountain tops, if we do not overtake the man and girl."

"What if we do overtake them?"

"It will be a good plan to freeze onto them, and hold them for the officers."

"No," cried Bart, sharply. "I will not agree to that."

"You will not?"

"No."

"Why not?"

"It would place the girl in peril. She would be——"

"That's where you're off, my boy. It might rescue her from peril. If she is in trouble, as we imagine, it would be the very best thing that could happen for her."

"How is that?"

"She could tell her story truthfully, and it might get her out of trouble by putting the man with the black mustache in a box. At the same time it would clear me."

Bart was obliged to confess that Frank had made a point, and still he did not like to think of turning the girl over to the officers of the law.

"Perhaps she would not 'peach' on the gang, if there is a gang behind her, which I doubt. She might keep her mouth closed, might swear she never let you have the queer money."

"And I can prove she did by the conductor of the Pacific Express. He saw me give her the small stuff for the two bills."

"Still, I do not feel like nabbing her and turning her over to the officers. We might not be able to nab her, anyway."

"That is true enough. I rather fancy her companion would be likely to put up a stiff fight. He looks to me like a dangerous man."

Frank fancied that he was beginning to understand Bart's feelings. He believed the boy was afraid the girl might prove to be one of a gang of counterfeiters, and he was so badly smitten that he did not wish to be instrumental in her arrest.

Frank, himself, had been highly interested in Isa Isban; but events had transpired which caused him to doubt that she was all her innocent face would lead a casual observer to believe, and his admiration for her had waned swiftly.

Having been brought beneath a cloud of suspicion, Frank was determined to vindicate himself in some manner. He sincerely hoped it might turn out that the girl was innocent. If she were innocent, then she must be in trouble, and he hoped to be instrumental in relieving her.

It was well the lads had obtained two good horses, for they were able to keep well in advance of the pursuers.

Once or twice they fancied they saw rising dust in the far distance, which led them to believe the man and girl were there.

If they were right, then the couple in advance were urging their horses to the limit, for they kept beyond view.

The road grew rougher and rougher. The mountains shut in on either hand, and still they climbed upward. The horses panted and perspired, while horses and lads were covered with dust.

"Do you know how far it is to the lake by this road?" asked Bart. "It can't be over ten miles."

"Well, it is the longest ten miles of road I ever passed."

The windings of the road shut the pursuers out from view. They were coming on when last seen, but had not seemed to gain in the least. At last an exclamation of satisfaction broke from Bart's lips.

"There they are!"

Far up the road, halted and looking back, were the man and girl, mounted on two dust-covered horses.

"Sure as you live!" cried Frank. "We have been gaining on them."

The boys were seen by the ones in advance, and the man made a gesture of rage, while the girl reached out and caught him by the arm, seeming to speak earnestly to him. He listened a moment, and then both touched up their horses, quickly galloping from view.

Now the chase became hot, although the road became more difficult and perilous. Several times the lads obtained glimpses of the man and girl.

Finally, with appalling suddenness, they came out upon the shore of Lake Tahoe, resting like a blue gem upon the mountain tops, upheld like a perfect mirror to a cloudless sky.

Cries of surprise and admiration broke from the lips of both boys, for never before had they beheld such a lovely sheet of water. The surface of the lake was unbroken by a ripple, and the water, into which the heated horses thrust their noses, was clear as crystal.

Afar, the mountain peaks rose like sentinels, their outlines softened to a purple shade. Along the shores were unmarred forests.

For a few seconds the boys sat silent, gazing in speechless admiration on the beautiful scene, and then Frank gave a start and drew the nose of his horse from the water, saying:

"Don't let your animal drink too much, Bart. They are very hot."

"That's right," nodded the dark-haired lad, following Frank's example. "But where are the man and girl?"

"They must have hidden up or down the shore of the lake. Look for the tracks of their horses."

It did not take them long to discover which direction had been taken, and away they went.

"I don't see how they are going to escape us," said Bart. "We have them cornered."

"And we must be ready to fight, for that man will raise a rumpus."

They looked at their revolvers, making sure they were in good working order. There was a look of resolution on Frank's face that contrasted strongly with the expression of doubt and uncertainty which had been growing on the face of his companion.

They rode round a point and came in view of a beautiful cove. Then they again uttered exclamations of surprise, for out of the cove a light canoe was skimming, and the canoe contained the man and the girl. The man was handling the paddle with strength and skill.

"Tricked!" exclaimed Frank, somewhat dismayed. "They have slipped us after all."

As he saw this, the expression of doubt on Bart's face turned to one of intense anger. He was enraged at being baffled. Riding his horse into the edge of the water, he drew a revolver, pointed it at the canoe, and shouted:

"Hold on, there! If you don't come back, you are liable to find yourself dodging bullets."

The reply of the man was a scornful laugh, the sudden uplifting of one hand, a puff of smoke, and the singing of a bullet that passed over Bart's head.

"Don't shoot!" cried Frank. "You might hit the girl."

Bart was in a white rage; he quivered with anger.

"Oh, I won't shoot!" he said; "but, if he were alone I'd give him a few lead pills, hang him!"

After the shot, which seemed flung at the boys in derision, the man resumed paddling, and the canoe glided on.

But that shot had aroused some on the opposite side of the cove, for a man came bursting out of the trees, rushed down to the shore, and stared after the canoe.

He was a gigantic fellow, being at least six feet and six inches in height, roughly dressed in woolen clothes, wearing long-legged boots and a wide-brimmed hat. He had a heavy mustache, and a long imperial.

Suddenly his voice rang in a roar across the cove:

"Hold on, thar! Whatever are you doin' with my canoe? Ef yer don't bring it back, burn my hide ef I don't turn a cannon on yer an' sink yer at sea!"

The man in the canoe made no immediate reply, but pulled the harder at the paddle.

"Derned ef yer don't git grapeshot an' canister!" howled the big man. "I'll riddle yer!"

Then the man in the canoe shouted:

"Don't shoot! You will find two horses hitched to a tree near where we obtained this canoe. They're yours in exchange."

"W'at do I want uv hawses!" roared the big man. "Bring back thet canoe instanter! I won't take yer hawses!"

But the man in the canoe continued to pull at the paddle, and the little craft glided straight out on the tranquil bosom of the lake.

# CHAPTER XLI.

## BIG GABE.

The big man roared and raged, but he did not do any shooting.

"I'll see yer ag'in," he shouted, "an' burn my eyebrows, ef I don't make yer settle fer this yar!"

Then he saw the mounted boys on the opposite side of the cove, and he stared at them inquiringly.

"Wa-al," he shouted, "who be you, an' what do yer want?"

"We will meet you and make an explanation," Frank shouted back.

The two lads began riding along the shore of the cove, and the big man moved to meet them, regarding them with no little suspicion.

They finally met at the head of the cove, where the giant stood, with folded arms, scowling blackly at them.

A short distance away two dust-covered horses were standing, hitched to trees, their heads hanging low, while they still breathed heavily.

They were the animals abandoned by the man and girl.

"Ef you youngsters want ter steal anything, ye'd best mosey outer this yar part uv ther kentry," growled the big man, sullenly. "First it's a gang uv pleasure seekers thet comes an' takes my sailboat, then it's a man an' gal thet kerries off my canoe, an' next it's two boys as ain't got anything yit, but looks like they want something."

"We do," palpitated Frank. "We want some kind of a boat in which to follow those people—the man and the girl."

"Wa-al, yer won't git it."

"We will pay you—we have plenty of money."

"Ter thunder with yer money! What duz Gabe Blake want uv money! All I want is ter be let alone. Ther fust crowd promised me money fer my boat, but I told 'em ter take her an' bring her back before night. They took her, an' I ain't seen hide ner ha'r uv 'em sense. Ther man an' ther gal took my canoe without askin' leave."

"They left those horses——"

"Burn their hawses! What do I want uv hawses! Hawses ain't no good harabouts. Ther fust gang left four hawses, an' I've got ther critters ter feed. Hyar's two more! Burn ther hawses!"

It was plain the giant was in anything put a pleasant frame of mind. He scowled blackly at the boys.

"If you will furnish us with a boat——" began Frank.

"Ain't got no more boats. Can't go out fishin'. An' I'm too blamed lazy ter build another boat. Built ther sailboat an' canoe afore I got lazy livin' hyar. Man thet lives hyar six weeks gits too blamed lazy ter work. What 'm I goin' ter do when I want ter go out fishin'?"

Bart Hodge made a gesture of dismay.

"Do you know where we can get a boat?" he asked.

"Thar's none round hyar."

"Then we cannot follow that man and girl?"

"Not 'less yer kin walk on ther water."

"It's hard luck," declared Frank. "I did not believe they would be able to slip us."

"What did yer want uv 'em?" asked the big man, his curiosity getting the better of his anger.

Frank dismounted.

"Might as well get off and give the horses a breathing spell, Bart," he said. "They are blowed."

"But the party pursuing us—what of them?"

"Let them come."

"Are you going to give up thus easily?"

"No; but I am not going to run like a criminal. Why should I? Let them come."

"You do not mean to fight?"

"Not if a regular officer attempts my arrest."

"What they goin' ter arrest yer fer, youngster?" asked the man, becoming still more curious. "Hev yer bin stealin' hawses?"

"No."

"Wa-al, yer needn't tell ef yer don't want ter!" resentfully said the giant. "I don't keer."

"I will tell you the whole story," said Frank. "When you have heard it you may be able to advise us about continuing the pursuit."

Bart dismounted, and the boys sat down on the ground. The man took a seat near at hand, and brought forth a cob pipe, which he leisurely filled and lighted. He was brawny, weather-tanned, and healthy in appearance. He did not look like a person who had ever seen an hour of illness.

"Fire away, youngster," he urged. "Somehow, I kinder take ter you. You've got an honest face on yer, burn me ef yer hain't!"

Frank expressed thanks for the compliment, and then, as concisely and plainly as possible, he told of his experiences since meeting the girl on the train.

The big man listened closely, his interest growing each minute. When the boy had finished, the man slapped his thigh and cried:

"Brand me deep ef I don't reckon ye've guv it ter me fair an' squar! I know somethin' about this yar gang uv queer-makers."

"You do?"

Both lads ejaculated the words.

"You bet!"

"What do you know?"

"I hev heard ez how they has a young gal who is queen uv ther band, an' she shoves ther queer on ther market fer them."

"Is that all?" asked Frank, with a trace of disappointment.

"Hold yer critters!" advised the big man, with a lazy wave of one hand. "Don't git too oneasy. I said I know something erbout 'em. What I told yer wuz what I had heard."

"Well, tell us what you know."

"See them mountains over thar, beyond ther lake, right whar I'm p'intin'?"

"Yes."

"Purty wild place over thar."

"Well?"

"Thet's whar ther den uv them thar counterfeiters is."

Frank clutched the man's arm, his face full of eagerness.

"How do you know?"

"I hev bin over thar."

"What did you discover?"

"Say, I don't keer ter mix in no rows, an' so I ain't troubled myself ter inform on 'em."

"But you will tell us what you discovered? We will pay——"

"Pay be derned! I tell yer I don't keer a hoot erbout money. Ef I git enough ter buy some terbacker an' clothes, an' sech provisions ez I want, thet's all I ask. I don't keer how much bad money is in circulation, an' thet's why I ain't meddled with them critters. Ef I blowed, they might take a notion ter call on me, some time, an' make it derned onpleasant fer me."

The hopes of the boys dwindled.

"But think what it may mean to me—my liberty, honor, everything!" cried Frank. "You must understand the situation in which I am placed."

"I do. Ef them critters hedn't run off with my boat, I might hev kept my mouth shet; but now, burn me deep, ef I don't git squar!"

The hopes of the lads rose again.

"I'll tell yer whut I found over thar," the big man went on, slowly. "I found ther place whar ther queer-makers hang out."

"You did?" fluttered both lads.

"Thet's whatever. Thar's a hidden cabin on a cliff, an' thet thar is their headquarters."

"Will you guide us there?"

"Wa-al, what do you two youngsters think you could do? Thar's a gang. You say yer wuz pursued by officers. Wa-al, I know Jack Long, ther sheriff, an' I kin fix it with him, ef he is in ther crowd. He wuz one as brought me hyar ter die uv consumption two years ago."

The boys looked at the giant in amazement.

"Brought you here to die of consumption?" cried Frank. "You— you? Impossible!"

The giant smiled lazily.

"I don't look like a consumptive, now, do I? Wa-al, ther doctors said thar warn't one chance in a thousan' fer me. They hed guv me up. I come hyar ter die; but I got well. This is ther greatest place I ever struck fer bracin' up a feller's lungs; but it takes all ther ambition outer him. It hes made me so I don't care ter do anything but be lazy. Let ther old world wag, Gabriel Blake won't bother with her none whatever."

"How can we reach the mountains over there?" asked Frank.

"Reckon we'll hev ter go round ther shore, thet's all ther way."

"And you will guide us?"

"Ef Jack Long shows up an' wants ter go, I s'pose so."

Blake said this somewhat reluctantly, as if he dreaded the exertion.

"If Long should not show up—what, then?"

"It won't be nary dern bit uv use fer one ur two uv us ter go rampin' off over thar. Ef Jack Long locates their hangout, he'll bring a posse an' scoop 'em."

The boys found the giant was set in his ways, and it was not strange that, as they were boys, he should consider them of minor importance in case of a collision with the counterfeiters.

He once more expressed his conviction that the lads were "squar," and it was his belief that he could thus convince Jack Long.

"Can we use our horses in getting round the lake?" asked Frank.

"Wa-al, I dunno but I kin pick out a trail fer yer; but fer me it'd be as much work ter travel hawseback ez afoot."

He then invited them to his cabin, and they followed him, leading the horses. He gave no heed to the animals the man and girl had abandoned.

Big Gabe's cabin was tucked away in a secluded nook, close to the shore of the lake, and not far from the cove. It was fairly comfortable in a rude way.

"Long will come hyar," he said. "Ef he wuz with yer pursuers he'll show up afore a great while. Make yourselves comfortable till he comes."

The lads did so.

# CHAPTER XLII.

## OVER THE PRECIPICE.

In time the sheriff appeared, but one man—a rough, awk-ward-looking fellow—was his only companion.

Long uttered a cry of satisfaction when he saw the boys.

"Well, I have caught you, after all!" he exclaimed. "The boys allowed you had given me the slip, and they went back."

His hands fell on the butts of ready revolvers, and he ordered them to surrender without resistance.

"Hold on hyar a bit, Jack," said Big Gabe, stepping between the lads and the officer. "Let's we hold a little plarver. You know me, I'll allow."

"To be course I do, Gabe, and I am mighty glad to see you alive and well. You once had the name of being the strongest man in Nevada; but you didn't look very strong when we brought you up here, two year ago. You'll be up to the old tricks again, before long."

The giant shook his head.

"I reckon not," he said. "Liftin' bolders an' wrastlin' with four men at a time is outer my line ferever, arter this. I'm too lazy, an' besides thet, I'll allow it wuz a strain I got at that business as brought on my first bleedin' spell arter I hed ther grip. I'm purty well, now, but I don't make no exerbitions uv my strength, burn me ef I do!"

"Wait till you get away from here. Everybody that comes here gets lazy, and stays lazy as longs as they stay here."

At this Big Gabe nodded.

"Thet's sure as preachin'. It's ther derndest place ter make a critter feel ez if he don't keer a hoot whether school keeps ur not!"

The sheriff had half drawn his revolvers. He now thrust one of them back into its holster, but motioned for Blake to stand aside.

"I judge you don't know the kind of youngsters these are as I have found here," said Long.

"And I judge I do," returned the big man, quietly. "I know all about 'em, an' they're all right."

The officer looked surprised.

"How does it happen you know about 'em?" he asked, wonderingly.

"They're old acquaintances uv mine," asserted Gabe, greatly to the surprise of the lads; "an' they're on the dead level. They came hyar to see me, sayin' as how they wuz in some trouble down at Carson over some counterfeit money as they hed got by accident."

Long was scowling and looking disgusted. He listened in silence, motioning for the giant to go on.

"I hev listened ter their story," said Blake, "an' knowin' 'em ez I do, I'll allow it's straight, an' you ain't got no cause whatever ter rope 'em, Jack."

"Mebbe you're right," admitted the sheriff, fishing in a pocket and drawing forth a paper; "but here is a warrant for the arrest of one Frank Merriwell, and I must serve it. It is sworn out by Ezra Coburn, a leading citizen of Carson."

"Burn Ezra Coburn!" roared Big Gabe, becoming somewhat excited. "Burn him and double burn him! I tell yer them youngsters is my friends, an' I'm standin' by 'em! You an' I don't want any trouble, Jack."

"No, we don't want any trouble; but, at the same time, I'll have to do my duty," came firmly from the lips of the sheriff.

"By thet yer mean yer'll hev ter arrest Frank Merriwell?"

"Exactly."

"Stiddy, Jack! Don't be too quick ter lay yer paws on ther boys. You know me."

"I do, and I do not fancy having trouble with you. At the same time I must do my duty."

"Wa-al, hold hard a bit. Don't be in a hurry about nabbin' them. I'll give yer my pledge as how yer kin hev 'em any time. Does thet go?"

The sheriff hesitated a bit, and then said:

"It goes, if you are responsible for 'em, Gabe."

"All right. Boys, this yar is Jack Long, sheriff from Carson, a white man clean through. He'll guv yer a squar' deal."

The boys shook hands with the officer, after which the latter said:

"This man with me is Silas Jones, of Michigan, relation to my wife, somehow or other. He is thinking of locating out this way."

Jones grinned all over his bearded face, shook hands in a strong, blundering fashion, and said:

"I swan if this ain't a great country, out here! Beats all natur! But I don't feel to hum, fer I was raised right in ther middle of the woods, an' there's too much open land out this way. I don't mean right round here, you understand; but I've seen more'n forty thousan' miles of prairie sence comin' out this way, an' it makes me lonesome."

Having expressed himself thus, he sat down on a box and relapsed into silence, listening to the others and grinning now and then, but seldom speaking unless addressed.

Big Gabe urged them all to sit down, and they did so. He then directed Frank Merriwell to relate to the sheriff the story of his adventures since meeting Isa Isban on the train, and the boy was obliged to go over the ground once more.

Bart was impatient, thinking how much time was being wasted; but he held himself in check as far as possible.

The dark-eyed boy noticed that Silas Jones listened to Frank's story with great attentiveness, apparently greatly interested in the narrative.

When the boy had finished, Blake explained how his sailboat had been engaged by a pleasure party of four persons, two men, a woman and a girl, and how they had failed to return with it, making it impossible for him to pursue the man and the girl who ran off with his canoe.

"Then you saw the man and girl?" asked Long.

"I did that," nodded the giant. "An' I said a few things ter them, but it wuz a case uv wasted breath."

The sheriff seemed to hesitate, doubtfully, and then Frank spoke:

"Mr. Blake believes he knows where the retreat of the counterfeiters is, and he has offered to guide us there."

"How about it?" asked Long, quickly. "Is it right?"

"Wa-al, purty nigh right. I reckon I do know whar they're located, an' I offered ter guide ther party ef you brung a good crowd with yer. You only brung one man."

"Here are five of us, in all," said Frank. "Two of us may be boys, but it is possible we can fight harder than you imagine."

"If such a thing can be avoided, we do not want to fight at all," said Long. "We want to take the makers of the queer by surprise and capture them in a strategic manner."

Silas Jones nodded.

"Either that or send for plenty of officers ter ketch 'em on ther jump," he said. "Ther United States Secret Service men would be mighty tickled ter git such a show."

Long gave Jones a peculiar look.

"The Secret Service men may be mighty glad if they get an opportunity to play second fiddle in this affair," he said.

Whereat the man from Michigan grinned, but made no further remark.

The sheriff was for taking the boys back to Carson, leaving them in custody, and then seeking the retreat of the counterfeiters.

To this Big Gabe would not agree.

"Give ther youngsters a show," he said. "I hev pledged myself ter stand good fer 'em. Take 'em erlong on ther expedition."

There was considerable discussion over this, and Long finally gave in, although he expressed himself as certain that the boys would prove a great incumbrance.

Both Frank and Bart resolved to show him his mistake, in case an opportunity was offered.

They made preparations for the trip, which Big Gabe declared would take the better part of four days, as they would have to pick their way carefully through the mountains.

The two horses left by the man and girl were brought up and stripped of their saddles, packs being substituted.

Big Gabe was almost entirely cleaned out of provisions, but he did not murmur because of that.

The giant insisted on making the jaunt on foot, saying he did not wish to be incumbered with a horse.

When everything was ready, they started out, Gabe in the lead, carrying his Winchester at his side.

It did not take the giant long to convince them that he was far from an invalid. He seemed built of iron, and he was sure footed as a mountain goat.

Before long they were forced back from the shore of the lake and compelled to pick their way through a rough and rocky region, where progress was exasperatingly slow.

It was midafternoon, when they halted at the beginning of a desperate and dangerous climb amid mighty bowlders, with yawning chasms on every hand.

Here they opened one of the packs and brought forth provisions enough for the party to satisfy their hunger, the food being washed down with water from a tinkling brook that ran toward the lake.

After they had satisfied their hunger, and allowed the horses to feed, the animals were saddled again, the packs made fast, and once more they started onward.

Although Big Gabe had explored the greater part of the rough region lying around the lake, he had never before attempted to find a road for horses along the precipices and black ravines.

After eating, they set about the most severe and dangerous part of the journey yet reached. Up amid the giant bowlders they climbed, at times working around some part of the mountain where there would be a bare bluff on one hand and a yawning chasm on the other.

The giant guide warned them to look out for the loose bowlders, saying that some of them could be sent crashing down the mountain almost by the pressure of a hand.

The dangers from these huge rocks were made apparent before they had passed beyond that region.

Frank's horse proved far more skillful in climbing, keeping close to Big Gabe's heels, and the others were left at a considerable distance, so it became necessary to pause once or twice for them to come up.

A nearly level bit of the mountain had been reached, and they were pausing before the next climb, when a rumbling jar was heard, and a cry of warning broke from the guide.

"Loose bowlder! Look out fer it, boy!"

The others were yet some distance away, so that Frank and Gabe were together, the boy being astride his heavily breathing horse.

With each moment the roaring grew louder, till it swelled to jarring thunder, and then past them shot a huge black mass, enveloped in a cloud of dust. This mass leaped down into the black depths of a great chasm that yawned close at hand.

Frank's horse was frightened and began to plunge. The boy tried to quiet the animal, which was no easy task. In its mad plunging the creature reached the edge of the chasm. Big Gabe leaped forward with a second shout of warning, but it came too late.

Horse and rider went over the brink!

# CHAPTER XLIII.

## A FRIGHTFUL PERIL.

ot a sound came from the lips of our hero as his horse went plunging into the chasm, although, in the moment when he went over the brink, the boy fully expected to be dashed to death in the dark depths below.

He saw Big Gabe leap to clutch him, but realized that the giant was too late.

In that fateful moment Frank cleared his feet from the stirrups and made a desperate effort to save himself.

Too late!

All he could do was to clutch at the high pommel of the Mexican saddle, to which he clung tenaciously.

A wild, half human scream of terror came from the throat of the horse.

"Whoa up, thar!" roared the giant, as he made a clutch at the horse.

By rare good fortune the man clutched the flowing tail of the animal fairly and firmly. His heels settled into a rift of the rocks, and he surged backward.

Over went the horse, dangling, head downward, above the terrible chasm, while the giant held it thus by clinging to the creature's tail!

And our hero held fast to the Mexican saddle!

Frank was amazed when he found the horse was not going downward, and, being unable to see the big man, he wondered what held the animal suspended in the air.

In a moment the man above cried:

"Are you gone, boy? Are yer done fer, youngster?"

"No," replied Frank, with sudden hope. "I am hanging to the saddle. Drop a rope to me, and pull me up—quick, before the horse falls!"

"Can't do it."

"Why not?"

"I'm holdin' ther critter by ther tail, an', burn me, ef yer both won't go to ther bottom ef I leggo!"

Then the boy realized what had saved him, impossible as it seemed, and he marveled at the astonishing strength of the strange giant who had been sent to Lake Tahoe to die of consumption.

"But he can't hold out long!" thought the lad. "He must give up in a moment, and then we'll go down to death!"

It was not a pleasant thought, and still Frank was not terrified. He wondered at his own coolness. He speculated on the length of time they would be falling. Would he be conscious when they struck, or would the fall rob him of his senses?

He looked down. Far below, ragged points of rocks jutted out from the chasm wall, seeming to beckon to him. They would bruise and tear him, and it seemed that they were awaiting, with impatience, for him to fall.

He could not see the bottom of the chasm!

"It is sure death!"

Without knowing that he did so, he uttered the words aloud.

"Not ef I kin hold on a little longer, boy."

The giant had heard him and made reply, much to his surprise, for he had seemed to forget that Blake was holding him from falling.

Then he marveled more than ever at the strength of the man, for it began to seem that he had been suspended thus many hours. Surely Gabriel Blake possessed supernatural prowess.

Something like a laugh came from the boy's lips.

"It is foolish to try to hold on longer," he said, a bit wildly. "Let go, before you, too, are dragged over to death."

"Hyar, hyar!" called the man from above. "Don't git nutty, boy! I kin hold yer some time yit."

Still Frank was sure it was all folly; it could only end in one way.

"I must fall at last!"

The giant heard these hoarsely muttered words, and he feared the boy would let go.

And now Bart Hodge and the two men had become aware of Frank's peril, and they were spurring their horses madly forward, having reached the top of the climb.

The giant saw them coming, and it gave him new strength.

"Hold fast, down thar, youngster!" Big Gabe shouted to Frank. "Thar's help comin' hot-foot an' hustlin'. We'll hev yer out uv thar in two shakes, brand me deep ef we don't!"

Still, Frank did not dare to hope. Once or twice it seemed that the horse, wild-eyed and snorting with terror, slipped a bit, and the boy fancied Gabe was losing his grip.

It was a fearful strain on the giant, but he held fast as if his own life depended on it. The cords stood out on his neck and forehead, and perspiration rolled down his face. He could hear his own heart thumping like a hammer in his breast.

The sheriff, Sile Jones and Bart Hodge came tearing up to the spot, flung their horses back with a surge at the bit, and leaped to the ground.

In a moment Jones had leaped to the side of Big Gabe and obtained a hold on the tail of the horse, relieving the giant a bit.

A lariat dangled from the sheriff's saddle, and this he had freed before he brought his horse to a halt. With it in his hand, he sprang to the ground and leaped toward the brink of the chasm, on which Bart was already kneeling.

"Hang on, old boy!" breathed the dark-haired lad. "The horse will not fall now. You are all right. We will have you out of that in a moment."

Frank looked up and saw Bart peering down. The sight of his friend's face gave the imperiled lad new hope.

"It's all right, if you say so, partner," he said, coolly. "But I don't care how quick you get me out of this."

Jack Long reached the brink of the chasm, lariat in hand.

"Say," he cried, "whatever are you trying to do, boy? Think you can slip me this way? Not much!"

He ended with a reassuring laugh, which was meant to encourage Frank. In a moment the rope was lowered, and the end dangled close by the boy.

"Catch hold!" cried the sheriff.

Frank did so, first getting a firm hold with one hand, and then with the other. By the time he had hold of the lariat Bart was ready to pull with Long.

"All right!" shouted Frank. "Lift away, up there."

They did so, carefully lifting him over the edge of the ledge, so his hold would not be broken, and he was drawn safely to the solid ground.

Some boys would have been completely overcome and unmanned by such a close call, but such was not the case with Frank. The moment all peril was past for him, he exclaimed:

"Save the horse!"

"Don't know as we can," said the sheriff, breathing heavily. "We'll try it. If we can get the beast up without strangling it we'll be dead lucky."

Long was skillful with the lariat, and he dropped the noose over the horse's head with a wide sweep. He did not draw it tight till the time came, and that was when every man and boy were ready to lift to the extent of their strength.

"Heave!" shouted Big Gabe, in a stentorian tone.

After a desperate struggle they dragged the horse up over the brink, but the unfortunate creature was more dead than alive, and nearly an hour passed before it recovered.

# CHAPTER XLIV.

## A GIRL'S MAD LEAP.

By nightfall they were encamped—or bivouacked—in a sheltered pocket, close by a clear bubbling spring. A fire was lighted, and, having eaten supper, they sat around and talked over the journey and adventures of the day.

The men smoked. The horses fed on some tender grass near at hand. Bart said:

"Do you know, Frank, I never touched a cigarette since you induced me to swear off at Fardale?"

"I am glad to hear that," said Frank. "There is nothing more hurtful than cigarettes used to excess, and one who smokes them regularly is almost certain to use them to excess, after a time."

"When you left Fardale I told you I feared I might fall back into my old ways—might become reckless and dissipated as I was before you gave me a helping hand and pulled me out. You remember it?"

"Yes."

"And do you remember that you said you were confident I would not go back—that you felt sure I had stamina of character enough not to take up with my old associates?"

"Yes."

"Well, Frank, by saying so you saved me. Whenever I have been tempted to do a mean thing, or to take up with any of the old gang, I have always thought of your words, and knowing you had faith in me has given me strength to resist."

"I am glad of it, old fellow. For all that we were enemies to begin with at Fardale, I found you had good stuff in you, and so I stood by you when others were against you."

"You stood by me when I was falsely accused of a theft, even though I had treated you shamefully, and it was that which made me ashamed and disgusted with myself. I saw you were white clean through, and I resolved to mend my ways if I ever pulled through the scrape I was in."

"You kept your resolution."

"With your aid. I did not expect you would accept me for a roommate, after what had happened, but you did. I do not believe I should have been able to remain in Fardale Academy but for that. Now——"

"Now what?"

"Well, it may sound like boasting, but you know I am not given to that, Frank."

"I know. Go on."

"Now, to a certain extent, I have taken the place you left vacant at Fardale. I was captain of the football team last fall, and we came out champions in the series we played. This year I was unanimously chosen captain of the baseball team, and we have had a most successful season thus far. The fellows who would have nothing at all to do with me originally are ready to stand by me to the last gasp now. All this came about through your influence, Frank."

"You make me blush," laughed our hero. "Don't tell me anything more, or you will give me a case of swelled head."

"There is no danger of that," Bart declared. "For a fellow who was so popular at school, you were and are reprehensibly modest. You had a way of holding your own, and still you never thrust yourself forward, which is something I cannot understand, for, as a rule, if a person does not push himself right ahead, he does not get there. Modesty may be all right, but, in most cases, the modest fellow gets left. Not that I believe in the braggart and blowhard, but a chap must have nerve to put himself ahead if he wants to keep in the game. I have seen lots of inferior individuals get a start on those with ability simply because they had the gall to sail right in and make their bluff. I believe there are two kinds of modesty, and one kind is closely allied to cowardice. The fellow who has confidence in himself, thinks he can do a thing, says he can do it, and does his level best to do it, is the one who will come out on top. If a chap wants an opportunity to try at anything, he makes a fool of himself if he says, 'I don't know, perhaps I can do it.' The one who says, 'I can and will' is the one people have confidence in, even though he may not be so smart as some modest coward."

Frank whistled softly.

"Hodge," he said, gravely, "you are a philosopher. Your philosophy may be a trifle mixed, but it will untangle itself later on. Such words from your lips rather daze me. I think I'll have to sleep and rest in order to recover."

He ended by a light laugh, in which, however, Bart did not join.

The dark-haired boy would have been glad to talk of the mysterious girl, but Frank rolled himself in a blanket, with his feet toward the fire and showed no desire to continue the conversation.

Bart soon followed this example, but the men continued to smoke and talk for some time.

Bart was awakened by feeling himself vigorously shaken, but, when he started to speak, a hand was over his mouth, and a voice whispered, in his ear:

"Easy, old boy; don't make a racket. We want to take a little stroll by ourselves, and there might be objections."

He knew it was Frank who spoke, although it was still dark, with just a hint of approaching dawn in the east.

When Frank was sure Bart understood he removed his hand from the latter's mouth, and the dark-haired boy crept softly from his blanket.

"Where are you going?" whispered Hodge, in surprise.

"Never mind," was the answer. "Take your rifle and come along."

The men were sleeping heavily. The horses stamped restlessly at a distance of two or three rods. The stars were fading before the gray light that slowly spread in the east.

Bart secured his rifle. Frank had his already, and they stole out of the bivouac.

Frank led the way, walking swiftly, and making no noise.

Bart wondered what the boy meant to do. Surely he did not think of skipping the party, for the horses were abandoned.

The dark-haired lad could not restrain his curiosity long, and he asked a question as soon as they were beyond earshot of the camp.

"What do you mean to do, Frank?"

"Take a morning stroll," was the laughing reply. "It is good for one's health. Why, it's a regular tonic."

Bart was puzzled, for he knew Frank was not out for his health.

"You are not skipping them?" he asked.

"Not for long," was the reply.

"But what will they think when they awaken and find we are gone?"

"I have left a note."

"Where?"

"Pinned to Big Gabe's breast."

"What did you say?"

"That we would be back, and for them not to think we were running away."

"They will think so, all the same."

"They are likely to."

"And I fail to see the object in this move. If they catch us before we return, Jack Long is liable to tie us up and take us back to Carson without delay."

Frank laughed softly.

"They will not catch us till we are ready to return. I will tell you just what this move means."

"Fire away."

"Last night, after we both seemed to be asleep, Big Gabe told his companions just where this hidden cabin of the counterfeiters is located. I was not asleep, although I seemed to be, and I heard every word."

"Well?"

"Well, we are going there."

"For what reason?"

"To see what we can do. I also overheard the men talking, and they seemed extremely doubtful as to our ability to do much of anything. In fact, they regarded us as an incumbrance. That touched my pride. I resolved to see if we could not convince them that they had made a mistake."

"Are you sure you can find this hidden cabin?"

"No; but I can try. I remember every word Gabe spoke, and I'll come pretty near it, you may bet."

"Go ahead. I am with you."

Bart did not question his friend further, although it seemed a foolish move to him. But he remembered that, in the past, Frank had seldom made a mistake when he set out to do anything.

Merriwell moved at a swinging pace, and Hodge held close to his heels.

The light in the east broadened, flushed, and rose to the zenith. The stars were blotted from the sky; but there were deep shadows far down in the ravines and gorges when the sunlight lay on the mountain peaks.

Having left the pocket, Frank led the way along a twisting ravine. Out of this he climbed at a certain point, and they made their way over a ridge into another ravine, from which they branched into yet another. Finally, with the bare face of a great mountain rising abruptly on their left, the boys advanced slowly.

"It cannot be far from here," said Frank, keeping his eyes about him. "We shall not be able to see the cabin from this ravine, but we may locate the cliff on which it is built."

"How can we locate it?"

"Big Gabe said there was a wide streak that ran perpendicularly in the rocky precipice not far from the cliff—and there it is!"

The boys fell back a bit, gazing intently at the wide, white strip that seemed to hang along the face of black stone, like a wide streak from a monster whitewash brush.

"I am certain we are very near the place," said Frank. "We will look for the cliff."

This they did, and, in a very short time, they fancied they had discovered it.

"There seems no possible way of reaching the ledge up there," said Bart, somewhat despondently.

"But there must be a way, if the hidden cabin is built there," declared Frank.

"I don't doubt it. At the same time, we are not likely to find it. Instead of making queer money in a city, where they would be in constant danger of discovery and arrest, they have come here to this wild region, where they are not likely to be discovered, and where there is very little chance that they will be arrested if they are discovered."

For some time the boys speculated concerning the possibility of reaching the ledge. They were about to seek a way out of the ravine when something happened that astonished them both.

"Look, Bart!" softly cried Frank, catching the shoulder of his friend—"look there!"

He pointed upward to the ledge.

On the very verge of the sheer descent a girl had suddenly appeared. In her hand she carried a huge umbrella, which she was struggling to open, her movements seeming to indicate that she was in great terror. Her unbound golden hair was falling over her shoulders.

"It's Vida!" palpitated Bart Hodge.

"It's Isa!" asserted Frank Merriwell.

"What does she mean to do?"

"Wait! Look!"

"Merciful goodness!"

Both lads were horrified, for, having succeeded in opening the huge umbrella, the girl suddenly turned, and, with a wild cry, leaped out into space from the edge of the ledge.

"Frank brought the butt of his Winchester to his shoulder, and began to work the weapon."

# CHAPTER XLV.

## QUEEN OF THE COUNTERFEITERS.

It seemed an act of madness.

A moment after she made the frightful leap a man came rushing to the edge of the ledge and clutched at her.

He was too late.

Already she was shooting downward toward the depths of the ravine.

With no small difficulty he saved himself from toppling over the brink.

Down in the ravine two boys gazed in unutterable horror at the falling form of the girl.

Then they beheld what seemed like a marvel.

To a certain extent the umbrella acted like a parachute, and, assisted by the girl's clothing, served to check the swiftness of her fall.

Down she came into the ravine, alighting within a few rods of the boys, collapsing in a motionless heap, while the huge government umbrella, which must have been stolen from its former owners, turned bottom up and rolled a few feet away.

Frank was the first to recover. With a low cry, he sprang toward the girl, knelt beside her, and lifted her in his arms.

"Is she dead?" fluttered Bart, over his friend's shoulder.

"I do not think she struck hard enough," said Frank. "No—she moves. She is alive!"

The beautiful girl, whose face was very pale, opened her eyes, caught her breath convulsively, looked straight past Frank, saw the face of the other boy, and murmured:

"Bartley!"

In a moment Bart Hodge was on his knees, and he almost tore her from Frank's hands.

"Give her to me!" he panted. "She knows me now! She will not refuse to recognize me here!"

Seeing how agitated his friend was, Frank surrendered the girl, asking:

"Are you severely harmed, Miss Isban?"

She looked at him in a bewildered way, but did not reply.

Bending over her, Bart echoed the question:

"Are you severely harmed, Miss Melburn?"

"I—I think not," she replied, faintly. "I lost my breath, and I feared I would lose my hold on the handle of the umbrella before I reached the bottom. I did not strike very hard, but everything seemed to float away when I knew I was at the bottom."

"It is wonderful—marvelous! What made you do such a mad thing?"

"The horrid wretch who insisted on making love to me! I became awfully afraid of him. He was pursuing me."

"But it seemed like a leap to certain death."

"I didn't care much. I was crazy with fear. I saw this old umbrella, and, remembering how I had once seen a man descend by means of a parachute from a balloon, I caught it up, rushed out of the cabin, slamming the door in his face, opened it, and jumped when he came hurrying after me."

"The brute!" grated Bart.

"He is a brute!" echoed the girl, "I had rather die than fall into his power again!"

"You shall not fall into his power. We will protect you."

"But how does it happen you are here?" she asked, bewildered. "I cannot understand that."

"This is no time or place for explanations," Frank cut in. "That fellow has disappeared from the cliff, but he will be back. We must get out of this."

To this Bart fully agreed, and he lifted the girl to her feet. She was rather weak, and so she was forced to lean on his shoulder.

They had moved but a little way when a shout came from the cliff, and they saw three men looking down at them. These men were armed, and Frank saw them taking aim with rifles.

"Look out!" he shouted. "They're going to send bullets after us!"

A second later the men on the cliff began shooting, the white smoke puffing from their rifles, the reports of which awoke the echoes.

The bullets whistled about the trio in the ravine.

"Run!" shouted Frank, wheeling and flinging his rifle to his shoulder.

He sent several bullets up at the cliff and then turned and dashed after Bart, who had lifted the girl in his arms, and made a rush for a place of safety.

The bullets spat spitefully against the rocks as he ran, whistled about him, dislodged pebbles and tore up little sprays of earth, but not one of them touched him.

The trio reached a turn in the ravine and passed beyond view of the cliff, so they were safe from the bullets of the men above.

For some moments they paused, panting from their exertions.

The girl looked at her companions in admiration.

"You are strong and brave," she said. "I feel that you will save me."

"But we are not out of the woods yet," said Frank. "Those fellows will be sure to give us a chase."

"How can they get down from the cliff?" asked Bart.

"There is a way to do that, you may be sure. As soon as we get our breath we must hasten on. We will be fortunate if we strike Blake, Long, and Jones without delay."

They did not wait long before hastening forward. The boys took the girl between them, both assisting her, sometimes carrying her over the worst places.

Her strength came back to her, after a time, and they were surprised by her skill and fleetness of foot.

Out of the ravine they made their way, and dropped over into the other, beginning to feel relieved by the non-appearance of their enemies.

But they were not to escape without a further encounter.

Five minutes after entering the second ravine they heard a clatter of hoofs behind them. There was no time to get out of the ravine, and it happened that they were unable to find a place of concealment in time to escape observation.

Six men came riding madly toward them, sending up a wild shout when they were observed.

"Behind these rocks here!" cried Frank. "We must stand them off. It's our only show. Put the girl behind that large one, so that she will be safe from bullets."

Bart was desperate. His teeth showed, his face was very pale, and he grated:

"They shall not touch her again—I vow they shall not touch her!"

Behind the bowlders plunged the trio, just as a bullet whistled over Frank's head.

Dropping on one knee behind a stone on which he could rest his elbow, our hero brought the butt of his Winchester to his shoulder, and began to work the weapon.

Even then Frank was not quite ready to shoot straight at the breasts of human beings, and so his first five shots brought down three of the horses, throwing the band into confusion.

Bart was more desperate, as his words indicated, for he half snarled:

"Don't kill the poor horses! Shoot the human brutes!"

Then he began firing, and, if his nerve had been as steady as Frank's, scarcely one of the six would have escaped. As it was, he quickly wounded two of them.

This was a reception the men had not counted on. Those whose horses had not been shot made haste to rein about and dash away, one with a dangling arm, while the others leaped to the shelter of the rocks.

"Now they have us cornered!" came fiercely from Bart's lips. "If you had not wasted your bullets, Frank, we would have the advantage now."

"Don't you care," laughed Frank, lightly. "We are hotter company than they were looking for, and I rather fancy we'll be able to give them a jolly good racket."

Frank was in a reckless mood. Danger ever seemed to affect him thus. A bullet tore his hat from his head, but he picked it up, laughing, as if it were all sport.

For some minutes the boys and their enemies popped away at each other, and then, from the opposite direction along the ravine, came the sound of galloping horses.

"Here come our friends!" cried Bart, joyfully. "We are all right now! Those chaps will have to take to their heels."

Suddenly a sharp whistle rang through the ravine from above, and the party below answered in a similar manner.

The boys looked at each other in astonishment.

"Shield yourselves as far as possible in both directions," cried Frank. "If I am not mistaken, we have enemies above and below!"

Crouching behind the rocks, they saw the second party dash into view—four in all. Three of them were men, but their leader was a girl, who wore a mask over her face.

"There!" exclaimed Frank—"there is the queen of the counterfeiters!"

# CHAPTER XLVI.

## AFTER THE FIGHT.

he masked girl seemed to have the eyes of an eagle, for she immediately located the trio behind the rocks. A wild cry broke from her lips, and then she caught the rein in her teeth, snatched out two revolvers, and charged straight down upon the boys and the girl they were defending, firing as she came.

The men followed her.

With hoarse shouts, the first party of pursuers joined in the charge, and the trio of defenders were between two fires.

"Shoot to kill! Shoot to kill!" screamed Bart. "Do not waste bullets now! It will be fatal if you do."

Only too well did Frank realize that he must seek human targets for his bullets. It was not the first time in his life that he had been compelled to do such a thing, but he always regretted the necessity, and did so only when forced to the last ditch.

It is a very easy thing to sit down quietly and think or write of shooting a human being in self-defense; but such a thing is not easy for conscientious persons to do. When the time comes, they either shoot in desperate haste, before they can think much about it, or hold off as long as possible.

Frank held off as long as possible, but now he realized it would not do to hesitate longer. Bart was shooting in one direction, and he began shooting in the other. Through the smoke that leaped from the muzzle of his rifle he saw one man fling up his hands and plunge forward on his face.

Either the men were utterly reckless, or they had not believed the boys would offer much resistance, for they exposed themselves fearlessly and rushed fiercely on the rocks behind which the trio crouched. It is possible they fancied that by shooting recklessly among the rocks they could keep the lads quiet till the barrier was reached.

This was a fatal mistake for some of them. The ones who were mounted came forward more swiftly, but some of them were toppled from the saddle, others were thrown into confusion, the horses were wounded and frightened, and the riders who could escape, reined about and made haste to do so.

All but the masked girl!

With the utmost reckless abandon, she charged right up to the rocks. Being a girl, neither of the boys had shot toward her, or her horse.

Now, however, Bart Hodge rose to his feet, took good aim at the animal, and shot it dead.

The creature fell, flinging the girl headlong.

She struck solidly, and lay still, in a huddled mass upon the ground.

"Hurrah!" cried Frank, seeing the enemy was repulsed. "I fancy they have had about enough of us."

He hastened to replenish the magazine of his rifle.

Bart's first thought, on seeing the fight was over, was of the girl they had been defending. He turned and found her safe where she had been placed behind the large bowlder, but she was still holding her hands over her ears, and her face was very pale.

Frank sprang outside the rocks, caught up the other girl, and leaped back quickly, placing her gently on the ground.

"I hope she is not harmed," he said, as he deftly removed the mask.

The moment the girl's face was exposed a shout of amazement broke from the lips of both lads. They stared first at one girl and then at the other, looking bewildered.

The girls were almost counterparts of each other!

"They are doubles!" exclaimed Frank. "Taken separately, it would be impossible to tell one from the other."

Then he turned on the girl they had been defending, stared straight into her face for a moment, and asked:

"What is your name?"

"Vida Melburn."

"It is not Isa Isban?"

"No, sir."

"Did I not change two fifty-dollar bills for you on the Pacific Express, shortly after leaving Ogden?"

"I never saw you till this morning."

"That settles it!" cried Frank; "the other girl is Isa Isban, and she is queen of the counterfeiters. She was the one for whom I changed the money, and she completely fooled me by her innocent face and manner."

"And I mistook her for Miss Melburn," said Bart. "Such a thing seems impossible, but it actually occurred."

"But how Miss Melburn came to be here is what I cannot understand," asserted Frank.

"I came up to Tahoe with my father, an uncle, and an aunt," said the girl, who was recovering from her terror. "My uncle and aunt live in Carson, and father and I were visiting them. We hired a sailboat of a big hermit who lives somewhere on the shore of the lake, and sailed over here, coming ashore to have a picnic dinner. The wind went down, and we could not get back. That evening I took a little stroll from camp, and I was suddenly seized from behind, nearly smothered in a blanket and carried away. I was held a captive in a cabin, far up on a high cliff. Back of the cabin was a cave through which the men reached the spot. Last night, or this morning, before daybreak, a man with a heavy dark mustache came to see me. I had not undressed, and he made me get up, so he could look me over. After some minutes, he cried, 'I swear she is handsomer than the queen!' Then he told me how he had seen me in Carson, and had mistaken me, at first, for some one else. How he found out his mistake, when he received a message from the other, who had been away to the east. How he vowed to know me better, and how, when he found our party were going to visit the lake, he sent word to friends of his to kidnap me. The monster! Then he tried to make love to me. I repulsed him, and he went away in an angry mood, swearing he would come back. He did so, in the morning, and once more tried to make love to me. I was filled with terror, and, clutching the big umbrella, I rushed out of the cabin. When he followed, I opened the umbrella and jumped from the cliff."

"You did not meet me in Reno, as you agreed," said Bart.

"Because father got hold of your letter, and he watched me constantly. I could not."

The other girl suddenly sat up. Her eyes had been wide open for some moments, and she had heard the whole of the story from the lips of her double, at whom she now stared, her face working strangely.

"So he made love to you—the traitor!" she cried, passionately. "Said you were prettier than I! I saw he had begun to tire of me! He would not let me see you; now I know why. You are a fine half-sister to steal my husband!"

"Half-sister!" gasped the other girl, shrinking back. "What do you mean?"

"Don't you know. Why, we are half-sisters. You are two years the older, although you do not look so. You do not remember your mother, for she left you when you were a baby. Your father must have kept the story from you. Mother told me everything. Your father has been forced to pay well to have the secret kept. He was proud, and his pride has been expensive."

Vida seemed dazed.

"I can scarcely believe it," she murmured.

Isa laughed rather harshly.

"I don't suppose it makes you feel any happier to know you have such a sister. What do I care! You robbed me of my happiness, for you made Paul fall in love with you."

"I repulsed him as best I could. He is repugnant to me."

"Well, I suppose you tell the truth. I was longing to strangle you till I heard your story. I shall not molest you now. Where is Paul? Where are the men?"

"Some of them are dead," answered Bart. "We did not wish to shoot them, but they forced us to do so in self-defense."

At this moment shots and cries came from up the canyon, and, a few seconds later, a man came into view and rode his horse down toward the bowlders which had served the boys as a fort.

It was Jack Long, the sheriff.

"Hurrah!" cried Frank, leaping to his feet and waving his hat. "Our friends are coming!"

Long rode up slowly, gazing in unutterable amazement at dead horses and men stretched on the ground.

"Well," he said, as he drew rein, "it looks like there had been a right smart scrimmage here. Who was in it?"

"We were attacked, and had to stand them off," explained Frank.

"You?" cried the sheriff, his amazement increasing—"you youngsters? Did you do all this shooting?"

"We didn't do all the shooting you may have heard, but we did some of it, and what you see shows we did not waste all our bullets."

"Holy smoke! We captured two fellows, back there, both wounded, and they said you boys did it; but I couldn't hardly credit that. You must have fought like wildcats! This knocks me. If I ever open my trap about kids again I hope I may choke!"

In a few moments Big Gabe and Sile Jones appeared, escorting the wounded prisoners, and the boys felt that there was no further danger of another attack from the counterfeiters.

Paul Scott, the husband of Isa, had been killed in battle. Great was her grief when she came upon his dead body.

The men slain in the struggle were buried there in the ravine.

The counterfeiters' cave and the hidden cabin were visited. Dies and presses, together with a large amount of "queer" money, were found. The counterfeiters who had escaped from the battle had taken to their heels, and they were not captured.

Then it transpired that "Silas Jones, of Michigan," was, in truth, Dan Drake, of the Secret Service, a fact which had been known to Jack Long all the while. Drake had been working for a long time to find the den of this band of counterfeiters.

On the return to the lake Vida Melburn's nearly distracted father, uncle, and aunt were found, and the girl was restored to them.

Then Bart Hodge and Frank Merriwell were introduced, and the girl somewhat maliciously informed her father that the person who had fought to save her from her kidnapers was the very boy he had forbidden her to see or correspond with.

It is needless to say that Bart and Frank were treated with great courtesy.

Drake did not wish to make anything unpleasant for Isa, so she accompanied the party as if she were one of them, although the detective tried to keep an eye on her. But she was shrewd, and she gave him the slip before Carson was reached. She was not overtaken and recaptured.

The detective was not forced to call Frank and Bart to testify against the captured counterfeiters, as both fellows confessed freely.

Big Gabe parted from Frank with a show of affection.

"'Low yer wuz squar' when I fust saw yer, burn me deep ef I didn't!" said the lazy giant. "I wuz right, too. No, I ain't goin' ter leave Tahoe. Reckon I'll live ther rest uv my natteral days hyar. Ef yer ever git round this yar way, don't yer fail ter call on Gabe Blake. Yer'll alwus be welcome at his shanty. Ef yer ain't, you may brand me."

When Frank left Carson City Bart was the guest of Vida Melburn's uncle. Vida and her father were stopping there, and Frank was urged to remain longer.

But Frank made haste to get away. He had a secret locked fast in his heart; he knew he, too, might become smitten by Vida's charms, if he remained, and he did not wish to "cross the trail" of his friend.

The boys parted with a warm handshake and a sincere wish to meet again, before long.

"And where will you go next?" asked Bart.

"To San Francisco, and from there to South America," answered our hero.

He told the truth, and his many adventures that followed will be related in the next volume of this series, entitled "Frank Merriwell's Hunting Tour." In this story we will meet not only Frank, but also many other old friends, and learn what they did while after big game.

And now good-by to Frank Merriwell, a typical American lad of to-day, as honest as he is brave.

# THE END

Lightning Source UK Ltd.
Milton Keynes UK
UKHW041114130920
369836UK00002B/5